FIGHTER PRED

BOOK 3

The Fighter Fred Series:

Fighter Fred and the Dungeon of Doom
Fighter Fred and the Wombat Wilderness
Fighter Fred and the Evil Temple of Evil

Other books by Jason A. Holt:

The Dragonslayer of Edgewhen
The Artificer of Dupho
The Klindrel Invasion
The Burglar of Sliceharbor
The Bladesman of Darcliff
Galaxy Trucker: Rocky Road

Visit jasonaholt.com.

FIGHTER FRED
AND THE
EVIL TEMPLE OF EVIL

JASON A. HOLT

Fighter Fred and the Evil Temple of Evil
Jason A. Holt

This is a work of fiction. All of the characters, organizations, locations, and events are either products of the author's imagination or are used fictitiously.

This is not a Dungeons & Dragons® product. Dungeons & Dragons® is a registered trademark of Wizards of the Coast. Although some Dungeons & Dragons rulebooks are briefly quoted or paraphrased for purposes of satirical commentary, no relationship between Fighter Fred and Wizards of the Coast is implied.

Copyright © 2019 by Jason A. Holt.

Fighter Fred illustration copyright © 2019 by Cory Thoman at 900foot.com.
Front cover design by James at GoOnWrite.com.
Back cover and interior design by the author.

Published by the author.
JasonAHolt.com

paperback ISBN: 978-1-950841-05-9
epub ISBN: 978-1-950841-04-2

Hear no evil. See no evil. You've failed your perception check.

Chapter One: In which our heroes visit the Den of Thieves.

The Den of Thieves was one of those taverns that didn't need a sign. If you couldn't find it, you shouldn't be there.

But Fred was no stranger to taverns—especially not to the taverns in Basetown. He knew his way through the twisting streets of the Thieves' Quarter. He found the dark alley between Good Neighbors Pawn Shop and the tailor's advertising *17 shades of black*. And in that alley, deep in the darkness, Fred found the stone steps that led down below ground level to the heavy wooden door.

"Is this it?" asked his friend Twilight.

"Yep," said Fred. "Pretty sure this is it."

"I feel like we shouldn't be here."

"It's fine," said Mak-Thar, the other friend who was standing in the dark alley with Fred. "You deposited your valuables in the bank, right?"

"Yes," said Twilight. "Except for the Amulet of Spring, of course."

"Please tell me you're not still wearing it," said Mak-Thar.

"It's a priceless family heirloom. If I'm not wearing it, I can't be sure it's safe."

"So you thought the absolutely safest thing to do was to wear it into a tavern frequented by every high-level thief in Basetown?"

"I sewed the amulet into my clothing," said Twilight. "If they want it, they'll have to steal my whole shirt."

"That is not beyond the realm of possibility."

Twilight considered this. "You think there are people in there who can take off my shirt without me noticing?"

"I'm sure the attempt would have negative modifiers," said Mak-Thar, "but that does not mean the probability is automatically zero."

Fred and Twilight were used to hearing Mak-Thar talk this way. He was a mage. They'd been on adventures with him before.

"If this place is so dangerous," asked Twilight, "why are you and Fred walking in with pouches of coins?"

"I have my reasons," said Mak-Thar. There was a smug smile in his voice. There was probably one on his face, too, but Fred couldn't see it in the dark.

"Did you bring your *Adventurer's Guide?*" Fred asked.

"Of course," said Mak-Thar.

"Can I borrow it?"

There was some puffing as Mak-Thar removed his enormous backpack and fished out his copy of *The Adventurer's Guide.* The book passed into Fred's hands.

"Shall I light a torch?" asked Mak-Thar.

"No thanks." Fred rapped his knuckles five times on the heavy wooden door. Then he pushed it open.

The noise of a dozen conversations spilled into the alley. Warm torchlight and the smell of ale washed over Fred's face. He smiled and strode into the tavern, raising Mak-Thar's book to deflect the knife that was thrown at his head.

The bartender called, "Relax. It's just Fred."

"Oh. Sorry, Fred!"

Fred waved at the thief who had thrown the knife and handed *The Adventurer's Guide* back to Mak-Thar.

The mage examined the cover anxiously. "It's scratched!"

"Wasn't that scratch there already?" Fred asked.

"Not that scratch. *This* one."

"Oh," said Fred. "Well, at least you'll know where you got it. It will make a good story."

Twilight followed them inside, but when he saw all the shady characters in the tavern, he hesitated in the open doorway. "Now I *really* feel like we shouldn't be here."

"We'll be fine," said Fred.

Reluctantly, Twilight shut the door.

Fred said, "They only throw knives if they think you're with the city guard."

Fred was not with the city guard. He carried a sword and walked around in steel armor, but he wasn't in the Den of Thieves to enforce any laws. He was there because he was an adventurer.

Mak-Thar and Twilight were adventurers, too, although Twilight would not always admit it.

Twilight could be odd sometimes. He insisted he was odd because he was an elf, but there was more to it than that.

Most elves in the adventuring business wore steel armor like Fred's. Twilight was wearing a frilly white shirt, a bright green vest, and matching green trousers. Twilight didn't go on adventures for fun and fortune. He went on "heroic quests" for noble causes. Fred wasn't sure this particular adventure would be up to Twilight's standards, but since nothing ever was, maybe it would all be okay.

Mak-Thar's standards were easier to meet because they were written down in *The Adventurer's Guide*. Mak-Thar didn't really care what happened on an adventure as long as the Mages' Guild would give him experience points for it. Fred wasn't entirely sure how that system worked, but it was all written down, and the mages liked that.

Mak-Thar murmured to Twilight, "Act confident. If you appear intimidated, they'll think you're an easy mark."

Fred chose not to contradict the mage, but he knew it didn't work that way. Even though Fred was never intimidated, someone always stole his gold. Then they'd buy him a drink and pay for it with his money. The trick was to bring only enough gold for a couple of ales.

Fred walked confidently toward the bar. Mak-Thar followed, looking like an easy mark.

Mak-Thar had so much stuff there was no way he could keep track of it all. First, there was his enormous backpack crammed full of everything an adventurer could possibly buy. Then there was the unwieldy amount of rope coiled about his chest and shoulders. Finally, there was his belt with a dozen pouches, not counting his coin pouch—which you couldn't count anyway because someone had already stolen it. People were fast in the Den of Thieves.

There was plenty of room at the bar. No one ever sat there. The patrons were the sort of people who prefer to sit in a dark corner. Most taverns have only four dark corners, but the Den of Thieves had lots. Each table was in its own little brick-walled alcove.

At the bar, they were in full view of every alcove in the tavern. Fred waved to some people he knew. They waved back.

"Why do you know so many thieves?" Twilight asked.

Fred shrugged. "If you adventure long enough, you meet all kinds of people."

The bartender ambled over. Fred reached into his coin pouch and discovered that someone had already sliced a hole in the bottom and taken the tip he'd been planning to hand over. Oh well.

"Hi," said Fred. "We're here for—"

"Those two will have to wait outside," said the bartender. "We don't serve their kind here."

Twilight's nostrils flared. "Excuse me?"

The elf actually put a hand on his sword, which is something you should definitely not do in the Den of Thieves.

"I think there's a misunderstanding," said Fred. "This tavern serves elves. Besides, Mak-Thar's not even an elf."

Mak-Thar had been a mule once, but never an elf.

The bartender grinned. He had a big face, so it was a big grin. "Aw, I'm jesting you! Fred's right. We serve all kinds. I just wanted a chance to use that line."

Twilight removed his hand from his sword and said, "It's not a very funny line."

The bartender laughed.

"This is Morc the Orc," said Fred. "They say he pours a fine mead, but I've never had any because someone always steals my money before I get to the bar."

Morc laughed some more. "Fred gets his money stolen because he doesn't know the secret knock."

"I knocked five times," said Fred.

"The secret knock is three short and two long."

Fred looked at his fingers. "I'm pretty sure that adds up to five."

Morc laughed.

"Fred is technically correct," said Mak-Thar. "A knock is a brief percussive sound, and there is no way to prolong its length."

"Who's this?" asked Morc. "Maybe I'll change my mind about serving him."

"You know me," said Mak-Thar. "And I won't order anything anyway. Someone has stolen my coin pouch." He did not sound particularly upset about this. In fact, he sounded smug.

Fred said, "We're here for a meeting in the back room."

Mak-Thar frowned with disapproval. "That was supposed to be a secret."

"Oh, right," said Fred. "We're here for a *secret* meeting in the back room."

"The back room is in the back," said Morc. He nodded his huge head in the direction of an unvarnished wooden door.

"Thanks," said Fred. They left the bar and headed for the back.

Twilight murmured, "It's not very nice to call someone 'the Orc' just because his face is disfigured."

"His face isn't disfigured," said Fred.

"He's horribly scarred and missing an ear," said Twilight.

"Oh, right." Fred had forgotten about the scars. On Morc's face, they were an improvement. "But he's called Morc the Orc because he's actually an orc. Well, half-orc."

Twilight's eyes went wide with astonishment. "What's the other half?"

"Human, I assume," said Mak-Thar.

Twilight contemplated this. "Um, so did … ?"

"What?" asked Fred.

"Never mind," said Twilight. "I don't really want to know where half-orcs come from."

"I think he's from Watergate," said Fred. Everyone in Basetown was from somewhere else. It was that kind of town.

They went down a few steps. Fred pushed open the door to the back room, and they went inside.

The room was already lit by lanterns hanging from iron hooks in the cobwebby ceiling. An old barrel and a serving girl stood in one corner. Chairs surrounded a table pitted and splintered with knife marks.

Fred nodded politely to the serving girl and sat down.

Twilight pulled up a chair beside him and said, "It looks like we're the first ones here."

"We're early," said Fred. "Helen will be on time."

"What about her friend?" asked Mak-Thar. "That thief she wanted us to meet?"

Fred shrugged. "She might be here already. I'm sure this meeting place was her idea."

"Should we ask if anyone has seen her?" asked Twilight.

"I could," said Fred. "What was her name?"

"I wrote it down," said Mak-Thar. He pulled a notebook out of a pouch and began leafing through the pages.

"It was something like Run," said Fred. "Or Ran."

"Ron?" asked Twilight.

"That sounds wrong," said Fred.

"Ren," said Mak-Thar. "Told you I wrote it down."

"It's Wren," said the serving girl. "The *W* is silent."

"What *W*?" asked Fred.

"Exactly."

"Where did *you* come from?" asked Twilight.

"She's been here all along," said Fred. He looked at the woman more closely: Nondescript face, slightly pretty if you bothered to look at it. Brown dress, neither fancy nor tattered. Sturdy boots that would be good for adventuring but also good for walking the dusty streets of Basetown. "You're Wren, aren't you?"

"Helen said you were smart," said Wren. "You must be Mak-Thar."

"No, I'm Fred," said Fred. He pointed at the mage with the scraggly beard. "He's Mak-Thar."

"And you may call me Twilight," said Twilight. "I apologize for not noticing you."

Mak-Thar frowned in confusion. "Were you hiding in shadows?"

"She wasn't hiding," said Fred. "She was standing in plain sight looking like a serving girl."

Mak-Thar said, "Well, according to *The Adventurer's Guide*, you should be unable to hide in shadows when people are looking at you."

Wren shrugged. "People don't look at me."

Indeed, there was something about her face that made Fred want to ignore it and go back to talking with his friends.

"Are you using some sort of enchantment?" asked Mak-Thar.

"No," said Wren. "I just have low charisma."

"Well, that's not true," said Mak-Thar. "You actually look quite nice."

A corner of her mouth quirked upward. "'Nice.' Not many people use that word to describe me."

Fred's buddy Helen had said that Wren was a high-level thief and a member of the Inner Circle of the Thieves' Guild. Fred wasn't sure what "Inner Circle" meant—he was from the Fighters' Guild, where everything was square—but he gathered that Wren was someone important. And you didn't get to be important, in any guild, unless you were dangerous. He hoped they hadn't offended her.

From the tavern came a shriek of pain, and the noise of conversation abruptly grew louder.

Fred glanced at the door. "Should I check on that?"

"Please do," said Wren.

Fred opened the door. A muscular woman in a plate-mail bikini was holding a scrawny thief in a painful wrist lock—at least, Fred *assumed* the wrist lock was painful, because the thief was on his knees with tears in his eyes.

"Hey, Helen," said Fred. "We're in here."

"I'll be there in a minute. I just need to break this guy's arm."

The thief whimpered.

"Please don't," said Fred. "That's my friend Louse."

"You have a friend named *Louse*?"

"I'm sure it's not his *real* name," said Fred. "That's just what his friends call him."

"He's pathetic," said Helen. She released Louse's wrist and shoved him over with a firm boot to the chest.

Louse crawled back to his alcove, where some of his friends were laughing at him.

Helen crossed the room to Fred. "He tried to steal from me."

"He's a thief," said Fred. "Thieves steal."

"Yes," agreed Helen. "But not from *me*."

Except for Louse, everyone in the tavern looked amused. *They* knew they weren't supposed to steal from Yellin' Helen.

"I mean," said Helen, as Fred let her into the back room and shut the door, "suppose fighters did that. Suppose we acted like it was okay to kill everyone we meet."

Twilight said, "You *do* act like it's okay to kill everyone you meet."

Helen smiled. "Hi, Twilight! Good to see you again."

Twilight returned the smile. "Good evening, Helen."

"So now we are four," said Mak-Thar. "Five. Sorry."

Wren accepted the apology with a nod.

"So you guys have all met?" asked Helen. "I don't need to do any introductions?"

"We've handled it," said Wren.

"Great!" said Helen. "Let's go overthrow that evil temple!"

Chapter Two: In Which Our Heroes Plot the Downfall of an Evil Temple.

"I THINK you're getting ahead of yourself," said Mak-Thar. "Did you not tell us that we needed Wren because she can devise a plan that is not suicidal?"

Helen looked to Wren. "You have a plan, right?"

Wren shook her head. "Not yet."

"Well, we can figure it out along the way," said Helen. "Let's go overthrow that evil temple!"

"Maybe you should sit down," said Fred. Helen could be quite excitable when presented with the opportunity to overthrow an evil temple. "And maybe you should offer to buy everyone a drink, since you seem to have kept your money."

"They took your money?" asked Helen. "Aw, you guys are chumps."

She sat down.

"They didn't take *my* money," said Mak-Thar. He was definitely smug. "They took my magically counterfeited money. I'm sure they will find themselves in deep trouble when they try to spend it."

"People in this place know how to launder counterfeit money," said Wren.

"They will have to do so soon," said Mak-Thar. "It will turn back into nightcrawlers by morning."

"I hope they don't try to launder the nightcrawlers," said Fred. "They don't last very long in water."

Wren fixed a bland gaze on Helen and asked, "So this is your team?"

"We're *your* team," said Helen. "But if you aren't interested in planning a heist, I'm sure Fred and I can plan a raid."

Helen's plans were always something along the lines of *We charge in and kill everybody*. She was a barbarian. Fred would not say that Helen had no imagination, but she did always imagine the same sort of thing.

"You know," said Fred, "I think Wren *is* interested in planning a heist, but she wanted us to plan it with her. Sort of like a teamwork thing."

"Oh," said Helen. She looked embarrassed. "Sorry. Was I being overzealous?"

"A bit," said Wren.

Fred said, "She gets like this on adventures with evil temples."

"Yeah," said Helen. "Sorry. Go ahead and do your planning. I'll keep calm."

Wren asked, "But if we mention the evil temple, will you go berserk?"

"No," said Helen. "I'm not that kind of barbarian."

"We wouldn't let a berserker in the party," said Mak-Thar. "We don't like people who might attack their fellow party members."

"All right," said Wren. "Let's try it, then. You can start by telling me everything you know about this temple."

They didn't know much. They had seen the temple during a previous adventure, but instead of investigating, they had continued on their main quest. Mak-Thar, in particular, had been opposed to anything that might sidetrack them, because he had been a mule at the time, and the object of the quest had been to restore him to his true form.

Later on that adventure, they had killed a few of the evil clerics in the desert. And at the end, right when Mak-Thar was about to regain his true form, they had confronted a small evil army and tricked them into not plundering a village.

But refugees continued to straggle into Basetown, telling stories from the villages that *had* been plundered. It seemed like those people from the evil temple were not very nice guys. They would confiscate a village's food and then burn all the cottages to the ground. And they'd done this sort of thing a lot.

They claimed to be worshipers of Toxia the Snake Goddess. Lots of them carried walking sticks that were carved to look like snakes. And all of them wore a tabard decorated with a green blob that was supposed to be a snake's head.

Their temple was in a swamp on the other side of the Impassable Mountain Range. They had some sort of relationship with the swamp's lizard men, who also wore the green-blob tabards, even though the clothing was not really compatible with their habit of slithering through the mud.

As Fred's friends filled in detail after detail, Fred realized that they actually knew quite a bit.

"Hm," said Wren. "You're right. You don't know much. None of you went inside the building?"

"It was heavily guarded," said Twilight.

"Well, you aren't thieves," said Wren, "so I can see why you let that stop you."

"We could have taken those guards," said Helen.

Wren frowned a moment, like she was working out a puzzle. "How did you stop Helen?"

"Helen's a team player," said Fred. "She wanted to attack the temple, but she had promised to help Mak-Thar become a mage again, so that's what she did."

Helen admitted, "It wasn't easy to leave."

"I really don't understand your obsession with this temple," said Twilight. "I concede that their actions are wrong, and I am pleased we are planning to remove them from a fragile wetland ecosystem, but in a world of injustices, why does this particular temple have such a grip on you?"

Helen shifted uncomfortably in her chair—her armored butt clanked against the wood. "I just don't like temples. That's all."

"It's a barbarian thing," said Fred.

"That doesn't really explain it," said Twilight.

"According to *The Adventurer's Guide*," said Mak-Thar, "barbarians hate all magic, all technology, and all signs of civilization. Since temples have a major civilizing influence on human society, it seems natural that barbarians would find them particularly hateful."

"Yeah," said Helen. "That's it."

Fred had the feeling that that was not it. Helen's hatred of temples was something he accepted, but it was not something he understood.

"I suppose we all have our quirks," said Twilight.

This was true. Twilight, in particular, knew all about quirks.

"I think we need to manage expectations," said Wren.

"What does that mean?" asked Fred.

Twilight said, "It means she doesn't think we can overthrow the evil temple."

"Well, I'm not sure we can 'remove them from the ecosystem,'" said Wren. "Also, the word 'overthrow' might be a little strong. Helen is correct: You don't need me to help you plan a raid. That's not what I do."

"What do you do?" asked Mak-Thar.

"I plan heists."

"I could be wrong," said Twilight, "but I don't think stealing a few coins will satisfy Helen's lust for destruction."

"But a heist doesn't have to be about money," said Helen. "Wren, tell them about the time you stole that sacred artifact and the entire temple collapsed."

"That was because I triggered a trap," said Wren.

"The trap made the entire building collapse?" asked Twilight.

"That sounds like shoddy engineering," said Mak-Thar.

"And she was chased by a giant boulder!" said Helen. "Heists don't have to be boring."

"A well-planned heist is never boring," said Wren. "But I prefer to be in control of the excitement."

"Me too," said Helen. "See? That's why I want Wren along. She and I think alike, but in completely different ways."

Fred thought that made sense.

"Did that make any sense?" asked Twilight.

"Well, enough about me," said Wren. "Why don't you tell me about your skills so I know what we have to work with."

Mak-Thar brightened up. "That seems like a good idea. As you may have guessed, I am a mage. At fifth level, I can cast one fireball per day. I am also very close to leveling up, which may entitle me to cast a second fireball during the adventure, although there are some who insist I should not use the new spell slot until my experience points have been Guild-certified.

"Among my other attacks are such useful spells as Sleep and Edwin's Weird Dweomer. Of course, I also have access to an array of specialized spells, which I can tailor to the particular adventure."

Wren held up a hand. "Mak-Thar, would I be correct in assuming that you have all this written down on a sheet of paper?"

"Not a single sheet. I keep my character information in a notebook."

"Ah. May I see it?"

Mak-Thar considered the question. "Well ... I suppose that *is* the most efficient way to transfer the information. Why don't I copy it down for you? Then you'll be able to refer to it later, if you need to."

"Excellent," said Wren. "Fred?"

"What?" asked Fred.

"What can you tell me about yourself?"

Fred shrugged. "Pretty much anything. I don't have a lot of secrets."

"What are your skills?"

"Skills?"

Wren gave up on Fred and turned to Helen. "*This* is the guy you think you can plan a raid with?"

"What you see is what you get," said Helen. "Fred's as strong as he looks, and he knows how to use his sword."

Wren gave Helen a dubious look.

"Fred is also a true friend," said Twilight. "Many a time he has rushed into danger to protect his weaker fellows."

Mak-Thar paused in his copying to say, "He can also carry a large amount of treasure. We want Fred along."

"Well, everybody is useful," said Wren. "But if the job goes smooth, then we don't need to hack anyone up. And if the job goes sour— I don't know. Fred's the sort of guy I would use for a scapegoat. I'd sacrifice him so the rest of us could get away."

Helen scowled.

Mak-Thar said, "I *do* hope your use of the subjunctive implies a counterfactual."

"What?"

"We aren't going to let you sacrifice Fred," said Twilight.

"I know. But when I look at him …" Wren shrugged. "That's just the first thing that comes to mind."

"Are you evil?" asked Mak-Thar. "I apologize for not stating this earlier, but I won't adventure with someone who's evil."

"I'm not evil," said Wren. "It's just … Look, I'm sorry if I offended anyone. We're supposed to be working together. So I want to be honest. With any job, it's important to be sure I have the right tools. And I don't know if I have enough to work with here."

Mak-Thar put down his pencil and drew himself up with a haughty air. "If you want to go on a thieves-only adventure, I am certain you can find plenty of like-minded individuals right outside this room."

"Eh, I've botched it," said Wren. She sighed and looked down at the knife-splintered table. "It's this stupid low charisma score."

"What are you talking about?" asked Twilight.

"Character theory," said Mak-Thar. "According to *The Adventurer's Guide*, every person is actually a character with six attributes."

"Seven," said Wren.

"Six," said Mak-Thar. He counted them off on his fingers: "Strength, intelligence, wisdom, dexterity, constitution—" he held up a thumb, "—and charisma."

One hand full of fingers and one thumb. Fred was pretty sure that was six.

"And comeliness," said Wren.

"Comeliness is apocryphal," said Mak-Thar.

"Comeliness is *essential*," said Wren. "You need to separate good looks from charisma. That way you can use charisma as your dump stat without being ugly."

"Who cares about being ugly?" asked Mak-Thar.

Wren said, "Women."

Helen nodded. "Women care a lot."

"Oh," said Mak-Thar. "Well, I've been female, and appearances never mattered much to *me*."

Twilight said, "But you were a female *mule*, Mak-Thar."

Mak-Thar considered this. "I suppose a human woman's perspective might be a little different."

"It is," said Wren. "If charisma and comeliness are the same thing, then a woman has to use something like wisdom for her dump stat. Or strength, I suppose. But this is not a good world in which to be weak."

Mak-Thar's eyes were glowing. Wren was talking in the language of *The Adventurer's Guide*. Mak-Thar *loved* to talk in the language of *The Adventurer's Guide*.

"Actually," he said, "the strength penalties can't hurt you if you never make melee attacks."

"I don't *enjoy* making melee attacks," said Wren. "But when I have to make them, I need them to be well-made."

"That's why you should bring along fighters," said Mak-Thar. "They deal damage so you don't have to."

"So is strength your dump stat?" asked Wren. "I've never met a guy with strength as his dump stat."

"Well, I certainly wouldn't pick wisdom," said Mak-Thar. "That would be foolish."

Twilight raised his hand and asked, "Is 'dump stat' one of those terms I'm going to be angry about as soon as you explain it to me?"

Fred nodded.

"The idea," said Mak-Thar, "is that one has only a limited amount of points to distribute among these six—or seven—attributes. For most people, being good at one thing makes them bad at something else. Fred, for example, is good at fighting. He deals a lot of damage because of his high strength. He can take a lot of damage because of his high constitution. Therefore, he must be bad at something else. That something else is his dump stat."

"Fred's dump stat is intelligence," said Wren.

"See?" said Mak-Thar. "That's a perfect example!" He was getting really excited. "What Wren said wasn't nice. So now you all like her less. That's a manifestation of low charisma! She gets minuses on our reaction rolls."

Twilight growled, "She's 'getting minuses' with me because she's saying mean things about my friend!"

Wren put her hands on her temples. "Right, right. I'm sorry. I'm so good at solo adventures, but working with other people is *hard*."

Fred tried to reassure her. "It's nice that you're getting some practice."

"The hardest part," said Wren, "is that I can't shake the feeling that I'm the only competent person in the room. I mean, I *suppose* everyone else must be useful too. I *suppose* my problems are caused by my low charisma. But I can't shake the feeling that everyone else is a bunch of imbeciles."

Mak-Thar reached out to her. For a moment, it looked like he was actually going to take Wren's hand! But he was sitting far enough away that all his hand could do was flop down in the middle of the table. "That's exactly the way *I* feel!"

"Oh," said Wren. "So it probably *is* just a low-charisma thing."

Fred said, "I think we'll be able to work something out. Twilight and I don't care about your charisma stats. And Helen can't even *add*."

"It's true," said Helen. "Barbarians don't need numbers."

Fred said, "Mak-Thar's the only one who cares about stats, and he—"

Fred looked at Mak-Thar. He was still sitting there with his outstretched hand flopped in the middle of the table, gazing at Wren with a face that was absolutely besotted.

"—I think he's fine with your charisma," Fred finished.

"See?" said Twilight. "That's another reason we need to bring Fred along. He always knows what to say to make everything better."

Was that what Fred had done? If Fred had realized he was supposed to be saying something to make everything better, he wouldn't have known what to say.

"The great thing about us," said Twilight, "is that we make up for each other's deficiencies."

"Oh, but I've left out the best part," said Wren. "Low charisma isn't actually a deficiency. The rules say that people with low charisma don't get noticed. I'm a thief. I don't *want* to get noticed."

Mak-Thar's eyes went wide. "That's brilliant!"

Wren grinned. "I know."

Mak-Thar asked, "So the only downside is that your colleagues don't notice you, and you occasionally offend people by telling them the truth?"

"That's right."

"That's wonderful!" said Mak-Thar. To the others he said, "I definitely think we should take her along."

"*I'm* deciding who we're taking along," said Wren. "You were writing down your character info for me."

"Oh, right." Mak-Thar went back to writing.

"You're taking all of us," said Helen. "Like I said: We're your team."

"Are any of them stealthy?" asked Wren.

"Twilight is as good in the woods as I am," said Helen. "I don't know how good he is at creeping around inside buildings."

Wren looked Twilight up and down. "He looks light on his feet. Is Fred as clumsy as he looks?"

"Absolutely not," said Helen. "He's only average-level clumsy. I'm not so sure about Mak-Thar. I've only been on the one adventure with him, when he was a mule."

"None of us can move silently," said Mak-Thar. "That skill is restricted to thieves only."

"All hunters know something of stealth," said Twilight.

"No they don't," said Mak-Thar. "Not according to *The Adventurer's Guide.*"

Wren said, "Mak-Thar, I know what it says in the *Guide*, but you don't always have to move 'silently'. Sometimes moving quietly is good enough."

Mak-Thar frowned. "What page is that on?"

"It's written in Wren's book of personal experience. Take Helen, for example. Can she hide in shadows?"

"No," said Mak-Thar.

"Can she move silently?"

"No. She's not a thief."

"And when you're in the wilderness, who do you want scouting for you?"

"Well, Helen, of course, but—"

"Helen *knows* things, Mak-Thar. She has skills that aren't explained by *The Adventurer's Guide*."

"I'm sure I could find them in a rules supplement."

"Sure," Wren agreed. "Her Stealth skill is written down *somewhere*, right?"

"Perhaps not literally," said Mak-Thar. "I seem to be the only one in the party who keeps his character information up to date. But yes, I concede that Helen does possess a certain amount of stealth, even though *The Adventurer's Guide* does not specifically describe the mechanism."

Twilight's mouth fell open. "How did you do that?"

"Do what?" asked Wren.

Twilight said, "I've been living with Mak-Thar—as man and mule—for two months now. I have worked on him ceaselessly, every day. And in all that time, he has never—*never*—admitted that there might be a reality that exists beyond *The Adventurer's Guide*."

"Twilight is prone to exaggeration," said Mak-Thar.

This was true, but in this particular instance, Twilight was not exaggerating much. Wren was getting through to Mak-Thar in a way that the rest of them could not.

"We need someone who can case the joint," said Wren. "I'm getting the feeling that the only one who can sneak in and get inside information is me. And I don't like sneaking in until I have inside information."

"You'll be fine," said Helen.

"I'll be even finer if we have an inside man," said Wren. "Anybody know one?"

Twilight frowned. "Are you asking us if we know an evil cleric who would be willing to betray his fellows?"

"We're looking for anyone with a connection to the temple," said Wren. "Maybe someone who made deliveries. Or a temple gardener."

"It's in a swamp," said Helen. "I don't think they have gardeners."

"Oh, right." Wren thought for a moment and then pulled a sheet of paper out of a pocket. "It's really hard to make a plan without a layout of the place. I'll ask around." She started writing on her sheet of paper. "Mak-Thar, am I correct in assuming that you keep track of the party's treasure?"

"I do," said Mak-Thar, quite proud of the fact.

"Are we starting out with any?"

"I do have some money set aside as initial capital, yes."

"Great. While I'm looking for an inside man, I need the rest of you to do some shopping."

CHAPTER THREE: IN WHICH OUR HEROES HYPOTHETICALLY DESTROY A TEMPLE.

DIRT CRUNCHED UNDER HELEN'S BOOTS. The dew was light this morning—just enough to keep the dust down. She could taste the moisture with every crunching step.

The rising sun was still low enough to cast long shadows tinged with haze. Warmth struck her bare skin, and she drank it in.

Her blade bounced gently against her back. Beside her strode Fighter Fred, the bravest, most honest, and most generous man in Basetown.

Mak-Thar and Twilight walked ahead of them, immersed in their incessant conversation. Twilight had recently bought a pair of tight green elf pants, and Helen appreciated the tailor's work.

Mak-Thar wore a robe—which was basically a dress. He had probably never washed it. The mage smelled of sour sweat and old smoke. His boots smelled of dung. Apparently, he had spent some time caring for the party mule this morning.

Mak-Thar had once been trapped in the body of that mule, and although he was a man again, he had retained some mulish traits. His scrawny frame carried a huge backpack stuffed so full that Helen could see the seams straining against the stitches.

Twilight was saying, "It's hard to believe Wren could think of something to buy that you don't already have."

Wren's shopping list crinkled in Mak-Thar's pencil-smudged hand. "I do have most of it. But there are a few nonstandard items we should seek. For example, we need to buy a butterfly net, some paint, and a telescoping ten-foot pole."

"We can cut poles in the forest," said Helen. *Most* of the things a person needed could be found in the forest, and Helen had never understood why people insisted on buying them in town.

Mak-Thar said, "Wren suggests we purchase a *telescoping* ten-foot pole. It will be easier to carry."

"Easier to carry than a ten-foot pole?" asked Twilight. "That's amazing!" The elf tended to be sarcastic.

Fred asked, "Is a telescopic pole one that you can see from a long ways away?"

Helen had been wondering the same thing. When Fred was around, she didn't feel stupid.

Mak-Thar said, "The pole is in segments that collapse into each other, in the manner of a telescope."

"Thanks for clearing that up," said Helen. Now she just had to figure out what collapsing segments were.

"Maybe we'll know it when we see it," said Fred.

"There's an illustration in the *Elite Dungeon Divers* rules supplement," said Mak-Thar. "In fact, most of this equipment is from there."

"It's not in *The Adventurer's Guide*?" asked Twilight.

"It is not."

"I can't believe she's actually convinced you to buy something that's not in *The Adventurer's Guide*!"

The elf was on the scent. Mak-Thar had definitely been giving Wren fawn eyes last evening.

Of course, Mak-Thar tried to deny it. "For your information, I have purchased many items that are not in *The Adventurer's Guide*."

"Name one!" said Twilight.

"Boots," said Mak-Thar.

"That's two," said Fred.

"Thank you," said Mak-Thar. "Your assistance with arithmetic is always appreciated."

That was disrespectful, but Fred wouldn't mind. Fred might not even notice.

"Boots aren't in *The Adventurer's Guide*?" asked Twilight.

"Prices for boots can be found only in rules supplements, such as *Elite Dungeon Divers*."

"You learn something new every day," said Twilight. "Something pointless, but at least it's new."

"Of course, the nonstandard items are more difficult to find," said Mak-Thar. "I believe we should visit the provisioner on Wattle Street."

Fred got a thoughtful look on his face and said, "Let's turn here."

"Don't be silly," said Mak-Thar. "The shortest route to Wattle Street is through the Temple Square."

"Oh," said Fred. "Okay."

Helen stretched her arms to loosen the muscles in her back. Fred shouldn't worry about her. She would be *fine* walking through the Temple Square. It was just another place in Basetown.

Like most of Basetown, the Temple Square was under construction. The former site of the vegetable market had been dug up, and great slabs of rock had been laid down to form a foundation for a new temple. Now the workers were raising tall pillars that thrust into the sky.

Helen could see the temple being built, right there in the middle of town. It occurred to her that the temple could also be knocked down, simply by doing everything in the opposite order.

Fred asked, "Helen? Where are you going?"

"I just want to see if I can push one of those pillars over. I'll be right back."

Fred's hand was on her arm—skin to skin. She looked at his meaty fingers, then up at his worried face.

Mak-Thar said, "That's an interesting question. I don't think the pillars are stable until they put the roof on top. And yet, the base is wide enough that any attempt to tip the pillar would have to lift the center of mass by at least a foot. If potential energy is mgh ..."

"We are not going to push any pillars over," said Fred.

"Well, of course not," said Mak-Thar. "This is the Temple of Law."

"They'd probably sue," said Twilight.

"But speaking purely theoretically," said Mak-Thar, "I'd guess that you can't get a good angle to apply enough torque. Now if you had a rope attached to the top ..."

"We also are not going to *pull* any pillars over," said Fred. "We don't overthrow temples in town. Someone might need them."

That was the big drawback of civilization—you had to share it with other people.

Helen nodded. Fred let go of her arm.

"On the other hand," said Mak-Thar, "who says you need to add all the energy in one go? If someone of sufficient strength were to *rock* the pillar, the energy could be added gradually to amplify the oscillation."

"Rock-a-bye temple?" asked Twilight. "Down will come pillar, temple, and all?"

"I think Wattle Street is that way," said Fred.

"But Helen makes a good point," said Mak-Thar as they started crossing the Temple Square. "Instead of stealing from the evil temple, we could just try to knock it down."

Helen hadn't been trying to make any point, but she liked where this was going.

"That doesn't sound very subtle," said Twilight.

"If the collapse kills enough people," said Mak-Thar, "then we'll get just as many experience points as we would for stealing treasure."

"The reason I agreed to this quest," said Twilight, "is that it's an *evil* temple. If we just drop it on everybody's heads, who's the evil one?"

"The ones inside the temple," said Helen. "That's why it's called an 'evil temple'."

"That stands to reason," said Mak-Thar.

"But if we kill them indiscriminately," said Twilight, "does that not make us evil, too?"

Mak-Thar frowned. "I don't think so."

He stopped in the middle of the square and pulled out his copy of *The Adventurer's Guide*.

"You can't find answers to moral questions in a rulebook!" said Twilight.

"Alignment is explained on page 11," said Mak-Thar. "Let's see ... Ah! It's in the example: 'After a battle with a band of goblins, the party has six prisoners. There is no local law enforcement, and the party has enough rope to tie up only four. An evil party member will see no need to take prisoners at all, and will offer to slit their throats. A good party member will take pity on them and argue that the two unbound goblins should be kept under constant guard. A neutral party member will allow the evil party member to kill two of the goblins and will then intervene to spare the lives of the other four, thus gaining approval from the good party member while allowing the evil party member an outlet for violence.'"

"Wow!" said Fred. "That neutral party member sounds like a real jerk."

Helen wasn't sure what she would do. The story left out important information. Were any of her friends lying dead on the ground, or was this just another good, old-fashioned butt-kicking? Sometimes she was good, and sometimes she was evil. She was a fighter—her job was to kill for money.

(Helen also had a steady income from underwear endorsements. That could have been neutral, but Nycadaemon Knickers made such comfortable underwear that Helen was certain her modeling career was purely good.)

Mak-Thar raised a finger. "Please note the assumptions built into this scenario: The party members—good, evil, and neutral alike—have already been fighting these goblins. Nowhere does it say that the good members objected to the battle. If one wanders into a dungeon, one must expect to fight goblins."

"And if one lives underground, one must expect to be attacked by a bunch of greedy, bloodthirsty adventurers," said Twilight.

Helen had the impression that Twilight thought this might be a bad thing.

"Certainly," said Mak-Thar, who understood that this was not good or bad—it was just the way the world worked. "And if one lives in an evil temple, one must expect that a well-equipped and tactically intelligent party will eventually be one's downfall—perhaps literally."

Twilight said, "So it's okay to kill any innocent scullery maids and gardeners in the temple, because they have it coming."

Fred frowned. "That doesn't sound right."

"Because it's not right!" said Twilight.

"We've already established that the evil temple has no gardeners," said Mak-Thar. "But if it did, I'm sure we could time the destruction to coincide with hours in which they would be working outside."

Fred said, "Before we destroy any temples, I think we should at least listen to Wren's plan."

"Yeah," said Helen. "I know she hasn't come up with much so far, but we should give her a chance."

Mak-Thar said, "I *will* be interested in hearing her thoughts on the matter."

Mak-Thar was interested in hearing Wren's quiet, feminine voice. He was thinking about the gentle way Wren filled out that little brown dress. Wren didn't have what it took to be a professional underwear model, but she had a lot going for her, if she chose to use it. Without even trying, she'd managed to get the attention of Mak-Thar!

Not that any woman would *want* the attention of Mak-Thar, but it was amazing that Wren could distract him. Helen had thought the mage was myopically focused on his rulebook and his quest for experience points.

"I *am* impressed with you," said Twilight. "I feared that bringing someone in to help with tactics would make you jealous."

"I admit I was a bit hurt when you all immediately rejected my inferno idea—"

Mak-Thar had suggested that Fred, Twilight, and Helen should charge in carrying six kegs of lantern oil.

"—but I approve of finding paths to success that do not rely on dumb, brute force. No offense, Fred."

"Huh?"

"In fact," finished Mak-Thar, "the Mages' Guild has been known to give bonus points for creativity."

Helen hadn't invited Wren for bonus points. She had invited Wren because Wren's plans *worked*. Helen's instincts told her that she and Fred should just rush into the evil temple and start hacking. But Helen's instincts told her that about *any* temple. They were walking past the Temple of Good right now, and Helen desperately wanted to charge in there and kick some clerical butt.

Helen's instincts were wrong. When it came to temples, she couldn't trust herself. She needed Fred to keep her head level. But she couldn't rely on Fred to come up with a plan. She needed someone smart.

Wren was smart—as smart as Mak-Thar. Either one of them

could have made an effective plan to destroy the temple. Helen had asked for Wren because she was also *competent.* Competence was what kept people alive.

And Helen wanted these guys kept alive. She wasn't willing to sacrifice them for her revenge.

Chapter Four: In which Mak-Thar is unpleasantly surprised.

Fred had been trying to avoid the Temple Square for a number of reasons. That number was three—Helen, Mak-Thar, and Twilight. Fred didn't know what his wisdom score was, but he thought it was unwise to talk about destroying temples so close to the future site of the Temple of Law. He'd managed to pull them away from there, but now they were at the opposite side of the square debating whether the Casino of Chaos was also a temple.

"If it's a temple," said Mak-Thar, "they shouldn't be coy. They should just come right out and call it a temple. But if it's a casino, they shouldn't be advertising so blatantly on the Temple Square."

Torchlit signs proclaimed, *Casino of Chaos! Where your soul is always a winner.* Fred wasn't sure why the signs were torchlit in the middle of the morning.

"It's not a temple," said Helen. "I'm not having any trouble controlling the urge to ransack it."

"Ah," said Twilight. "So perhaps it is not a temple, but it *is* a holy place of worship."

"There's nothing holy about gambling," said Mak-Thar.

"Not to you or me," said Twilight. "But to those who are devoted to chaos—"

"Chaos isn't even an alignment!" said Mak-Thar. "*The Adventurer's Guide* lists good, evil, and neutral. That's it!"

A short woman dressed in snug black leather armor with a

cute pleated leather skirt stepped out of the casino. She stared at Fred in surprise. "Wow. It's you."

Fred beamed. "Nightshade! Great to see you again!"

"Yeah. You too." She gestured at the casino. "I was in there praying for good fortune, but I didn't realize it would work."

"Did you win a lot of money?" asked Mak-Thar.

"I lost fifty gold pieces, but now that I've run into you guys, I guess I'll count it as a donation."

Fred said, "Yeah we were just going ..."

"Shopping," said Helen. "We're going shopping. How have *you* been?"

"Pretty good!" said Nightshade. Then she thought about it and said, "And kind of not so good. I took a lot of disadvantages to pump up my character for my adventure with you guys, and now they're kind of biting me back."

"What sort of disadvantages?" asked Mak-Thar.

"Sort of like bad things in my back story."

"Your super-secret back story?" asked Twilight.

He was mocking her. Everyone liked Nightshade, but she also had a number of unpleasant habits that irritated people. She even irritated Fred, sometimes, but he knew she was just a kid with a lot to learn, so he didn't hold it against her. She certainly tried hard to be likeable.

"Yeah," said Nightshade. "Has anyone told you my secrets yet?"

"If they are secrets," asked Helen, "how could anyone else know them?"

"Word's starting to get around." Nightshade's lips sagged into a glum look. "I think I'm gonna have to leave town."

A man dressed in a black silk shirt and leather pants stepped out of the casino and stabbed Nightshade in the back. Then a lot of stuff happened at once:

Nightshade gasped and looked over her shoulder.

Fred drew his sword and sidestepped around Nightshade so he could get an angle on the assassin.

Helen drew her humongous sword from her back scabbard, swung the blade over her head, and yelled, "Duck!"

And during this brief moment of time, Mak-Thar, the awkward academic, stepped around Nightshade, drew his dagger, and stabbed the assassin in the chest multiple times.

"Die, die, die!" screamed the mage, as he stabbed the surprised assassin over and over. He left Fred no clean angle of attack. Helen's eyes bulged with the effort of holding back her two-handed, over-the-head death-cleave.

After three seconds of being attacked by a scrawny mage striking with the rapidity of a murderous woodpecker, the assassin managed to push himself away, and this gave Fred an opening in which he delivered the killing thrust. The assassin fell dead in the Temple Square with his black silk shirt in ruins.

"Wow," said Nightshade. "That was intense."

Mak-Thar fell to his knees beside the assassin and resumed his woodpecker stabbing. "Die, die, die!"

"Mak-Thar," said Helen, "he's dead."

"Die!" said Mak-Thar.

Twilight put a hand on Mak-Thar's shoulder and helped him to his feet. The mage's hands were shaking. He'd left his dagger embedded in the assassin's chest.

"Wh—?" asked Mak-Thar. "Wh—?"

Fred wasn't sure how to answer that question.

"Thanks for defending my honor," said Nightshade.

"He was defending your life," said Twilight. "That's not the same as your honor."

"Oh," said Nightshade. "What's my honor?"

Helen snickered.

"What just happened?" asked Mak-Thar.

Fred said, "Someone tried to kill Nightshade, and you stabbed him a lot in the chest."

Fred approved. That was what you were *supposed* to do when someone attacked your friend. But he'd never seen anyone do it with a small dagger. He'd certainly never seen a *mage* leap into close-quarters combat like that.

Mak-Thar was still shaking. "That was scary!"

"Well … yeah," Fred admitted.

"I was scared!" said Mak-Thar.

"Uh huh."

"It was scary!"

"You mentioned that."

"Battles aren't supposed to be *scary!*"

Fred felt like the conversation was slipping away from him. He looked around for guidance.

"I think that was Mak-Thar's first real battle," said Twilight.

"But we've been in battles before," said Fred.

Twilight said, "Before he was killed, he didn't think the battles were real."

"He was a pretty good fighter as a mule," said Helen.

"Yes," said Twilight. "But this was his first battle as a man again."

Mak-Thar looked to Fred with haunted eyes. "Is it always going to be this way?"

Helen sheathed her humongous sword and laid a hand on Mak-Thar's shaking arm. "You'll be okay."

"But what about next time?"

It was a good question. Adventurers had to expect *lots* of battles.

Mak-Thar asked, "Am I a berserker?"

Helen grinned. "Maybe you were, for just a moment."

"I don't want to be a berserker. It's not compatible with my character class!"

"You won't be a berserker." Helen's voice was soothing. "He just took you by surprise, that's all."

"I don't like surprises!"

"No, you don't." Helen patted his arm. "I think the assassin knows that now."

Fred and Twilight exchanged a concerned glance. Mak-Thar had once been killed by surprise. His dying words had been *I'm not surprised, and I draw my dagger.* Apparently the assassin had run into Mak-Thar's unfinished business.

Poor guy.

Twilight shook his head, as though trying to clear out the

memory of that ill-fated adventure. "Forgive me, Nightshade. How badly are you wounded?"

"He mostly stabbed my backpack," she said. "More good luck from the Chaos Goddess! I only lost four hit points. Unfortunately, as a first-level thief, that's almost enough to kill me. Good thing I pumped up my constitution stat."

Twilight rolled his eyes. "You'd better let me look."

"Um, he stabbed me in the *back*. That's like *under* my shirt. I'm not taking off my shirt for you."

"If you take off the leather, I can cut away the cloth."

"I guess that would work. I'll have to buy a new shirt anyway."

A person could just buy a new shirt? Why had Fred never thought of that? His clothes were full of mended holes.

While Fred pondered this, Twilight cleaned and disinfected Nightshade's wound. Helen calmed Mak-Thar down and helped him stop shaking. As Twilight started sewing Nightshade's skin back together (because she couldn't buy a new skin) two guards approached.

"Hey! What's going on?"

Twilight stopped his stitching and looked guilty. It's not a good idea to look guilty when the city guard shows up.

"Our friend was attacked by this assassin." Fred gestured to the body lying in the dust. "So we killed him."

"Hm," said the other guard. "Someone *really* doesn't like assassins."

Helen said, "We don't hang out with people who really *do* like assassins."

"Good point. Do you want to press charges?"

Twilight gaped like a fish.

"Maybe later," said Fred. He had a feeling that Nightshade shouldn't be talking to the city guards. "There's no point right now, is there? Why don't you just contact me if someone revives him? My name is Fred. You can leave a message at the Fighters' Guild."

The two guards exchanged glances and decided that Fred's suggestion sounded good.

One of them took out a piece of paper and wrote a note that read, *If body revived, contact Fred at F.G.* They pinned the note to the corpse's holey shirt and pulled out Mak-Thar's dagger because it was in the way.

"Here's your dagger," one of them said.

Fred took it.

The guards lifted the assassin between them and carried him off to the city morgue.

"That was *amazing!*" said Twilight. "How did you do that?"

"Do what?" asked Fred. He handed the dagger back to Mak-Thar, who took it and numbly returned it to the scabbard on his belt.

"How did you convince them that he was the murderer and not us?"

"I just told the truth," said Fred.

"Yeah," said Helen. "He was obviously an assassin. He wore black."

"Nightshade also wears black," said Twilight.

"It's okay for *me* to wear black," said Nightshade. "I'm too cute to be an assassin."

Twilight said, "They came to a crime scene, took statements from only *one* witness, and then they handed back evidence."

"Well what did you *want* them to do?" asked Helen. "Should they have arrested us for preventing a murder?"

And so Fred's friends argued about police procedure for a time, while Twilight stitched up Nightshade's wound. That had been a nasty attack, but Fred was grateful for one thing: It had distracted Nightshade and kept her from asking about their plans.

And this was good, because if Nightshade found out they were going somewhere, she would probably want to come along. Helen wouldn't like that, but Fred wasn't sure he could tell Nightshade no.

Chapter Five: In which Nightshade joins the party, just like you knew she was gonna.

As an adventurer, Helen had spent a lot of time underground. She was *used* to musty rooms with cold, damp walls and spider-infested ceilings. But this wasn't the sort of place she would choose for holding meetings.

Helen and the boys were once again sitting around the table in the back room of the Den of Thieves. Instead of planning, they were waiting for Wren.

Wren was late. Helen had never known Wren to be late, but tonight she was late.

This made Mak-Thar anxious. "You say she's never late?"

"I didn't say she's *never* late," Helen reminded him. "I just said I've never *known* her to be late. Maybe some business came up at the Thieves' Guild."

"We should search the room," said Mak-Thar.

"This room?" asked Helen.

"Yes. Maybe she's hiding in shadows again."

Helen looked around the tiny room. "There's nowhere to hide."

"Except that barrel." Mak-Thar pointed at an old barrel standing in a shadowy corner. "I'll search there. Fred, you look under the table. Twilight, check for secret doors."

"I think she's just late," said Twilight. "Why are you expecting a thief to be reliable?"

"Good point," said Fred.

"No it's not!" snapped Mak-Thar.

Twilight blinked at him.

Mak-Thar looked sheepish. "That is, Helen has assured us that Wren is reliable, and her word is good enough for me."

Helen said, "I know you haven't run into any thieves you can trust, Twilight, but there are all kinds of thieves, just like there are all kinds of clerics and all kinds of fighters."

"Yes," said Twilight. "You and Fred are so different from each other and not stereotypical at all."

"Is the elf in the frilly shirt going to lecture *me* on stereotypes?"

Twilight looked down at his embroidered green vest and his frilly white shirt with the poofy sleeves. "Well, that cuts a little close."

"Wait," said Fred. "Is Twilight saying you and I *are* different or that we're not?"

"I was attempting to make a little jest," said Twilight. "But it seems everyone is on edge."

Was Helen on edge? Yeah, maybe she was. She could hear someone standing silently on the other side of the door.

"Wren's here," said Helen, a split-second before the door opened.

"Sorry I'm late," said Wren. She came in and closed the door. "I was waiting for our inside man, but she hasn't shown up yet."

"Our inside man is a woman?" asked Twilight.

"Yeah," said Wren. "It's just an expression."

"An innocent scullery maid?" asked Mak-Thar.

"No," said Wren. "She's actually a new member of my guild."

Oh no, thought Helen.

"What a coincidence!" said Fred.

"Yeah," said Wren. "She ran across the temple on an adventure last month, and she's already cased the joint."

Twilight pursed his lips thoughtfully.

"So ... not a scullery maid," said Mak-Thar.

Wren shrugged. "It's kind of hard to find former employees of evil temples. Unless you animate their corpses. But this is the next best thing—she knows the place inside and out."

"*Inside* and out?" asked Helen. Maybe Wren *wasn't* talking about Nightshade.

"Inside and out," said Wren.

There was a knock at the door. Nightshade poked her head in and said, "Hi, I'm here for— Wow! Twice in one day. This must be fate."

Helen said, "Nightshade does *not* know the temple inside and out."

Wren's gaze flicked around the room. "You guys all know each other?"

"Why don't you come in and close the door?" Fred suggested.

Helen did *not* want Nightshade to be invited in. She gave Fred a look.

"Well," said Fred, "this *is* supposed to be a secret meeting."

Nightshade came in and closed the door. Fred scooted his chair over to make room for her, and Nightshade sat down beside him.

Wren bit her lip and looked at Helen. "Is this going to be a problem?"

"No problem," said Mak-Thar. "We've worked with Nightshade before."

"Yes," said Twilight. "On our last adventure. When we did *not* go inside the temple!"

Wren looked at Nightshade. The girl just sat there with her folded hands on the table, like Miss Prissy.

"Nightshade?" asked Wren.

"Yes?"

"Is there something you want to tell me?"

Nightshade blinked. "About what?"

"You told me you know the temple inside and out."

"I do," said Nightshade. "We all do."

"But *they* say you never went in."

"Well, we didn't. We decided not to."

"Stupid dump stat," muttered Wren. "I'm sure if I had more charisma I'd get a straight answer."

Twilight said, "If you haven't been in the temple, you should not have claimed to know the place inside and out."

"Well, I'm sorry, okay? That's just an expression. Like if

Mak-Thar knows the rulebook inside and out, that doesn't mean he's literally *inside* the rulebook."

Twilight turned to Helen. "This is why I mistrust thieves."

But not all thieves were flakes—certainly not as flaky as Nightshade. Women could have lots of reasons for being thieves instead of fighters. Maybe they couldn't take a hit, or maybe they didn't *like* taking hits. Some women prefer to kill from a distance or from the shadows. Helen *admired* sneaky, ruthless women—just so long as they were also ruthlessly loyal to the party.

Nightshade wasn't exactly *disloyal*, but …

"I would have been here earlier, but I had to buy a new shirt, okay? I got *stabbed* today, if you remember."

Mak-Thar went glassy eyed.

"We remember," said Helen.

"I need to get her out of town," said Wren. "She's in hot water."

Fred raised a hand.

"Yes, Fred?"

"Is 'hot water' like 'deep doo doo'?"

"Yes, Fred."

"She can't tell you any more about the temple than we did," said Twilight.

Wren said, "She *did* tell me it had a red dome on white pillars with a black foundation."

"Like a scoop of Neapolitan ice cream," said Nightshade.

"Neapolitan ice cream," agreed Wren. "Look, if you guys don't want her, I understand. But she's a baby thief, and I gotta watch out for her. You *know* how hard it is to get a thief to second level."

Mak-Thar said, "Actually, thieves level up more rapidly than any other character class."

"Yeah," said Wren, "but we're mostly useless until we do."

"I'm not useless," said Nightshade. "I've been practicing my pickpocketing. So what I'll do is, I'll find the guard and then steal his keys, and then we can all sneak into the temple at night."

"I'm sure no one will be doing anything in an evil temple at *night*," said Twilight. "Thanks to your clever stratagem, our victory is ensured."

"In point of fact," said Mak-Thar, "your chance of successfully picking someone's pocket does not go above fifty percent until you reach seventh level."

"Seventh?" asked Nightshade. "Are you sure?"

"Look it up."

Nightshade reached into her cute little backpack and pulled out a dainty, pocket-sized *Adventurer's Guide*. That was the *real* reason Helen disliked Nightshade: She was cute and dainty and perky and everything else that Helen was not. She could even *read*. Having Nightshade in the party was like having a living catalog of Helen's shortcomings.

"Wow, you're right," said Nightshade. "About the only thing a first-level thief can do is climb walls. This character is *lame*."

"You're pretty good in a fight," said Fred.

"But don't rush into melee," said Mak-Thar. "First-level thieves can't take a hit."

"Oh, that's another reason I want to go with you guys. Twilight said someone will have to take out my stitches."

Wren asked, "What do you say, Helen? I know she can't pull her own weight yet, but if you had to babysit a first-level fighter, wouldn't you want to keep her close?"

It wasn't that simple. Nightshade was worse than just a beginner—not worse in a fight, really, just harder to get along with. Wren was standing up for Nightshade only because she didn't know her yet.

Helen looked at Fred—big-hearted Fighter Fred. *He* wanted Nightshade along. Mak-Thar also had a soft spot for her, because when he'd been a mule, Nightshade would write stuff down for him and hold his *Adventurer's Guide* so he could read it.

Helen looked at Twilight. The elf shrugged. He was willing to leave the decision up to Helen. She could nix the deal right here and send Nightshade out onto the street.

Where she would probably get murdered by an assassin.

Helen asked, "Who hired that guy that Mak-Thar stabbed twenty-two times this morning?"

"Twenty-two?" asked Mak-Thar. "Are you certain?"

"I just made it up," said Helen. "Is twenty-two a real number?"

"Yes. It's an integer, in fact."

"Oh," said Helen. "Well, I'm sure its mother is very proud. But I still want to know who hired the assassin."

"Okay," said Nightshade. "Time to reveal my big back story: The assassin was sent by the mage I apprenticed under when I lived in Watergate—a wizard named Blackleg."

"His name is 'Blackleg'?" asked Twilight. "Seriously?"

Nightshade asked, "Did you know that 'Zauberei' is just the German word for 'wizard'?"

Twilight winced.

"Blackleg's not a big player in the Mages' Guild," said Wren. "But he can afford to send more assassins. He has a lot of cash."

"And he had a lot of magic scrolls," said Nightshade, "until I stole them."

"Ah!" said Mak-Thar. "Now all is clear."

"Weird," said Twilight. "Your super-secret back story actually *does* explain how you got all that equipment for our last adventure."

"Yeah, well, if you remember, when I drank from the magic spring and took my true form—" she gestured to indicate her cute leather outfit, "—everything in my Backpack of Holding disappeared, including the magic that made it a Backpack of Holding."

"Oh," said Fred. "So you can't make the wizard happy just by giving everything back."

"Nope. But giving stuff back was never the plan. I ran away to Basetown hoping that he couldn't track me."

"If I had ever owned a Backpack of Holding," said Mak-Thar, "I would track it down to the ends of the earth. In fact, I would track it down to the Negative Material Plane, if necessary."

"Yeah," said Nightshade. "So that's why I'm on the lamb."

"You're 'on the lam'," said Wren.

"The *W* is silent," said Fred.

"There is no *W*," said Wren.

"Actually," said Mak-Thar, "it's *B*."

"What's *B*?" asked Fred.

"The letter that isn't."

Helen was *so* glad she had never learned to spell. She asked, "Are you lying about this wizard?"

"No," said Nightshade. "I mean, I'm thinking of changing my alignment to chaotic? So I might start lying about stuff, like for practice? But I'm totally not lying about my back story."

"Chaotic is not an alignment," muttered Mak-Thar.

"And anyway, I'm planning to still be good," said Nightshade. "So I won't lie to you guys unless it's for a really good reason, like—I don't know—if your dog gets run over by a cart, and I'm not sure Twilight can save him, I might say your dog died, just so you don't get your hopes up. But otherwise—"

"Please shut up before I change my mind about letting you into the party," said Helen.

"I'm in?" asked Nightshade.

Wren smiled. "You're in, kid. Now don't louse it up."

Fred said, "Oh, you've been on adventures with Louse, too."

"So now we are six," said Mak-Thar. "And we have purchased our equipment. Should we discuss our plan?"

"Well, we still don't have any inside info," said Wren. "So we might need a plan for casing the joint, and then we can make another plan for doing the actual job."

"That seems very wise," said Mak-Thar.

"Really? Wisdom is my secondary dump stat."

"Are you sure?"

"Yeah," said Wren. "You only use it for saving throws, anyway."

"I suppose," said Mak-Thar. He sounded doubtful.

"But I *have* found somebody who knows a shortcut through the Impassable Mountain Range," said Wren.

"We followed that shortcut, too," said Helen. "Sage the Sage told us it goes only one way."

"How can a shortcut go only one way?" asked Wren.

"How can you hear silent letters?" asked Twilight. "This world is full of mysteries."

"She's not talking about *our* shortcut," said Nightshade. "I think she means a *different* shortcut."

"Oh." Helen was embarrassed. "So who's the person who knows a shortcut through the Impassable Mountain Range?"

"His name is Ludo," said Wren.

"And is he planning to join us?" asked Mak-Thar.

"Not yet," said Wren. "But I think he probably *will* join us once we break him out of jail."

CHAPTER SIX: IN WHICH OUR HEROES ATTEMPT A JAILBREAK.

IT WAS AFTER MIDNIGHT IN BASETOWN. All the fighters were in bed or in a tavern. All the mages were in bed or in a library. All the clerics were in bed or in a weird midnight ceremony. And all the thieves were on their way to work.

"This is so *cool!*" said Nightshade. "I didn't know you could do adventures in *town!*"

"But you *should* know," said Mak-Thar. "You got stabbed in town just this morning."

"Oh yeah. But that was more like *his* adventure than mine, you know?"

Fred was glad Nightshade had joined the party. He had taken her out on her first wilderness adventure, and he knew she was still trying to figure out how to fit in. He was glad to have a second chance with her. He felt like her education was only half baked.

Well, you couldn't bake education, of course. Fred was being— What was he being?

"What's that word that means when you say something's a cake even though everyone knows it's not?"

"If it's not a cake, why would you say it is?" asked Mak-Thar.

Twilight asked, "Are you speaking metaphorically, Fred?"

"No," said Fred. "I was just *thinking* metaphorically."

"You know," said Wren, "if everyone would think instead of speak, we'd be a lot quieter."

"Right!" said Nightshade. "Total silence. Stealthy like a cat!"

"That's a simile," said Twilight.

"It's pronounced 'smilodon'," said Mak-Thar.

"What's pronounced 'smilodon'?" asked Helen.

"The giant cat with long teeth," said Mak-Thar.

"I thought it was pronounced 'sabre-tooth tiger'," said Helen.

"'Smilodon' is a synonym," said Mak-Thar.

"So I was thinking cinnamon-ly?" asked Fred.

"You were thinking synonymously," said Mak-Thar.

"No he wasn't," said Twilight. "He was thinking metaphorically."

"Okay," said Fred. He was glad they had cleared that up.

"So if we're supposed to be quiet," said Nightshade, "does that mean you're going to narrate the plan while we act it out?"

"What?" asked Wren.

"You know: 'Once invisible, Nightshade will sneak past the guards.' And then cut to a visual of me sneaking past the guards."

"You can't cut to a visual of someone invisible," said Wren.

"Oh. I guess you're right."

"You can't 'cut to a visual' at all!" said Twilight. "This is a jailbreak, not a movie of a jailbreak!"

"Which is another reason I won't be narrating the plan as you act it out," said Wren. "A third reason I won't be narrating is that my part requires me to be quiet. I won't be doing things that might draw attention, like shouting 'Jailbreak!' in the middle of the night."

"Will you at least tell me why I'm carrying this sack of

potatoes?" asked Mak-Thar. "Or why you're wearing a fake beard?"

"Oh, you noticed?" asked Wren.

It was hard not to notice a woman wearing a bushy, brown beard.

"Yes," said Mak-Thar. He smiled. "It looks very attractive."

Mak-Thar continued to walk along the street. After about five steps, he stopped and turned around.

"Why did you all stop? And why are you all staring at me?"

"Sorry," said Fred. "I was just trying to figure something out, and I didn't know where to start."

Mak-Thar said, "Sometimes when I'm stuck on a problem, it helps to write down the variables."

"Yeah," said Fred. "I'll try that."

They started walking again.

A few minutes later, they passed the bank.

"Oo!" said Nightshade. "When we're done with the jailbreak, can we knock over the bank?"

"What?" asked Mak-Thar.

Helen moved very swiftly.

"Urk!" said Nightshade.

"Helen," said Wren, "would you please let go of Nightshade's throat?"

Helen let go of Nightshade's throat.

"Player-on-player contact is not cool," said Nightshade.

"Sorry," said Helen. "Reflexes."

"Reflexes made you grab my *throat*?"

Helen looked guilty. "Yeah, um, what I meant to say was that if any of you hear someone is thinking of attacking the bank, I'd like to know about it."

"That's what you meant to say instead of grabbing Nightshade's throat?" asked Twilight.

"Yeah."

"I don't think anyone would try to hit the bank," said Wren.

"The Mages' Guild would fall on them like a ton of books," said Mak-Thar.

"That's a smilodon," said Fred.

"Or we'd be on them like a smilodon," agreed Mak-Thar.

"The Thieves' Guild also needs a safe place to keep cash," said Wren. "It's not like we can trust our treasurer."

"Oh, okay," said Nightshade. "So no bank robbery, then."

"No bank robbery," said Helen.

Fred was surprised that Helen was so defensive of the bank. The fighters *did* trust their treasurer, and most of them kept their money at the Fighters' Guild—on the theory that anyone who was gutsy enough to steal from a building full of fighters would probably be fun to fight. But maybe Helen was just showing her civic pride.

Their arrival at the bank meant that they were now at Basetown Square. The bank was on one side of the square. The town hall was on another side. The side opposite the bank had the city guard headquarters. This included the jail, which had been built at Basetown Square possibly to deter bank robbers or possibly to deter the city council from becoming corrupt enough to get caught.

There was supposed to be a building opposite the town hall, too, but Basetown was still pretty new and they hadn't yet gotten around to figuring out what should be on the fourth side of the square. Did that make it a triangle?

Anyway, opposite the town hall was a sign that said *Future site of important civic building*. Behind the sign stood a clump of shacks hastily erected to take advantage of the location—a pawn shop, a bail bond joint, and offices for various private investigators and bounty hunters. One office advertised the services of a *Criminal-Defense Attorney*. Beside it was the office of a *Criminal Defense-Attorney*.

All the buildings were conveniently made of dry, flimsy wood, so the city council would be able to incinerate them all with one glowing ember, if they ever got around to deciding what they wanted to use the space for.

The three official buildings, by contrast, were made of stone. That made it harder to break into the bank or break out of the jail. Fred wasn't sure why the town hall needed to be made of stone. Were the walls there to protect the council members, or were they there to protect Basetown *from* the council members? Maybe both?

Someone had started a paving project. New cobblestones surrounded each building, giving the impression that the stone was seeping out of them and beginning to creep toward the center of the square.

"What are all these rocks on the ground for?" asked Helen.

"Those are cobblestones," said Nightshade.

"Are those like kidney stones?" asked Helen.

"No," said Twilight.

Wren asked, "Honestly, you've never seen pavement before?"

Helen shrugged. "I'm a barbarian."

"But I thought *everyone* had been to Watergate," said Wren.

"Oh," said Helen. "Is this how they did the streets of Watergate?"

Nightshade asked, "You thought they just found a plain of rocks and built the city on it?"

"Well, yeah."

Wren waved to get their attention. "Hello? Focus, please. I think we should get started. Does everyone know their part in the plan?"

"I need to make Nightshade invisible, and then continue carrying this sack of potatoes," said Mak-Thar. "But I still don't know why."

"Well, you're about to find out," said Wren. "Is everyone else ready?"

They were more-or-less ready.

"Okay. Do it, Mak-Thar."

"I'm going to intentionally fail my saving throw so the Invisibility spell works on me," said Nightshade.

"You don't need to fail the saving throw," said Mak-Thar. "The spell just works, assuming you don't resist."

"Okay, so I'm like totally unresisting, then. I look at my arm.

Am I invisible?"

"I have not cast the spell yet."

Twilight asked, "Can you also do a spell like Invisibility, but for sound?"

"I still have my super silent elf boots," said Nightshade.

"Can you wear them on your mouth?"

"Do you guys always argue this much?" asked Wren.

"Always," said Fred.

Wren shook her head. "This is why I go solo."

* * *

The second step of the plan was to wait around. Fred and Twilight had to wait with invisible Nightshade while Wren, Helen, and Mak-Thar got into position.

"Has it been three minutes yet?" asked Nightshade.

"I don't know," said Fred.

"As an immortal being, I experience time differently from humans," said Twilight.

"Oh yeah," said Nightshade. "Me too. That's why I was asking. Because as an elf, I wouldn't know."

"You're not an elf," said Twilight.

"I'm a round-eared elf," insisted Nightshade. "I'm just as short as you, and just as bad at telling time. *And* I've got elven boots."

"Which you stole from a human wizard!"

"Nope. My elven mom knitted them for me. Says so in my back story."

"Moms can't knit boots!" said Twilight.

"They can knit baby boots," said Fred.

"She's wearing *leather* boots."

"Oh, I think he's right," Fred said to the patch of air that was probably Nightshade. "I don't think it's possible to knit leather."

"Well maybe she *made* them, then. I don't have to be an expert on arts and crafts to wear boots."

"So your mother's a cobbler," said Twilight.

"No. She's a bootmaker."

"That's what a cobbler is!"

"A cobbler makes cobblestones," said Nightshade. "Duh."

"My mom bakes fruit cobblers," said Fred. "So maybe a cobbler is more than one thing. Anyway, it's been three minutes."

"Oh, goody! Okay, guys, do your diversion. I'm going in!"

They waited for Nightshade to approach the city guard headquarters. After a few moments, Twilight said, "Well, she must be gone. I can't hear her chattering."

"I heard that!" called Nightshade.

"You're supposed to be quiet!"

"I am! I'm as silent as a simile!"

Fred shrugged. "I guess it's our turn."

Twilight put a hand on Fred's shoulder and looked into Fred's eyes. "Let's do this for Ludo."

"For Ludo," agreed Fred.

They walked over to a window of the city guard building.

"Do you know Ludo?" asked Fred.

"Never met him," said Twilight.

"Me neither," said Fred. "I hope he didn't do anything too bad. Sometimes people are in jail for a reason."

"Wren wouldn't ask us to free a convicted murderer," said Twilight. "Would she?"

"Well, she probably wouldn't ask us to free an *evil* murderer," said Fred.

"Are there good murderers?"

"I dunno," said Fred. "Everyone assumes *I'm* good, but I've killed a few people. In fact, I killed a man just this morning."

"But he was an assassin," said Twilight.

"Sure," said Fred. "He was a bad murderer, and I'm a good murderer."

"You did what had to be done," said Twilight. "You can't let it haunt you."

Fred shrugged. "Killing people doesn't haunt me. But maybe it should."

"Sometimes I still see Paul's face," said Twilight.

"So do I," said Fred.

Paul had been the thief on their first adventure together. He had killed Mak-Thar, and then Twilight had killed Paul.

Paul was probably still dead. He wasn't the sort of guy that you would haul into a temple and cast Raise Dead on.

Mak-Thar had been reincarnated as a mule, which had led to their second adventure, but the point was that Twilight had been forced to kill a man who had pretended to be their friend.

"The worst part," said Twilight, "is that sometimes I'm sorry I killed him, and sometimes I'm glad."

"I think I'm glad," said Fred. "Someone had to stop him, and I couldn't."

Twilight gazed across the square up at the starry sky. "What pain it is to be immortal in a world where life is cheap!"

"Guys?" asked Nightshade. "Diversion?"

"Oh, you're back!" said Fred.

"Well, I was waiting inside, but you were taking an *hour*, so I thought I'd better come back and check on you."

It wasn't an hour. Fred was pretty sure it hadn't been more than three minutes.

"Sorry," said Fred. "We're ready now. For Ludo."

"What?"

"For Ludo," said Fred. "That dwarf we're trying to rescue."

"Oh, him. Yeah. For Ludo."

Fred waited to see if Nightshade was going to say anything else.

She didn't.

It was weird talking to someone invisible.

"Is she gone?" he asked.

"I hope so," said Twilight.

"I heard that!" called Nightshade from the entrance of the building.

Twilight rolled his eyes. "We'd better do it. She's going to need all the diversion we can give her."

Fred looked up at the window. The headquarters was one of those fancy places where you had to walk up steps to get inside.

This meant that the entry floor was above ground level, and thus the windows were so high that you couldn't see into the building from the street—although people inside could look out just fine.

No one was looking out right now, even though Fred and Twilight had been talking directly under their window. That was good. Guards should not be diverted until you were ready to make your diversion.

Wren had described Fred's part of the plan as a supporting role. Specifically, he was supposed to support Twilight's weight on his shoulders while the elf looked through the window.

"I'm ready," said Fred.

"May Selene watch over us," said Twilight.

"Yeah," said Fred. "Unless Ludo was arrested for mugging old ladies or something. In which case, I hope Selene will look the other way."

"Do you really think—?"

"Diversion," said Fred.

"Right." Twilight swallowed. "Diversion."

The elf placed his hands on Fred's head and gracefully vaulted onto Fred's shoulders.

Fred grabbed Twilight's ankles to steady him. The elf's weight shifted as he unslung his bow and drew an arrow from his quiver.

"Actually," said Twilight, "this isn't right. Archers don't face their targets head on. Could you turn?"

Fred turned.

"No. Other way."

Fred turned the other way. Twilight wobbled, then steadied himself.

"Good. Stop."

Fred stopped.

Twilight fitted the arrow to his bowstring.

A guard walked by on his way to work.

"Evening, Fred."

"Evening, Cuthbert."

"You're out a little late this evening."

Fred tried to shrug, but he had an elf on his shoulders, so he tried to shrug with his eyebrows. "Town adventure."

"Oh." Cuthbert looked up at Twilight.

"This is Twilight," said Fred. "He's on the adventure with me."

"I gathered that."

Fred said, "Twilight, this is Cuthbert. He used to be a fighter before he joined the city guard."

"Um ... pleased to meet you?"

"Likewise," said Cuthbert. "Fred, you aren't planning anything that will make us charge out and get killed, are you?"

"What? No. This is a nonlethal diversion."

"Oh. I see." Cuthbert looked up at Twilight again. "But ..."

"Yes?" asked Fred.

"Well, see here. If I catch you making mischief outside our building, I have to try to arrest you, see?"

"Oh," said Fred. "Is that how it works?"

"Yeah."

"Oh. Sorry. I'm new at crime."

"But Fred, we'd really appreciate it if you didn't go *into* crime. A little disorderly conduct is fine, now and again, but if the Fighters' Guild is going to start raiding HQ, things could become awkward."

Fred thought about this. "I see what you mean. You guys could get hurt."

"We could," said Cuthbert.

"Twilight was just going to shoot an arrow to knock over an oil lamp," Fred explained. "You have a stone floor, so we figured you'd be able to put out the fire pretty quick."

"That's still vandalism and attempted arson."

"It is?"

"It is," said Cuthbert.

"Gee," said Fred. "That sounds pretty bad."

"Should I put my arrow back?" asked Twilight.

"I think so," said Fred. "Maybe we haven't thought this through."

Twilight shifted his feet, and Fred heard the clink of arrows.

"Should I come down?" asked Twilight.

"Yeah," said Fred.

Twilight climbed down.

"Hello, again," he said, now that he and Cuthbert were both standing on the cobbles together.

Cuthbert nodded.

"But disorderly conduct is fine?" asked Fred.

"This is Basetown," said Cuthbert. "Disorderly conduct is practically required."

"Okay," said Fred. "Thanks."

"No problem," said Cuthbert. "Can I ask one more favor?"

"Sure," said Fred.

"Could you do your diversion before I have to go on duty?"

CHAPTER SEVEN: IN WHICH OUR HEROES WORK THROUGH SOME BARS.

YELLIN' HELEN, barbarian warrior of the wild steppe, was crouched in a dark alley helping Wren saw through the bars of a basement window. Helen was a long-limbed woman who liked having room to swing her two-handed sword. In order to fit the tiny saw between the bars, she had to crouch knee-to-knee and shoulder-to-shoulder with Wren. The position was not very comfortable.

However, it was a good opportunity. In her product-placement voice she said, "In this dark alley, I feel confined. Luckily, I have underwear that sets me free. Nycadaemon Knickers: They're like a jailbreak for your skin."

"Do you have to do that *now*?" asked Wren.

"Yeah. On a one-shot, I like to get my product placement in before the action starts."

"Helen is a professional underwear model," said Mak-Thar.

"I know," said Wren. "Every woman in Basetown knows. That's how they pay her salary—because we all buy their underwear."

"Oh," said Mak-Thar conversationally, "are you wearing Nycadaemon Knickers?"

Wren's body tensed and there was a pause in her sawing. "Did you just ask about my knickers?"

"Well, Helen brought it up," said Mak-Thar, somewhat flustered. "I was just being polite by engaging in the conversation."

Wren said, "When *we're* talking about knickers, that's girl talk. When *you* talk about knickers ..."

"What?"

"Hey," said Helen, "why don't you ask Mak-Thar about *his* knickers? Then you'd be even."

Mak-Thar's eyes went wide enough that Helen could see them in the dark alley. (She could see his eyes, not his knickers.)

"Aw, I guess I should cut him some slack," said Wren. "Sometimes I forget that other people also have low charisma." She went back to sawing.

"I try to overlook low charisma scores," said Mak-Thar, "except in cases where the rules state that a negative reaction is mandatory."

"Isn't he sweet?" asked Helen. "That's why we like adventuring with him."

"And I enjoy adventuring with you, too," said Mak-Thar, "despite the fact that you insist on mocking me."

Helen had been afraid that mocking Mak-Thar would be more difficult once he'd stopped being a mule, but in some ways, it was actually easier.

The bar she was sawing started to wiggle, which meant that she had sawed most of the way through. Helen slid the tiny saw free and rested it on her boot. Then she seized the bar and ripped it out of the window.

"Hey!" said Wren. "That deforms the metal!"

"So?" asked Helen. "It's not like you need this bar."

"We need to put them back when we're done," said Wren. "If they don't notice that the bars are damaged, we might be able to use this window again."

"Use it for what?" asked Helen.

"For breaking into or out of jail," said Wren.

Helen was not planning to break into or out of jail, but Wren had an entire guild of thieves to consider.

Mak-Thar said, "I must admit I am a bit perplexed about this part of the plan. I thought Nightshade was supposed to get the dwarf out through the front door."

"There's no way a first-level thief can pull that off," said Wren. "Nightshade is just a diversion."

"I thought Fred and Twilight were the diversion," said Helen.

"They're a diversion, too," said Wren.

"You can never have too many diversions," said Mak-Thar.

"Does Nightshade *know* she's the diversion?" asked Helen.

"Oh, don't tell her!" said Wren. "I don't want her to think I don't have confidence in her."

"But you don't," said Helen.

"No," said Wren. "Should I?"

Helen wasn't sure.

Wren said, "Look, if she gets Ludo out by herself, that's great, right? Then this window is just our backup plan. But I didn't get to eighth level by relying on other people to get the job done."

"You're at eighth level?" asked Mak-Thar. "That's very impressive!"

"Thanks," said Wren. "I put a lot of work into it."

Over the patient sound of Wren's sawing, a melody floated through the air.

"Is that a flute?" asked Wren.

"I believe so," said Mak-Thar. "And as an eighth-level thief, you have a four-in-six chance of being able to hear it."

Helen could hear the flute even without being a thief. And now she could also hear Fred singing:

In Scarlet Tooown, where I was born,
There was a faaair maid dwellin'.
Made every laaad cry "Well-a-day!"
For love of Barrrb'ra Allen.

Wren asked, "Are your boys improvising?"

"I wouldn't exactly call it improvisation," said Mak-Thar. "Although Fred *is* using a touch of rubato."

Wren shrugged. "This might be better than a fire, anyway. The song should cover our noise."

Helen thought the sound of their sawing was already safely covered up by the prisoner's snores. She'd never known a dwarf who didn't snore.

Helen started on the next bar. The music paused for a moment, as though the first verse had just been a warmup. When the song resumed, it had different lyrics:

In dear Basetooown, where I call home,
There is a strooong girl dwellin'.
Makes all the monnnsters run away
For fear of Yellllin' Helen!

That was pretty good, Helen thought.

"*Now* Fred's improvising," said Mak-Thar.

There was another pause, during which Helen could imagine Fred and Twilight consulting on the lyrics.

'Twas on a verrry sunny day
A day when feeeet start smellin'.
Some goblins thooought that they would play
With our barbarrrian Helen.

And Helen swiiiftly drew her sword.
And swiftly sheeee did stab them.
And when they diiied, she took their coins.
As fast as sheeee could grab them.

Yeah. Helen was liking this.

And from their graaaves, their corpses rose.
But Helen's sworrrd rose higher.
Those zombie goooblins died again.
They could not paaacify her.

And that's the waaay I'll end my tale
Of dear old Yellllin' Helen!
Now bring me wiiine or bring me ale,
Or else it werrren't worth tellin'.

Helen found the song very inspiring. She had already sawed through the bottom half of her bar.

A quiet and excited voice echoed off the stone walls inside the basement: "Once past the guards, Nightshade will use her awesome dexterity score to silently remove the key ring from its hook."

Keys clinked.

"Then she'll noiselessly approach the cell where the prisoner lies sleeping."

"Nightshade!" Wren hissed. "Don't narrate!"

Unlike Nightshade's voice, Wren's was probably not loud enough to be heard above the snoring.

"At the jail cell door, Nightshade will pad her experience points by attempting to pick the lock."

"Should she be doing that?" asked Mak-Thar. "How long does lock picking take?"

"Usually one to four combat rounds," said Wren.

"Oh," said Mak-Thar. "That's not as bad as I thought."

The snoring stopped. A worried voice inside the jail cell asked, "Who's there?"

"I'm Nightshaaade! I'm here to rescue you. Just let me finish failing this Lock Picking check. There! Failed it."

A moment later, the keys jangled and the lock clicked open.

Out in Basetown Square, Fred started to sing again.

Alas, my elf, you do me wrong
To cast your spell so discourteously.
Now I must love you all day long
Delighting in your company.

"Wow, that guy sounds really good," said the dwarf.

"Do you like him?" asked Nightshade. "He's our diversion. We need to get out of here before he runs out of songs. Follow me."

"I can't even see you."

"Oh, right. Mak-Thar? Are you out there?"

"Yes," said Mak-Thar, in the hoarse voice of a guy who's trying to shout really quietly.

"How do I turn off my invisibility?"

"According to *The Adventurer's Guide*, you remain invisible until you attack or cast a spell."

Charm Person was my downfall.
Charm Person was my delight.
Charm Person made me fall
In love with the elf who cast Charm Person.

"You can't go wrong with the classics," murmured Mak-Thar.

"What?" asked Nightshade. "Did you say I need to attack the dwarf?"

"Let's not be hasty!" said the dwarf. "I'll just follow the sound of your voice."

"No talking!" said Wren.

"Right," said Nightshade. "We have to be as silent as two sabre-tooth tigers. … Can you see these keys?"

"Yes. They appear to be floating in midair."

"Cool! You can just follow them, then."

Alas, dear mage, you do me wrong
To cast your spell so discourteously.
Now I must stand here all day long,
Forced to endure your company.

"This verse always bothers me," said Mak-Thar. "Hold Person doesn't really last 'all day long.'"

"Unlike Invisibility?" asked Wren.

"Unlike Invisibility," agreed Mak-Thar, "which could theoretically be permanent."

Only theoretically. Helen had never known an adventurer who could go very long without attacking someone.

Hold Person was my downfall.
Hold Person was my demise.
Hold Person made me stand still
At the mercy of he who cast Hold Person.

A jangling of keys indicated that Nightshade had returned. "Wren? We got a problem."

"Spill it."

"That's so cool! I love the way you talk thieves' cant."

Wren sighed. "Nightshade, please tell us the problem."

"Okay. So, like, we went to the front door? But it was totally crowded. Everybody's out on the steps watching Fred and Twilight."

Evil cleric, you do me wrong
To cast your spell so discourteously.
Now I fight monsters skinny and long
Writhing so very disturbingly.

Helen couldn't blame the guards. If she weren't so busy sawing through bars, she'd be out there, too.

"No problem," said Wren. "We just go to the backup plan."

"Cool! What's the backup plan?"

"You guys come to the back, and we lift you up. That's the plan."

"Oh, that makes sense," said Nightshade. "I wondered what you guys were doing by the window."

Wren said, "Helen, I need you to drop in there and give the short people a boost."

Helen grinned. "Sounds like fun!"

Sticks to Snakes was the cleric's delight.
Sticks to Snakes was my demise.
Sticks to Snakes was too much too fight.
Beware of the one who turns sticks to snakes.

Helen ripped out the bar she had been working on and slid through the window. Her boots landed on a stone floor, gritty and damp.

She said, "Ludo's first."

"Whoa! What in the world are you?"

"I'm Yellin' Helen."

"You're darn near naked! Invisible girl, are you an amazon, too?"

"No way," said Nightshade. "I'm an elf."

"I'm not an amazon," said Helen. "I'm a barbarian."

From the alley—which was now at Helen's eye level—Mak-Thar said, "Technically, 'amazon' just means 'breastless one', so it should be obvious that Helen isn't an amazon."

"What are you talking about?" asked Wren. "Amazon means 'female warrior'."

"A warrior is any second-level fighter. No gender distinction is made. The word 'amazon' derives from the erroneous belief that a woman could not use a bow unless she removed her breasts."

"Ew!" said Nightshade. "Content flagged as inappropriate!"

Wren said, "Please go stand over there until I need your potatoes."

Alas, red dragon, you do me wrong
To cast your spell so discourteously.
Now I am trapped here in your lair,
Where I fear you'll devour me.

Helen laced her fingers together to make a stirrup. "So do you want to be rescued, or not?"

"Er, rescued, of course. I'm supposed to put my foot in your hands?"

"Yep. Then climb up my shoulders and out through the window."

"How do I do that without touching your skin?"

"It's just skin!" Why was he making such a big deal of this? "Pretend I'm a horse."

"Or you could pretend that you're a monkey climbing up her shoulder," suggested Nightshade.

"You amazons are better at pretending than I am," said the dwarf. But he put his boot in her hand.

Helen couldn't really see him. He could see *her*, of course—dwarves can see in the dark—but Helen couldn't see him. She could smell him, though. He'd been in jail long enough to get musty, but not long enough to grow moldy. His leather boots and belt had recently been treated with a nice grease that would keep them supple. And there was something on his hands that reminded her of silver polish.

Wizard Lock was my downfall.
Wizard Lock was my demise.
Wizard Lock blocked my escape
From the dragon who cast Wizard Lock.

Ludo's boots were on Helen's shoulders when they heard the voice from the hall:

"Ludo? You awake?"

"I'll hide in shadows!" said Nightshade.

"You're invisible," said Helen.

"Oh. Right. *You* should hide in shadows, then."

"Ludo?" The call came from the hall outside. Lantern light flickered against the bars of the tiny window in the prison door.

Ludo ducked his head back inside the room and called, "Jerry? What's up?"

"There's a fighter out in the square singing folk songs."

Alas, storm giant, you do me wrong
To blow me off so discourteously.
When I've been climbing for so long
Just to share in your company.

"Yeah I hear him."

"An elf is accompanying him on the flute," said the guard, who was now right outside the door. "You can come watch if you promise not to escape or anything."

Helen wasn't sure what to do. This looked like it was about to turn into a fight, and Helen did not want to fight with a dwarf on her shoulders. It would be awkward.

"Eh," said Ludo. "You know what? By the time we get the manacles on, they'll probably be done. Why don't you go back and enjoy it? I can hear pretty good from inside."

"You sure?"

"Yeah, I'm sure."

Summon Storm was my demise.
Summon Storm was my downfall.
Climbing cliffs is most unwise
When the storm giant casts Summon Storm.

The lantern light grew dimmer as footsteps receded down the hall.

"Wow, that was close!" said Nightshade. "I thought I was gonna have to blackjack him."

Helen helped the dwarf crawl out the window.

"Hi. I'm Wren."

"Nice beard," said Ludo.

"It's fake," said Wren.

"I should hope so," said Ludo.

"We're looking for a mountain guide."

"So you're not just rescuing me out of the goodness of your hearts?"

"Wren and I are neutral," said Mak-Thar.

"And we have low charisma," said Wren. "So it would be really nice if you would take that into account if you're feeling any negative reactions toward us."

Inside the cell, Helen said, "You're next, invisible amazon."

"No, you go ahead. I got this."

Helen couldn't see Nightshade, but she knew how tall she wasn't.

"You sure?"

"I need to practice my Climb Walls skill."

"Okay." Helen reached a hand out through the window. "Ludo? Little help?"

The dwarf took her hand. Using his leverage, Helen climbed out of the jail cell.

"And then Nightshade sneaks out the back window and we make our getaway!" said Nightshade, still inside the jail cell.

"Wait!" said Wren. "The potatoes!"

"So *now* you need the potatoes?" asked Mak-Thar.

"Yes. Drop them down to Nightshade."

"Very well." Mak-Thar did so.

"And you'll need this," said Wren. She removed the fake beard and dropped it through the window as well.

"What do I do with them?" asked Nightshade.

"I have to spell it out for you?" asked Wren. "You put the potatoes in the bed."

"Wren," said Helen, "that's not nearly as obvious as you just made it sound."

"Are you sure?"

"I'm sure."

"Oh, sorry. Nightshade, you put the potatoes in the bed and then give them the beard. Now do you see?"

"I see that you think a dwarf looks like a sack of potatoes with a beard," said Ludo. "We are going to get along so well."

Chapter Eight: In which our heroes hire a mountain guide.

ON THE FOLLOWING DAY, Fighter Fred was once again walking down that dark alley by Good Neighbors Pawn Shop. Even at noon, the alley was full of shadows. Yellin' Helen was in the lead, walking with cat-like grace—if you consider a sabre-tooth tiger to be a cat. Fred had never seen a sabre-tooth tiger, but if he saw one right now, he wouldn't be worried, because Helen looked like she could deal with it.

They were not attacked by a sabre-tooth tiger. Helen found the steps, went down, and pushed open the door to the Den of Thieves.

Morc the Orc shouted, "Don't throw! It's Helen!"

Fred followed her in and shut the door. "Sorry. She doesn't know the secret knock."

Helen glided through the tavern like water flowing downstream. On her way past Morc, she rapped on the bar: *Knock, knock, knock. Knock. Knock.*

Morc grinned. "She knows it. She just don't use it."

"*That's* the secret knock?" asked Fred.

"Three short and two long."

That wasn't how Fred would describe it. He rapped a rhythm on the bar: *One-and-two, three, four.* "Like that?"

"Fred learned the secret knock!" Morc's scarred face glowed with pride.

"Drinks on the house!" shouted a high-level thief, using Ventriloquism to make his voice seem to come from the bartender.

"Drinks are on Louse!" said Morc.

"Why me?" asked Louse.

"Because you're the one who just stole Fred's coin pouch."

Fred left them to their argument and followed Helen into the back room.

Have you ever ducked inside a building just as the rain starts to come down? You know that feeling of coziness you get when you hear the rain smacking onto the roof? Well, this was nothing like that, because there was an argument going on in the back room, too.

"That's outrageous!" said Mak-Thar, in a voice that reminded Fred of the days when Mak-Thar had been a mule.

"You're overreacting," said Wren, in a bland sort of voice that no one was paying any attention to.

"How could anyone be so irresponsibly selfish?"

Mak-Thar's outrage was focused on the dwarf they had stolen from the town jail. He wore a dainty blue hat that sat atop his head like a pancake. His beard was brushed and lightly oiled. His vest was trimmed with silver buttons. His boots, by contrast, were heavy clomping things designed for tramping over mountains.

Twilight said, "I can't believe they arrested a jeweler just for doing his job."

"His job?" asked Mak-Thar. "Destroying our entire economy is his job?"

"Hey, catch us up," said Helen. "What did Ludo do?"

"He sold rings," said Twilight.

"He sold *gold* rings," said Mak-Thar.

"That he made himself," said Twilight.

"From …" said Mak-Thar.

"From what?" asked Helen. "From lead? From tin? From his toenail clippings?"

"It's Twilight's turn," said Mak-Thar. "I say, 'From …' and then Twilight is supposed to tell you."

Twilight shrugged. "He was selling gold rings he made from gold."

"Made from gold *pieces*," said Mak-Thar. "He was taking *one* gold piece and making it into a ring that he would sell for *three hundred*."

"Cool!" said Fred. "Then you could make three hundred more rings!"

Ludo gave Fred a satisfied smile and nodded.

"Destroying the economy is *not* cool!" said Mak-Thar.

The door opened and someone moving very quietly came in, shut the door, and sat down in a chair.

Everyone stared at the chair, which still looked empty.

"What are you staring at me for?" asked a voice from the seemingly empty chair. It was Nightshade.

Helen said, "We're staring because we've never seen an invisible woman come late to a meeting before."

"My thief isn't late. She's been sitting here the entire time. You didn't notice her because she's invisible."

Twilight said, "But we just saw you walk in the door!"

"You're supposed to keep player knowledge separate from character knowledge," said Nightshade.

"What are you talking about?" Twilight was exasperated.

"There's no way you could know it was me who opened the door," explained Nightshade. "If I say I was sitting here the entire time, you have to take my word for it."

Mak-Thar said, "In the first place, he doesn't have to take your word for it. I'm sure he should be allowed a wisdom check—and with substantial bonuses because *we all saw you walk in the door.*"

"But you didn't! I'm invisible!"

"In the second place," said Mak-Thar, "'player knowledge' does not refer to conclusions that any reasonable person could deduce from available information. 'Player knowledge' refers to information that can be found in *The Adventurer's Guide*. So anyone who tells you to ignore player knowledge is essentially telling you to play suboptimally and die."

"I'm pretty sure ignoring player knowledge is good role-playing," said Nightshade.

"Argh!" said Twilight. "We aren't *playing!*"

"We're arguing," explained Fred.

"We're supposed to be planning," said Wren. "Could we start, please? Mak-Thar has a map."

"Yes I do," Mak-Thar said, somewhat stiffly. He reached

into a pouch, found a piece of paper, unfolded it, and spread it on the table. "We are here." He put his finger on a hexagon labeled *Basetown*. "We want to be here." He put his finger on a hexagon labeled *Got Lost*.

"We want to get lost?" asked Fred.

"No," said Nightshade. "That's where we got lost and found the evil temple. But there wasn't enough room to write all that down." (Nightshade had been making notes for Mak-Thar because he had been a mule at the time.)

"Between here and there, you will note a mountain range, labeled *Impassable*." Mak-Thar looked at Ludo. "Am I to understand that this is a misnomer?"

"Is that a geological term?" asked Ludo. "I learned geology in dwarven."

Mak-Thar asked, "Is the Impassable Mountain Range actually passable?"

"I see," said Ludo. "You're looking for a shortcut."

"Yes," said Mak-Thar. "Because we don't want to combine the temple heist with a full-blown wilderness adventure."

"We'd like one that's only half blown," explained Fred. "Or even one-quarter blown, if you can manage it."

Ludo put a stubby finger on the map. "What does this shape mean?"

"That's a hexagon," said Mak-Thar. "Surely you've seen hex paper before."

Ludo carefully removed his finger from the map and backed away. "Is this witchcraft?"

The term *hex* had once confused Fred as well. "Hex paper just means 'paper with shapes on it.' It's not magical."

Mak-Thar pursed his lips. "I confess I am having misgivings."

"Is that like bunions?" asked Helen.

"No," said Twilight.

"I was quite pleased with how smoothly everything went last night," said Mak-Thar. "But instead of getting a mountain guide, we seem to have freed a criminal who can't even read maps."

"I can read maps," said Ludo. "But real maps have runes and

actual drawings of what the mountains look like. The mountains on your map all look like little triangles. How can you tell them apart?"

"Maybe the map wasn't the best idea," said Wren. "Maybe we should just let Ludo lead us through the mountains, and when we get to the other side, we can look for a landmark you guys recognize."

"That should work," said Fred. He wasn't the best at reading maps, but it was obvious that a shortcut through the mountains would make the journey shorter. In fact, that was probably why it was called a *short*cut.

"I suppose that could work," said Mak-Thar. He turned to Ludo. "You *do* know a route through the mountains?"

"I do." The dwarf was quite proud of his expertise.

"Then let us address the issue of compensation," said Mak-Thar. He reached into his enormous backpack and pulled out *The Adventurer's Guide*, which he opened to the page entitled NPM Retainers. "Let's see ... I don't think you're a mercenary. Are you a member of the Sages' Guild?"

"I'm not in any guild."

"Not even the Jewelers' Guild?" asked Mak-Thar.

Ludo shook his head. "They hate me."

Wren looked over Mak-Thar's shoulder. "How about 'Navigator'? He's kind of like a navigator, but for mountains instead of oceans."

"How much does a navigator get paid?" asked Ludo.

"One hundred fifty gold pieces per month," said Mak-Thar.

"I earn twice that on a single ring," said Ludo.

"Yes, but that's not *legal*," said Mak-Thar. "Guiding people is legal."

"Is that supposed to be a plus?" asked Ludo. "Maybe I want to keep breaking the law so I can join the Thieves' Guild."

"Dwarves can't be thieves," said Mak-Thar. "Dwarves are either fighters or NPMs."

"Okay. So, what if I decide to be a fighter?" asked Ludo. "Do I get paid more?"

Wren checked *The Adventurer's Guide.* "Dwarven mercenaries cost five gold pieces."

"Ah," said Mak-Thar. "So over a month, that would be one hundred fifty gold pieces, the same as it is for navigators."

Wren shook her head. "Not five per day. Mercenaries are paid five gold pieces per month. Or ten for hazardous duty."

"Really?" asked Mak-Thar. "I can't even eat *breakfast* for ten gold pieces a month."

"Couldn't Ludo just join the party?" asked Twilight.

"I'm afraid not," said Mak-Thar. "We already have six."

"A party can't have seven?" asked the dwarf. "Seven seems just right, to me."

"Seven is too many," said Mak-Thar.

"Seven is better than thirteen," said Twilight. "I think dwarves prefer larger parties than you are used to."

Mak-Thar frowned and flipped to a different section of *The Adventurer's Guide.* "No. It says here that dwarves travel in groups of one to six."

"What does it say about elves?" asked Twilight.

"Parties of elves are one to four," said Mak-Thar.

"Well, that's ridiculous," said Twilight. "Four elves isn't a party. It's not even a clique."

Ludo said, "I'm thinking the secret way through the mountains is valuable information. It seems like the sort of thing you should pay three hundred gold pieces for."

"Three hundred gold pieces is quite a lot," said Mak-Thar.

Wren shrugged. "Well, if the guards haven't noticed what we did to the bars, I suppose we can put him back the way we got him out."

"One fifty sounds very fair," said Ludo. "When do we leave?"

Wren smiled. "I'm ready to go now."

"Me too," said Fred. "I lost my lucky walking stick on my last adventure, so I don't need to go back to the Fighters' Guild for anything—as long as Mak-Thar will let me borrow a treasure sack."

"Of course," said Mak-Thar. "I need to stop by the stables to pick up our mule, but otherwise I am ready to go. All my spells are fully prepared."

"Everything I own is in this backpack," said Nightshade. Presumably she gestured at her backpack then—they still couldn't see her. "So I'm always ready!"

Twilight said, "I, too, am but a wanderer in these lands."

"That means he's ready," said Fred.

Helen grinned. "Let's go overthrow that evil temple!"

Chapter Nine: In which Mak-Thar is Mak-Thar and Nightshade is invisible.

And so the brave adventurers set out on their journey. Ludo had put away his blue pancake hat and was now wearing a green alpine hat with a brown feather. Helen walked in front with an easy, loose-shouldered gait. Wren and Nightshade trailed behind, discussing levels and advancement in the Thieves' Guild. Twilight looked at wildflowers growing in the meadows along the road. Cows looked at Twilight.

Fred just walked. It was a nice day for a walk, and he liked being outdoors with his friends.

"I recommend a pentagon-and-two formation," said Mak-Thar.

"Really?" asked Helen.

"Yes. You should take point because you have a lot of hit points, and because your Woodcraft skill might give you plusses when checking for surprise."

"I bet you say that to all the girls," said Helen.

"I'm not sure what you're implying," said Mak-Thar.

"He's never said that to *me*," said Wren.

"Do you have a Woodcraft skill?" Mak-Thar asked.

"Helen was jesting you," explained Fred.

"Jesting is fine," said Mak-Thar, "as long as it does not impair her perception checks. Fred, I want you and Twilight guarding the rear. Twilight's Woodcraft skill—and his enhanced elven senses—will give him advantages in detecting potential ambushes."

"Can we take turns?" asked Helen. "Ever since he bought those green elf pants, I've been wanting to guard Twilight's rear."

Wren and Nightshade giggled.

Mak-Thar was thoroughly confused. "They are just regular pants, as far as I know. His armor class has not improved, and so he is still not well-suited for going in front."

"I think he's very well suited," said Helen.

"Is that some sort of double entendre?" asked Mak-Thar.

Wren said, "That whooshing you hear is the sound of everything going over Mak-Thar's head."

Fred didn't hear any whooshing, so he assumed that Wren was speaking … metamorphically? That didn't sound right.

Fred asked, "Is *metamorphic* a word?"

"It's a type of rock," said Ludo.

Well, that made sense. Helen's jokes were like rocks whooshing over Mak-Thar's head.

"The thieves should be on the flanks," said Mak-Thar. "Now, Nightshade probably needs to be protected, so we'll put her on the left side, in front of Fred."

Fred wasn't sure how to protect Nightshade when he couldn't see her, but he approved of the principle.

"That leaves Wren and Twilight on the right," said Mak-Thar.

"Right," said Wren.

"As specialists," said Mak-Thar, "Ludo and I should go in the middle. Ludo should be on the left because the Impassable Mountain Range is on our left." He pointed at the mountains in the distance.

"It doesn't matter," said Ludo. "We're still a day away from the trailhead."

"I think it's very important for you to accustom yourself to this marching order," said Mak-Thar. "It will help you keep your bearings. Also, while you are watching the mountains, you will be able to simultaneously help watch our left flank, because you will be able to see through Nightshade."

"I'm still imagining her as this nine-foot-tall chick in spiky battle armor," said Ludo.

"Gee," said Fred. "You're going to be disappointed."

"Spiky battle armor sounds kind of cool," said Nightshade. "But it's not my character's style. Nightshade is all about basic black."

"And all about referring to herself in third person," said Twilight. "I thought we cured you of that."

"Sorry," said Nightshade. "I'm still getting used to playing a thief."

"*Being* a thief," said Twilight. "You're *being* a thief."

"That's what I said. So, Ludo, imagine this cute and perky round-eared elf dressed in stylish black leather."

"Well, at least you're dressed," said Ludo.

"I don't think your marching order will work," said Helen. "Ludo won't be able to handle looking at my legs all day."

Ludo shrugged. "If the sight of your skin gets to be too much for me, I'll walk behind the mule."

"Yes, I'll have Evenstar," said Mak-Thar. "I forgot to mention that, but I have it written down."

He didn't need to mention it. Everyone could see that he was holding the mule's rope.

"This is just like old times," said Twilight.

And so the brave adventurers continued setting out on their journey, but now they had a marching order. Fred did not think it a coincidence that Mak-Thar had put himself next to Wren.

* * *

Walking behind Nightshade was really cool!—not for any reason that Helen might turn into an inappropriate comment, but rather because Nightshade was invisible. Fred was fascinated by the way her footprints appeared on the road. Occasionally, she would bend a branch or walk through the grass, and it looked like the plants were moving themselves!

Fred was theoretically supposed to be guarding the rear, but he was pretty sure Twilight could handle it. Anyway, nothing ever attacked from the rear unless you were running away.

They camped in the same place they had camped on their last visit to the Wombat Wilderness, and they got attacked by skeletons again. Maybe they were even the same skeletons. Fred didn't know. He was pretty good at recognizing faces, but he wasn't so good at recognizing skulls.

Twilight drove the skeletons away almost immediately by waving his arms and acting holy. Ludo was impressed. So everything got off to a good start.

However, on the following morning, things got weird. Nightshade's black leather pants walked into camp wearing a bra.

Well, pants can't wear bras, of course. It was Nightshade wearing the bra. But all they could see was her boots and pants with the bra floating above.

"Why are you all staring at me?"

Evenstar the mule saw the floating bra, snorted, and shied away.

"Easy there!" said Mak-Thar, firmly holding the mule's rope.

"Um," said Helen, "let me guess. You went off into the woods to change your underwear."

"Of course," said Nightshade. "But I don't see why it's any business of yours."

"Oh that makes sense," said Mak-Thar. "When you took off your pants, they became visible again."

"Yeah," Nightshade admitted. "I couldn't figure out how to change without taking off my pants and boots. But I'm still invisible from the waist up!"

Wren said, "Your bra strap is showing, dear."

"It is? Eek!" The bra changed shape as Nightshade tried to cover herself. "Eek! My hands are invisible! Don't look." Nightshade turned her back, which meant they could all see her bra from the inside. And Fred didn't *want* to look, because that was really creepy. But when something is creepy, it's kind of hard not to stare, you know? That's how medusas get most of their victims.

Nightshade's pants and bra ran off into the forest.

"What I don't understand," said Mak-Thar, "is why her shirt did not become visible also."

"She changed her bra without taking her shirt off," Wren explained.

"How is that even possible?" asked Mak-Thar.

"If you don't know that," said Helen, "then I guess you didn't learn anything from being female."

"I was a female mule," said Mak-Thar. "We don't wear bras, do we, Evenstar?" He patted the mule on the shoulder.

A few minutes later, Nightshade came back with everything visible—except her hands and her head. "Boy, I'm glad you guys can't see how embarrassed I am."

Helen asked, "So now if you want to be invisible again, you're just going to take off all your clothes?"

"I don't think I'm comfortable with that plan," said Ludo.

"Being invisible is kind of a pain," said Nightshade. "Are you sure I have to stay invisible until I attack?"

"Until you attack or cast a spell," said Mak-Thar. "That's the rule."

"Weird. Okay, Twilight? The next time skeletons ambush us in our sleep, I want you to let me attack one before you turn them away."

"The goddess Selene and I will keep that in mind."

"Cool! Thanks."

* * *

Later that morning, Ludo found a trail branching off toward the Impassable Mountain Range. At least, everyone said that was what he had found. Fred just kind of followed along. Worrying about maps and directions was for other people.

Twilight asked, "Is this the trail that the refugees have been following to get to Basetown?"

"I hope not," said Ludo. "This trail is supposed to be secret dwarven stuff."

"We are most grateful that you choose to share such secrets with us," said Twilight.

"I'm grateful to be busted out of jail," said Ludo. "So I guess we're even—except for the hundred and fifty gold pieces you owe me."

"Has anyone ever seen refugees in Basetown?" Twilight asked. "Or has it just been *rumors* of refugees?"

"There must be refugees," said Nightshade. "How else would you get the rumors?"

"Not all rumors are true," said Mak-Thar.

"We've met beggars who said they were refugees," said Fred.

"Oh, that's right," said Twilight. "Still, it seems a little thin."

"Because they don't have much to eat," said Fred.

"No, I mean the story is thin," said Twilight. "We really haven't had a defining moment when we're forced to confront the evilness of this temple. Mostly we're just doing this because Helen wants to."

"That's a good reason," said Helen.

"We've been over this," said Mak-Thar. "We know they're evil because they attacked us in the desert after they discovered that you and Fred are good. Also, they serve Toxia the Snake Goddess, who is listed as evil in the *Cosmic Compendium*."

"You have the *Cosmic Compendium*?" asked Nightshade.

"It's in the Mages' Guild library."

"Attacking us just because we are good is obviously evil," Twilight agreed, "but it's so obvious, it's almost cartoonish."

"I'm cool with fighting cartoon evil," said Nightshade. "If this turns into grimdark evil, I'll find a different campaign."

Twilight shook his head. "I'd just feel better if we met some refugees on the way, so we know what we're fighting for. And the fact that the refugees start with an impassable mountain range between them and Basetown severely undermines the story's believability."

Mak-Thar asked, "What if it's not a story, Twilight? What if it's real life?"

"Ah, *touché*, my friend. *Touché*."

Helen asked, "Is that the elven word for tush?"

"No," said Twilight.

"Oh."

"I think they flew," said Ludo.

"Who flew?" asked Fred.

"The refugees," said Ludo. "I heard things got so bad that some giant eagles swooped in and started carrying people off to Basetown."

"Giant-eagle bad is pretty bad," said Twilight.

"Why would the eagles do that?" asked Mak-Thar.

Twilight said, "If your heart is pure and your cause is just, sometimes the eagles will aid you out of the goodness of their hearts."

"I'm fairly certain that eagles' hearts are neutral," said Mak-Thar.

"No way," said Twilight. "They're practically an allegory for divine grace."

"We could look it up," said Mak-Thar.

"In the book that says elves always travel in groups of four?" asked Twilight.

Mak-Thar shrugged. "Well, perhaps giant eagles are as good as you say, yet so haughty that they are effectively neutral for game purposes."

"I guess that makes sense," agreed Twilight.

"Take a left at the boulder," said Ludo.

They all took a left. And then they all stopped because they were confronted by a five-hundred-foot-high granite cliff. Directly in front of them was a wide wooden door.

"Oh," said Fred. "When you said, 'through the mountains,' I was imagining something different."

CHAPTER TEN: IN WHICH LUDO LEADS OUR HEROES THROUGH THE MOUNTAINS.

THE DWARF LOOKED UP at the sheer granite cliff face. "You thought we were going to climb that?"

"No," said Fred. "I was just imagining a trail."

"Trails go *over* mountains," explained Ludo. "To go *through*, you need a tunnel."

Twilight asked, "Does this tunnel lead to caverns that were once the stronghold of your ancestors but have, over time, become infested by goblins and possibly balrogs?"

"Isn't a balrog just a goblin spelled backwards?" asked Ludo.

"I don't think so," said Twilight.

"Look, it's a tunnel," said Ludo. "And there weren't any goblins in it last time I was here. Why don't we go in and you can take a look?"

He opened the door.

"That's it?" asked Twilight. "You just turn the knob? You don't have to solve a riddle while a lake tries to eat us?"

"You'd have to be right daft to build a tunnel next to a carnivorous lake," said Ludo.

"I'm not sure we're prepared for a dungeon crawl," said Wren.

"Of course we are," said Mak-Thar. He tried to pat his backpack meaningfully, but his arms wouldn't bend that way. So instead, he flailed at his backpack meaningfully. "I'm always prepared for a dungeon crawl."

"You won't have to crawl," said Ludo. "Our ceilings are high."

In fact, the ceiling was not *very* high. It looked like Evenstar the mule could fit in without ducking, but—

"I don't think there's room to draw my sword," said Helen.

"It does seem to be short of the ten-foot ceiling recommended in *The Dungeon Digger's Handbook*," said Mak-Thar.

"But it's not a dungeon," Ludo repeated. "It's a tunnel. Are you guys coming or not?"

Helen shrugged. "I guess I can draw my sword if I drop to my knees. I'm in."

"I'm in!" said Nightshade. "Dwarven tunnels sound like fun!"

"I think we're all in," said Fred.

He looked at Wren. She met his gaze and nodded.

Mak-Thar got out his tape measure and asked Nightshade to hold one end.

"Twenty feet wide," he announced, once he was done measuring. "And seven-and-a-half feet tall at the apex. The curved ceiling will make it difficult to compute the cross-sectional area. Is that a circular arc? Any idea what its radius might be?"

Ludo said, "I'm a jeweler, not an engineer."

"Ah." Mak-Thar pulled out his notebook and began to draw. "We can establish lower and upper bounds by approximating with a triangular and a rectangular ceiling."

"We can?" asked Ludo.

"Are we going to do this now?" asked Wren.

"I don't want to be trapped in a corridor of unknown cross-section," said Mak-Thar. "It's definitely in our best interests to know a fireball's blast distance before we go in."

Twilight explained, "Sometimes Mak-Thar spontaneously bursts into math. It's like a musical, but with equations instead of show tunes."

They waited while Mak-Thar mumbled. Finally, he was satisfied with his estimates.

"I recommend a three-one-three marching order," said Mak-Thar. "Ludo should go in front, between Fred and Helen. At the first sign of anything amiss, Ludo retreats to the second rank with me. Our rear will be protected by the elf and the two thieves. Note that this formation is fairly open, and Ludo is short. This should give our archers several firing lanes."

Ludo raised a hand to his green alpine hat. "I don't think I want a firing lane over my head."

"Is this your first dungeon?" asked Mak-Thar.

"It's not a dungeon," said Ludo. "It's a tunnel."

They got into Mak-Thar's marching order. Fred discovered that the formation was not as "open" as Mak-Thar had thought. Because of the curve of the ceiling, Fred and Helen had to walk more toward the middle if they did not want to scrape their heads. Ludo got ahead of them as they went in.

"I light a torch," said Mak-Thar.

"We know," said Twilight. "We can see you lighting the torch. You don't have to tell us."

Ludo stopped and looked back over his shoulder. "You guys did say you were coming, right?"

"We should advance no faster than sixty feet per turn," said Mak-Thar.

"What does that mean?" asked Ludo.

"It's about two steps per minute," said Fred.

"Really?"

"It's ridiculous, we know," said Twilight. "But someone wrote it down in *The Adventurer's Guide*, and Mak-Thar likes to follow rules."

"Well, if you want me to be your guide, you're going to have to keep up."

"The cautious movement rate gives us time to search for secret doors and traps," explained Mak-Thar.

"What traps? It's a tunnel!"

"Also, it minimizes the risk of alerting monsters. Parties who exceed the recommended movement rate never achieve surprise."

"Well *I'm* surprised," said Ludo. "I'm surprised you think you can walk six miles through a mountain at a rate of two steps per minute."

"Hm," said Mak-Thar. "How long would that take?"

Wren asked, "Ludo, do we have your word that this tunnel has no monsters or traps?"

"Of course it doesn't. It's a tunnel!"

Mak-Thar said, "You keep saying that word like it explains something."

"If I may," suggested Twilight, "perhaps Ludo does not see a tunnel as an opportunity for an underground adventure. Perhaps for dwarvenkind, tunnels are simply roads that go through mountains."

Mak-Thar asked, "Are you suggesting we could walk through the tunnel as though it were a road?"

Twilight nodded. "Hard as it is to believe, being underground has no effect on our legs."

"This is very irregular," said Mak-Thar. "But I suppose it's all right—only because we have a dwarven guide."

"Wonderful," said Ludo. "So we can go?"

Fred nodded.

"Okay. Don't forget to shut the door."

Ludo turned and they all followed him, this time at an easy walking pace.

"Mind you," said Mak-Thar, "this is only allowed because Ludo is an NPM. A full member of the party would be bound by the same rules as we are and would not be allowed to confer any movement bonus."

"Is he always like this?" Wren asked.

"Always," said Twilight.

"Like what?" asked Mak-Thar.

"Like Mak-Thar," said Twilight.

"How tautologous!"

"Is that a type of rock?" asked Fred.

Ludo shook his head. "Not as far as I know."

* * *

It was weird to be walking underground with no one searching for traps. There were no doors to listen at. There were no corners to look around. There was nothing but straight corridor as far as the eye could see—which wasn't very far, because Mak-Thar's torch illuminated only thirty feet.

Fred's eyes were telling him that they were in a moderately long dungeon corridor, and it was only after an hour of walking that his brain finally began to understand that they were not in a dungeon. As Ludo had said, they were simply in a tunnel.

"On your left, please note the stone wall," said Nightshade. "This was carved by dwarfs before you were born. On your right, same thing. Now come ahead with me and we'll see more stone wall."

"What are you talking about?" asked Ludo.

"I think she's being a tour guide," said Twilight.

"I'm being sarcastic," said Nightshade. "Walking through a stone tunnel is boring."

"We could have left you in Basetown," said Wren. "Being pursued by assassins is a lot more exciting."

"Okay, fine. Yippee. Dwarf tunnel. When do we get out?"

"About seven days," said Mak-Thar.

"Seriously?" asked Nightshade.

"Relax," said Ludo. "We'll be out before nightfall."

"Perhaps," said Mak-Thar. "But if we were to walk six miles at the recommended pace, we would still get out by the end of the week, so it's not nearly as ridiculous as you all seem to think."

"I don't want to spend a week down here," said Nightshade. "We elves are forest creatures."

"You're not an elf," muttered Twilight.

"I think I might be an Arctic elf," said Nightshade.

"A what?"

"Well, if Arctic foxes have round ears, then maybe Arctic elves do, too."

Twilight said, "So you're proposing that your round ears are an adaptation to prevent frostbite?"

"Seems plausible," said Mak-Thar.

"Seems ridiculous," said Twilight.

"As ridiculous as spending seven days in a tunnel?" asked Nightshade.

"We won't spend seven days in the tunnel," said Ludo.

Twilight said, "Friend dwarf, you seem quite knowledgeable

about this place. To help us pass the time, could you tell us something of its history? Or perhaps you could tell us why a Basetown jeweler knows secret paths under the mountain?"

The dwarf glanced over his shoulder. "Oh, you want my back story?"

"Or the tunnel's back story," said Twilight. "Or both."

"Well, okay. I guess we got time."

* * *

As long as there has been land here, there have been dwarves. Some say the land made the dwarves, and some say the dwarves made the land. But it doesn't matter, because we both showed up at about the same time.

Don't scoff, elf. You're the one who asked for my story.

Right. Anyway …

In the old days, the land was different, and the Impassable Mountain Range wasn't impassable. But a thing happened—which is a different story all in itself, so I won't go into it now—and after the thing happened, half the range was impassable and the other half had become a bottomless gorge.

None of this mattered to the dragons and hippogriffs and giant eagles and cockatrices and other flying creatures, but the dwarves were people of the earth, so the Impassable Mountain Range got in their way.

In those days, there were two great dwarven cities—Kalamazoo and Alakazam. One was out there where the western desert is now, and the other was somewhere in the Wombat Wilderness. When the mountain range rose, the two great cities were cut off from each other.

But even in those days, the dwarves were a wise and clever people. They realized that if they couldn't go over the mountains, they ought to go through. So the people of Kalamazoo started digging a tunnel. And the people of Alakazam started digging a tunnel. And when the two tunnels met, each city wanted to charge the other a toll. But there was a wise old dwarf who knew arithmetic, and he pointed out that no one would walk three miles under a mountain just so they could use half a tunnel. Anything one city charged for their half of the tunnel would be canceled by what they paid to use the other half. So both sides agreed to share the tunnel toll-free, and for a while, both cities continued to prosper.

That was long ago. Over time, both cities declined. Some say it was because of orcs. Some say it was dragons. Personally, I suspect climate change. You can't really sustain a city in a desert—even the most industrious dwarves can only import so much ale. Once the city in the desert was gone, the one in the wilderness probably died from loneliness—and don't ask which city was which, because it doesn't matter now.

Although the cities were gone, dwarvenkind persisted in isolated villages. And when humans and elves and half-pints finally moved in, we were glad for the company. The Wombat Wilderness grew up around the abandoned city of Alakazam or Kalamazoo, and everyone forgot about it because they were too busy farming or mining.

Anyway, about three hundred years ago, most of the dwarves on the east side left to go build Watergate—you wouldn't believe how many cobblestones that city has—so those of us on the west side stopped using this tunnel, except to send an occasional trade caravan to the human lands.

About ten years ago, a caravan set out and discovered that someone had built a nice little inn just south of the Wombat Wilderness. So the caravan stopped there, and some dwarves had too much to drink, and a big fight broke out, and the whole inn burned down. When the caravan got to Watergate, they told everyone how much fun they'd had, and soon everybody was coming to that little village looking for a good time. And that was pretty much the start of Basetown.

Now on my side of the mountains—the west side—we have quite a few jewelers, but not much market for jewelry. Most people are agriculturally oriented, and they worry about getting a neck chain caught in a hoe and such-like. For jewelers, Basetown was a great opportunity. I was able to earn nice commissions by taking jewelry through the tunnel to sell in Basetown, and for a long time, that was how I made my living.

Of course, the Jewelers' Guild wanted their cut. But I'm an independent operator. We've been feuding for a while, now. They tried to stop me a few times, but a dwarf has a right to sell jewelry. Any law that could stop me would also stop adventurers from selling their loot, and the Jewelers' Guild isn't powerful enough to take on all three adventurers guilds at the same time.

So this tunnel was a modestly profitable trade route for a few years. But, when the evil temple moved in, things got bad … as you might expect. Once they started razing villages, my people got all frowny and serious and started making weapons instead of brooches. When I lost my suppliers, I started punching holes in gold coins to make ends meet.

The Guild caught me, and now I don't know what to do. The west side of the mountains has gone all grim and depressing, but the east side wants to lock me up.

* * *

Fred thought that was a pretty good story. Apparently Twilight did, too, because he said, "Alas, you have my sympathies, dear dwarf. I hope our quest to overthrow this evil temple will bring you some small solace. If there is anything else we can do for you, you have but to say the word."

"We've agreed to pay him one hundred fifty gold pieces," Mak-Thar said. "Isn't that enough?"

* * *

After a few more hours, Wren said, "You know, I'm starting to think that a hundred and fifty gold pieces is quite a bit to pay someone for guiding us through a straight tunnel with no side passages."

"There must be some side passages," said Mak-Thar.

"Why would we have side passages?" asked Ludo.

"If there are no side passages," asked Mak-Thar, "then how could we get lost?"

"Why would you want to get lost?" asked Ludo.

Wren tried to clarify. "We're trying to figure out why we need you to guide us through the tunnel."

Ludo shrugged. "It was your idea. I'm just glad to have an excuse to get out of Basetown for a couple days. The Arctic elf isn't the only one who has to lie low."

Helen laughed.

"What?" asked Ludo.

"Sorry," said Helen. "I thought you were making a height joke."

"I wasn't." Ludo sounded cross.

"Forgive her," said Mak-Thar. "Barbarians have a questionable sense of humor."

Ludo grunted. Helen laughed again.

"So we could have just hired you to take us to the entrance?" asked Wren.

"I suppose so. But this way, if we run into any dwarves, I can say, 'It's okay. They're with me.' Otherwise, someone might get upset and you might get an axe in your knee."

"Well, I certainly don't want an axe in my knee," said Wren.

Helen asked, "Are there other dwarves up ahead?"

"I was speaking hypothetically," said Ludo.

"Is that also a type of rock?" asked Fred.

"Not as far as I know."

"Well *I'm* not speaking hypothetically," said Helen. "I smell cooking."

Ludo sniffed. "There shouldn't be anyone cooking in here."

Fred could smell it, too, now. "That doesn't smell right."

"Oh," said Ludo. "You're right. It's not right."

Ahead of them, something hissed. The tunnel was suddenly filled with the sound of clawed feet coming rapidly closer.

"That sounds like monsters," said Wren.

Ludo's eyes went wide. "It's monsters."

Chapter Eleven: In which our heroes fight a battle, because spending all day in a tunnel without fighting any monsters would just be wrong.

Hissing voices, scrabbling claws, and a faint whiff of swamp mud—even before their scales gleamed in the torchlight, Helen knew what they were. "It's lizard men!"

Helen dropped to one knee and drew her humongous sword.

"It's lizard men!" squeaked Ludo.

"Spread out to open up firing lanes!" shouted Mak-Thar. "Protect the mage!"

Wren said, "Eat steel, lizard man!"

Wren's arrow whizzed between Helen and Fred and struck a shadowy figure. The monster stumbled and fell into the torchlight with an arrow in its eye.

"Wow, that's so cool," said Nightshade. She shot an arrow and said, "Eat feathers, lizard man! Get it? Because I've got feathers on the end of my arrow? So it's, like, going in even deeper than steel."

Twilight shot a lizard man in the shoulder, saying, "Fight now. Make pithy comments later."

Helen glided forward. A lizard man's club slid off her blade. She struck, recoiled, struck again, and slipped between the falling bodies of her foes.

A lizard woman raised a club with fear in her eyes. Helen slit the monster's throat, whirled to take out the knees of the one trying to outflank her, blocked a club with her crossguard, jabbed an elbow into a scaly face, and lunged at a shadowy figure on the edge of the torchlight.

The figure turned, nearly sweeping Helen's legs with its tail. It emitted a shrill hiss, and the tunnel filled with the smell of reptilian panic. Scaly claws scrabbled on stone floor as the lizard men ran away. An arrow flashed by and vanished into the darkness.

"Wait," said Fred.

Helen stopped, two steps into her pursuit. "Wait for what?"

"Wait for the lizard men to run away so we don't have to fight them in the dark."

Helen's heart pounded. Blood was on her sword and the thrill of battle was in her veins. Fred wanted her to stop? Fred *always* wanted her to stop.

Helen didn't want to stop. Helen wanted to spend every second of every minute feeling this good.

Maybe she *was* a berserker. Would that really be so bad?

A crack of light appeared in the darkness, seeming to float right in front of Helen's eyes. The optical illusion resolved itself into distant reptilian silhouettes escaping through an arched doorway.

"Our combat radius is only thirty feet," said Mak-Thar. "To optimize our tactics, the vanguard needs to stay comfortably within the torchlight."

"Uh huh."

"Did you understand what he just said?" asked Fred.

"Yeah," said Helen. "He said wait for the lizard men to run away so we don't have to fight them in the dark."

"Wow," said Nightshade. "Helen was slicing and dicing!"

Wren said, "She even makes French fries!"

"What are French fries?" asked Fred.

"They're the chips you get with your fish and chips," said Twilight.

"Are they like wood chips?" asked Fred.

"No," said Twilight. "Why would anyone eat wood chips?"

"I don't know," said Fred. "I don't eat much fish, either."

The dwarf was staring at the dead bodies, mouth open in horror.

Nightshade asked, "Does Ludo get experience points for this battle? I don't think he did anything."

"Everyone gets experience points," said Mak-Thar. "But

Ludo gets only a half-share because he's an NPM."

Helen looked for a scrap of cloth to clean her sword. There wasn't one. She asked, "Weren't they wearing clothes last time?"

"They were," said Twilight.

"These guys are naked," said Helen.

"Not everyone wears clothes around the house," said Wren.

"What?" asked Nightshade.

"Do tell!" said Twilight.

Wren rolled her eyes. "*I* wear clothes around the house. I'm just saying that some families are closet nudists."

Fred frowned. "They take off all their clothes and go into a closet?"

Ludo turned his horrified gaze from the dead bodies to the low-charisma thief.

"It's just something I read about once," Wren mumbled. "I'm sorry I brought it up."

Twilight elbowed Nightshade. "Forget the mages and their *Cosmic Compendium*. Sounds like you should be checking out the library at the Thieves' Guild."

Nightshade rolled her eyes.

"Hey!" said Twilight. "You're visible again!"

"I am? Oh, cool! I am."

Fred said, "Now you can eat fish and chips without biting your fingers."

"Which brings us back to those mysterious cooking smells," said Twilight.

Soup. It had smelled like a strange sort of soup.

Helen couldn't smell it anymore. The corridor now smelled like fear, death, and the insides of lizard men. ... But also wood smoke.

Yeah. Like a campfire. Smoke lingers.

They advanced toward the end of the tunnel. Light shone in the open doorway, turning cold and pitiless as it seeped along the stone floor.

In the shadows between the doorway and Mak-Thar's torch, hot coals glowed faintly red. As they drew closer, the flickering torchlight illuminated the wall behind an iron cookpot black as the darkness. A dozen wooden bowls were stacked beside it.

"The tunnel has a kitchen!" said Fred.

"Look at the bones!" said Twilight. He pointed at a chalky white heap against the wall.

"What a hideous skull!" said Fred.

"That's a deer skull," said Helen.

"Oh. I thought some poor elf had grown antlers."

"But *that* skull isn't a deer skull," said Twilight. "And *that* skull isn't a deer skull. And *that* skull …"

"Hey, we get the point," said Ludo.

Fred frowned. "The lizard men have been eating human noodle soup?"

"Possibly without the noodles," said Twilight.

"That's barbaric!" said Fred. "Sorry, Helen."

Helen shrugged. "No, you're right. We don't put noodles in *any* of our soups."

Ludo asked, "Do you put humans in soups?"

"Only if they had it coming." Barbarians didn't *really* eat humans, but neither did they have an obligation to reassure people who thought they did.

"I wonder if these people had it coming," said Twilight.

"Maybe so," said Nightshade. "Check this out!"

She kicked her cute little boot at a pile of clothes. Helen came over to inspect the find and to get a cloth to clean her sword. She picked up a tabard with a green blob on it.

"See?" said Nightshade. "Snake-head serapes!"

Fred said, "I still think the green blob looks more like a beetle."

"Hm," said Twilight. "So either these tabards belong to the lizard men, and they all came in here to get naked and have some soup …"

He looked pointedly at Wren.

Wren shook her head. "You're not going to let that go, are you?"

"Or," said Twilight, "the lizard men have been eating priests from the evil temple."

"It must be the naked closet thing," said Fred. "We know the lizard men and the temple are on the same side."

That was true. On their previous visit to the swamp, a party of lizard men wearing tabards like these had tried to carry Twilight away in a sack. Helen had killed those lizard men, too.

"I don't think it's the naked closet thing," said Twilight.

"I didn't mean they were literally in a closet," said Wren, in a voice that was easy to ignore.

"Yeah," said Nightshade. "I'm with Twilight. I think the lizard men have been chowing down on evil cleric."

Fred frowned. "So they're on our side now?"

"Lizard men are on their own side," said Mak-Thar. "*The Adventurer's Guide* says they're neutral."

Twilight asked, "So the monsters who boil and eat people are the same alignment as the giant eagles who rescue heroes in their moment of greatest need?"

"Yes," said Mak-Thar.

"Don't you think your alignment system might be a little broad?"

"Like Nightshade," said Helen.

"What about Nightshade?" asked Fred.

"She's a little broad," explained Helen.

"Ah," said Mak-Thar. "You are using 'broad' as a slang term for woman. I get it." He glanced at Wren. "I disapprove, of course, but I get it."

Helen thought the joke had been funnier than that, but people didn't always get her sense of humor.

Wren asked, "Does *anyone* use 'broad' as a slang term anymore?"

Mak-Thar blinked virtuously. "I certainly don't."

"You're all crazy," said Ludo.

"We are," admitted Twilight. "But you'll get used to us."

"Actually," said Mak-Thar, "he's done with us."

Fred looked at the tunnel's exit. "Oh. I guess you're right."

"I wish I'd left you ten minutes earlier," said Ludo. "Piles of bones and dismembered lizard men were things I did not need to see."

"Oh, friend dwarf," said Twilight, "forgive us for our mirth in this somber setting! In truth, it is the only way we can cope with the horrors that we have already witnessed."

Ludo gave him a skeptical face.

"I see you do not understand," said Twilight. "Very well. I pray that you never do."

During this time, Mak-Thar had been counting out coins, and he now presented the dwarf with fifteen pounds of gold. "One hundred fifty gold pieces, as agreed."

Ludo gave each person a frown, then he took the gold from Mak-Thar's hands.

"Don't forget to shut the door on your way out," he said.

"We won't," said Fred.

"And if you meet any dwarves, tell them the tunnel has lizard man problems again. They'll know what to do."

Helen was pretty sure *she* knew what to do, too. In fact, she'd already done it. If Fred hadn't held her back, she could have chased the lizard men down and finished the job. It wasn't right to kill fleeing enemies, but it was fun. Helen was pretty sure that made her a bad person. That was one of the reasons she liked hanging out with Fred—he held her back.

CHAPTER TWELVE: IN WHICH OUR HEROES SCOUT THE SWAMP.

AFTER SAYING FAREWELL TO LUDO and remembering to shut the door, Fred and his friends wandered away from the mountains and into a swamp. Normally, travelers try to avoid swamps, but this swamp was special because it had an evil temple in it.

Nightshade soon started to complain. "Why did they build their temple in a *swamp*? Couldn't they have built it in one of those villages they terrorized?"

"I think the swamp is their base of operations," said Helen.

"You gotta start somewhere," said Fred.

"But why a swamp?" asked Nightshade.

"Perhaps the swamp is sacred to their goddess," suggested Twilight. "Or perhaps it's just one more illogical thing that this shoddy excuse for a world expects us to unquestioningly accept."

Mak-Thar raised an eyebrow. "How can the world 'expect' something, Twilight?"

"He means the GM," said Wren. "He's criticizing the GM's worldbuilding—which is something I definitely would not do while I'm in a swamp that very likely has poisonous snakes."

"Don't give the GM ideas," said Nightshade.

In a honey-coated voice, Mak-Thar said, "But Twilight doesn't *believe* in the GM."

Twilight sighed. "You're right. I don't."

"So it must be the sacred-to-goddess thing," said Fred. "That makes sense."

"Don't forget that the mountains have a large supply of temple-building rock," said Helen.

"That could also be a reason," Twilight admitted. "I apologize for my cynicism. When presented with plausible explanations, I should be grateful, not skeptical."

"Skepticism is good," said Wren. "But I don't see how you can be skeptical about the GM. That's not safe."

"So you believe in the GM?" asked Mak-Thar.

"Let's just say you won't get me to admit that I don't."

"Ah," said Mak-Thar. "Then let me ask you this: Do you believe in a fair GM, or an unfair GM?"

Wren rolled her eyes. "The smart play is to say the GM is fair. If he exists, you don't want to be on his bad side."

"Or *her* bad side," said Nightshade. "I think the GM and the Chaos Goddess are the same person. That's why *The Adventurer's Guide* spends so much time talking about dice."

"Oh dear," said Twilight. "There's so much wrong with what you just said that I don't even know where to begin."

"Let us assume a fair GM," said Mak-Thar. "What does *fair* mean in this context?"

Fred was pretty sure Mak-Thar was talking about the *justice* type of fair, and not the type of fair where you could bring your chickens, but before Fred could speak up, Mak-Thar answered his own question:

"*Fair* means the GM follows the rules."

Wren considered this with a thoughtful frown.

"And do the rules say we must worship the GM?" asked Mak-Thar. "Do the rules say we must be careful invoking the GM's name? They do not. The rules do not even mention the GM! Therefore, we must conclude that a world run by a fair GM will be unaffected by our belief. No matter what we say, the GM will follow the rules."

Nightshade asked, "So you're saying that, because the GM is fair, I can raise my finger like this and shout, 'To heck with the GM!' without any consequences?"

"Precisely," said Mak-Thar.

Fred was puzzled. "Is that finger obscene in your culture?"

Nightshade shook her head. "No. *This* finger is the obscene one. I just didn't want to offend Twilight."

Helen snickered.

Twilight said, "Thank you for your consideration."

Mak-Thar continued to pursue his argument. "So you see, Wren, a world run by a fair GM is indistinguishable from a world with *no GM at all*! The world simply follows its rules. Belief is irrelevant, and no GM is required."

Wren gave Mak-Thar a skeptical look. "You think the GM always plays by the rules?"

"I think there is no GM," said Mak-Thar. "Because when I died—"

"Mak-Thar died and got reincarnated as a mule!" said Nightshade.

"I know," said Wren.

"Oh."

"When I died," said Mak-Thar, "I did *not* see the GM. And I am beginning to realize that there does not need to be one. The rules of the universe are powerful enough to enforce themselves."

Fred lifted a boot out of the swamp muck so he could climb over a fallen log. Fred didn't get into Twilight and Mak-Thar's metaphysical discussions, but he appreciated the distraction from the fact that they were wading through ankle-deep water.

"Uh huh," said Wren. "Well, kissing up to the GM has gotten me this far in life, so I'm not going to stop now." She scowled at a snake that was watching from the branch of a mossy tree. "By 'this far', I'm not actually referring to this swamp. When we were planning this job, I didn't realize it would be so wet."

* * *

The swamp was wet. And it was confusing. Fred assumed that Helen and Mak-Thar had some sort of plan for finding the evil temple, but after a while, he realized they were just wandering until they found something hopeful. That wasn't a real great plan, because hope is scarce in a swamp.

Finally, Helen called a halt and put everyone to work chopping down trees. Wren and Mak-Thar had loaded one of Evenstar's packs with several useful tools. Fred and Helen got the axes. Wren and Nightshade worked at either end of a two-woman saw. Mak-Thar tried to chop down trees by burning them (it didn't work) and Twilight sloshed around looking mournful while asking forgiveness from his nature goddess.

When the work was done, they had a platform of logs that would keep most of their stuff dry while they slept.

Mak-Thar said, "We should plane a few boards so Evenstar can have a platform, too."

"She can sleep standing up," said Helen.

"She can," admitted Mak-Thar. "But she wants dry feet as much as we do."

"Don't you have a foot-drying spell?" asked Nightshade.

"Fireball?" suggested Helen.

Everyone scowled at her and told her that wasn't funny. Poor Helen.

"Actually ..." said Mak-Thar.

Fred didn't like the sound of that.

"... we are nearing the end of the day, and it is kind of a waste to leave my Fireball spell unused ..."

"Are you thinking what I'm thinking?" asked Nightshade.

"I think I am," said Mak-Thar.

"What are you thinking?" asked Twilight.

"I wasn't thinking anything," Nightshade admitted. "It just seemed like Mak-Thar wanted a set-up line."

Mak-Thar pointed at a nearby thicket of willows. "Those shrubs have formed a small hillock. That might be a good place for Evenstar to stand, once I've reduced the shrubs to ash and scorched the mud underneath."

"Cool!" said Nightshade.

"What do you think?" asked Mak-Thar. "Should I save the spell in case we need it? Or should I cast it now?"

"Oh, do it," said Wren. "I wanna see you cast a fireball."

These words erased all of Mak-Thar's misgivings. With a dramatic wave, he announced, "Then stand back!"

They stood back. Mak-Thar frowned with concentration and wiggled his fingers. A ball of flame appeared in his hands, and he threw it at the unsuspecting willows.

When Fred was about eight, he'd wandered over to the hearth to check on the pot in which his mother was stewing a chicken. Prudently wrapping his hand in a rag, he had seized the lid, leaned over the pot, and lifted the lid to release a blinding blast of scalding steam. Mak-Thar's fireball was a lot like that.

Flames expanded to engulf the willows. The water *shrieked* in the sudden blast of heat. Mud and steam exploded from the ground, coating all onlookers in a fine layer of scalding, wet ash.

Wren spoke for all of them when she said, "Ow, my face."

Well, Wren spoke for all of them except Helen, who was also scalded on her knees, thighs, belly, shoulders, and arms.

"Yeah," said Helen. "I should have seen that coming."

Evenstar the mule, wide-eyed with shock, was attempting to bolt from the scene, but she'd stepped on her rope. She couldn't run because she was desperately trying to pull her head away from her own foot.

Twilight took the rope and tried to calm the mule down.

Mak-Thar, who was probably best protected of them all, thanks to his scraggly beard, said, "Ah. Interesting. Apparently a fireball impacting wet ground has a secondary blast radius which does 1d4 scalding damage."

He pulled out his notebook and wrote this important information down.

* * *

Fred awoke the next morning with an aching stiffness in his back. It was the sort of stiffness one would expect to get from sleeping in a steel cuirass on a bed of hard, round logs. Under the circumstances, Fred supposed he should be grateful that he wasn't waking up in a bowl of human noodle soup. But no matter how much he tried to look on the bright side, Fred couldn't shake the feeling that he preferred the sorts of adventures that allowed him to wake up in a bed.

Helen looked frightful. Normally, she had an easy-going grace that allowed her to look good anywhere, anytime. But this morning, her skin was covered with popped blisters from Mak-Thar's fireball and pockmarked with impressions from the bark of the trees she had slept on.

Mak-Thar assured them that *The Adventurer's Guide* mentioned no penalties for sleeping on hard, round trees, so apparently they were all okay and ready to fight. But they didn't fight, because nothing attacked them. Instead, after a breakfast of probably-not-poisonous snakes, they were slogging through the swamp, ready to scout the layout of the evil temple.

The first step to scouting the layout was to find the temple. Fortunately, they knew that the lizard men had made very obvious paths that led straight to it. All they had to do was find one of those paths and then hope they didn't find any lizard men.

The lizard-man situation was confusing Fred. Last time, lizard men wearing temple-issued green-blob tabards had tried to kidnap and eat Twilight. But now it looked like the lizard men were eating the green-blob clerics. Did that mean there were two groups—evil lizard men and evil-eating lizard men? Fred decided not to worry about it. There were smart people in the party who would give him the answer once they had figured everything out.

It took Helen about an hour to find a lizard man trail, but once she did, they found the temple in only ten minutes. In the bright summer sunlight, it didn't look all that evil. Proud and solid, shiny and clean, the temple rose above the swamp as though a divine hand had reached down and said, *Here there will be order.*

An odd place to impose order. Trees and cattails had been cleared all around it to form a very shallow lake. A wooden walkway allowed people to approach the temple without getting their feet wet. Fred had to approve of that.

The walkway also allowed *lizard men* to approach without getting their feet wet—which was wasted effort in their case, because they were just going to slink back into the swamp anyway.

From their hiding place on the edge of the lake, Fred and his friends watched as a group of lizard men in muddy green-blob tabards discussed something with human green-blob priests. The scene was very similar to what they had seen on their previous visit.

Wren seemed uninterested in the lizard men. She was focused on the temple's red granite dome.

"How far can you throw a grappling hook?" she asked Helen. "Do you think you can hit the dome from here?"

"I doubt I can throw that far."

"It goes farther if you swing it," said Wren.

"Give it a whirl!" said Nightshade.

Mak-Thar asked, "Wouldn't it be a higher-probability throw if you were to sneak closer?"

"I suppose," said Wren.

"Getting closer means wading out into the lake," said Twilight.

Nightshade wrinkled her nose. "This place is so gross."

"Let me think," said Wren. She pondered the temple in silence for a minute. Fred was impressed that the rest of his friends were able to stay silent that long.

Wren shook her head. "Even if we get across the lake, we still don't know what we'll find inside. Someone has to case the joint."

"Right," said Nightshade. "Case the joint."

"Should we come back at night?" asked Helen.

"Once again," said Twilight, "I must caution against the assumption that evil clerics are at a disadvantage at night."

"Right," said Helen. "Good point."

"What if Nightshade just walked in?" asked Wren.

"Then they'd kill me and eat me for supper?" suggested Nightshade.

"Evil clerics wouldn't eat you," said Twilight. "They'd use your still-beating heart in some ghastly ritual."

"Oh. That's comforting."

Wren said, "I'm just thinking that Nightshade gives off the vibe of the permanent newbie. If she simply walked up and asked to join their temple, they might let her in."

"Wow," said Nightshade. "That sounds ... audacious."

"Good word!" said Fred.

"Thank you."

"It *is* audacious," agreed Wren.

"I don't like it," said Mak-Thar. "She has fewer hit points than any of us. One wrong move, and she's dead."

Wren said, "Not even Helen would survive if every cleric in the place suddenly turned against her."

"I would if I had my sword," said Helen.

"Okay," conceded Wren. "*Maybe* Helen would find a way to survive, but my point is that the plan only works if it works. If it doesn't work, it fails catastrophically."

"Oo," said Nightshade. "High stakes. Okay. I'm in!"

"What?" asked Twilight. "You can't be serious."

"No, it's cool," said Nightshade. "I'll just put my soul in the hands of the Chaos Goddess."

Twilight rolled his eyes. "I don't see how *that* could go wrong."

"I'll go with her," said Fred.

"Me too," said Helen.

"No," said Wren. "We're standing in a swamp full of snakes and lizard men. We can't send away all our fighters."

"Never split the party," said Mak-Thar.

"Why not?" asked Wren.

"Um … it's a basic maxim of adventuring. I thought that's what you were saying."

"What page is that on?" asked Wren.

"Well, it's not written down …"

Wren gave Mak-Thar a serious look. "Splitting the party might be our best bet. We need an inside man."

"Inside woman," said Nightshade.

"It's just an expression," said Wren.

"Challenging gender defaults is important," said Nightshade.

"Inside people," said Fred. He really didn't like the idea of Nightshade scouting the evil temple alone.

Wren considered this. "Okay. Yeah. Inside people."

"Which people?" Helen asked.

Wren said, "I'm thinking Fred, Nightshade, and Mak-Thar."

"Why them?" Helen asked.

"Because this is our team," said Wren. "Right? This is our team?"

"This is our team," Helen agreed.

"And I'm sure you've noticed that some members of our team are quiet enough to sneak into the temple, and some members of our team are not."

Helen frowned.

Wren said, "This is a way to get them inside. They don't have to move silently. They can just walk in. And if it doesn't work, Fred starts hacking off limbs, Mak-Thar tosses a fireball, and they all run away."

"Good backup plan!" said Fred.

"Well, it's more fleshed out than our usual backup plans," said Twilight. "I'm not sure that makes it good."

"Twilight is super good at sweet-talking people," said Nightshade. "He should come inside too."

"No," said Wren. "Three go in. Three stay out."

Mak-Thar looked worried.

"It's risky," Wren admitted.

"But you can't win if you don't play!" said Nightshade.

"I've never tried to talk my way past guards before," said Mak-Thar.

Wren said, "I'm a city-based, solo-adventuring cat burglar hanging out with five other adventurers in a *swamp*. For this team to work, we all have to push against our comfort zones." She reached out and touched his arm. "Are you in?"

Mak-Thar looked at the hand on his arm. "I suppose I'm in."

Wren smiled. "Great! Because I know a role that would be perfect for you."

Chapter Thirteen: In which Fred, Nightshade, and Mak-Thar attempt to talk their way into the evil temple.

The next morning, Fred, Nightshade, and Mak-Thar climbed out of the swamp onto the wooden walkway. They passed between the cattails for a few minutes until they came to the edge of the clearing, where they stopped in full view of the evil temple.

"Okay," said Mak-Thar. "Remember the backup plan."

"I fight off the guards, you lob a fireball, and we all run like crazy," said Fred.

"Right."

"If you're worried about your lines," said Nightshade, "maybe we should switch roles. I have high charisma."

"We are not switching roles," said Mak-Thar.

"You're too perky to be an evil priest," Fred told her.

"Evil priestess," said Nightshade. "And the priestesses of

chaos are perky. So perky should be okay for evil priestesses, too. Plus, I'm wearing black."

Mak-Thar frowned in confusion. "Aren't you wearing a snake-head tabard just like Fred and me?"

"Yes," said Nightshade. "But underneath that, I'm wearing black. Definitely cool, high-level priestess here."

Mak-Thar shook his head. "Wren said I'm in charge, and that's final."

"I think Wren has a good plan," said Fred. "And remember, if we do what she says, she can't blame us when it goes horribly wrong."

"It'll work!" said Nightshade. "Don't be negative!"

By this time, they had the full attention of the man and the woman standing guard at the temple entrance.

"We should probably go talk to them," said Fred, "before they ask why we're just standing here."

Mak-Thar took a deep breath. "Very well. I just wish I had the Acting proficiency."

"You'll do fine," said Fred. "Just remember to act pompous and bossy."

"I'll do my best," said Mak-Thar.

If the whole plan hinged on whether Mak-Thar could be pompous and bossy enough, then it was sure to work. And if the plan failed spectacularly, then they would all have something to talk about when they got back to Basetown.

Mak-Thar took the lead. Fred and Nightshade followed behind. They were all wearing green-blob tabards that they had collected from the dwarf tunnel. At least, Fred and Mak-Thar were wearing green blobs. Nightshade had declared that her tabard was "gross", and by the time she had finished washing and scrubbing, her green blob had worn off. Once the tabard had dried, she'd tried to paint the green blob back on, but instead of an amorphous green blob, she had painted a snake's head. Fred hoped that her painting skill would not get them into trouble.

"Halt!" said the female guard. She was short and shaped like a dumpling. "Who goes there?"

Her voice was loud, but not quite strong. Fred could tell she was shouting to hide the fact that she was confused.

Her partner put his hand on the hilt of his sword and frowned with worry. He was a young man with a long neck and not much experience with a sword. Helen would have carved through these two without stopping.

"Allow me to introduce myself," said Mak-Thar. "I am Sauron, the evil cleric. This my acolyte, Belladonna, and my bodyguard ... um ... Diabolicus Maximus."

"Hi." Fred waved. "You can call me Fred."

Mak-Thar scowled. He didn't want Fred to be called Fred. Well, Fred always tried to get along with Mak-Thar, but he drew the line at using a fake name he couldn't pronounce.

"If you're a cleric," asked the dumpling woman, "where's your snake staff?"

"Oh," said Mak-Thar. "Um, er ..."

"He lost it in the swamp," said Fred. "He was using it as a walking stick and *sploosh!* it was gone."

Dumpling woman eyed their muddy boots. "Why did you leave the walkway?"

That was an interesting question. Fred realized that the evil clerics wouldn't want to walk through miles of swamp to get to their temple. The walkway probably led out of the swamp to dry ground.

Nightshade rolled her eyes. "We're traveling in mixed company. Sometimes you have to leave the walkway to get a little privacy."

The long-necked guard frowned as he tried to work out what Nightshade might be implying.

"Call of nature," Fred explained.

"Oh," said the long-necked man. He nodded his thanks for the explanation.

His hand had drifted away from his sword, too. This was working!

"Why are you here?" asked dumpling woman.

"Isn't it obvious?" asked Mak-Thar. "We've come to join your temple. Now let us in!"

"Is there a problem?" A frowning young man appeared in the doorway. He carried a war hammer on his belt—possibly because he wasn't important enough to have a snake staff. Fred recognized him. This was Bradly.

Fred and Bradly had met in the desert—just one adventuring party crossing paths with another, except that Bradly's party had been composed entirely of evil clerics. Fred's party had pretended to be neutral, but Bradly had cast Detect Good. The result had been a battle in which Fred had driven his sword all the way through Bradly's body. This had made Bradly die.

Shortly thereafter, the evil clerics had surrendered and demanded that Fred and his friends help them haul the dead bodies to the road so a wagon could pick them up and take them to be resurrected. Fred had thought that was fair, so they had hauled the bodies. Fred was glad to see Bradly alive again— hauling his corpse across the desert had been hard work, and Fred was glad the hard work had not been wasted.

Fred was about to say, *Hey, Bradly, remember me?* when he realized that being recognized might make it harder for them to infiltrate the evil temple.

But Mak-Thar was thinking fast. (Well, faster than Fred.) He pointed a finger at Bradly and said, "You there! Cast Detect Good on this guard! She's behaving suspiciously."

"What? I'm not—"

Bradly mumbled some words and touched the dumpling woman.

She glared at Mak-Thar, but apparently she had to put up with being Detected because Bradly outranked her.

Bradly withdrew his hand. "She's not good. What's the trouble?"

"Well, maybe she's neutral, then," said Mak-Thar. "Someone *evil* should want new recruits for your *evil* temple. But she won't let us in."

"He claims to be an evil cleric," said dumpling woman. "But something's not right about them."

"*Nothing* is right about us!" said Mak-Thar indignantly. "We are all bad, unjust, and wrong. How dare you suggest something might be right!"

"Please calm down," said Bradly. "I'm sure she didn't mean it that way."

"Hmf!" said Mak-Thar.

Bradly asked, "What level did you say you were?"

"Fifth!" said Mak-Thar.

"Oh, so you're a vicar." There was a sly smile in his eyes, as though he had just set a trap.

"I'm not a vicar!" said Mak-Thar. "I'm a curate! Even an adept should know that a fifth-level cleric is a curate! What are they teaching you at this temple?"

"He checks out," said Bradly. And everyone relaxed a little bit.

That was nice. For a moment, Fred had been afraid that Mak-Thar and the evil people would have trouble getting along.

Bradly gave Mak-Thar a polite nod. "Please accept my apologies, curate. The guards were only doing their job."

"Well, no harm done, I suppose." Mak-Thar sniffed. "And really, that's unfortunate, because I enjoy harm. Do you suppose anyone would mind if I cast Cause Light Wounds on her?"

Dumpling woman looked worried.

"It might be better if you didn't," said Bradly. "The Council prefers to let the sergeant-at-arms discipline the guards."

"Oh?" asked Mak-Thar. "Is the sergeant-at-arms good at torture?"

Bradly studied Mak-Thar with a thoughtful look. "Funny you should mention torture. We have an opening for a torturer in our dungeon."

"Oh really? You have a dungeon?" Mak-Thar was intrigued.

"Yes. If you will all follow me, I'll help you get registered."

* * *

Considering it was in the middle of a swamp, it was a really nice temple. The floor was a polished black granite that felt solid against Fred's wet and squishy boots. The space under the red marble dome had been partitioned with walls of wood and plaster. There was no ceiling. The walls just stopped ten feet up so you could admire the dome high above. Fred imagined that a light-footed woman like Wren could run all around the temple on the tops of the walls without ever needing to touch the floor.

There wasn't much decoration. The walls were there to separate the hallways from the rooms. The floor was there to keep your feet out of the swamp. There were no mosaics, frescoes, or paintings—which was just as well, considering how bad the clerics were at painting their uniforms.

They passed several closed doors, and none of them were labeled. Fred wondered what was behind them, and he got his answer when one of them opened.

A grouchy-looking cleric stepped into the hallway, his snake staff thumping into the granite like a third foot. He scowled at them and said, "Adept, close that door for me."

"Yes, curate." Bradly closed the door.

The curate ignored them and thumped away in the opposite direction. As Bradly resumed walking, Fred heard the curate knock on another door and say, "It's time for the reckoning."

If he got a reply, Fred didn't hear it. Bradly led them around a corner.

Here, the hall was wide enough to accommodate a writing desk. Behind the desk sat a balding little man who didn't look up until Bradly said, "These three are reporting for assignments."

"Oh!" The balding man jumped and nervously fluttered some pages in a ledger. Fred was reminded of a chicken dusting her feathers.

The balding man blinked at Mak-Thar. "Um … name?"

"Sauron the Evil," said Mak-Thar. "Curate of Toxia."

"A curate! Oh, um …"

"I suggested he could be assigned to the dungeon," said Bradly. "He seems to enjoy torture."

"Oh! Well, somebody has to do it, right? Heh, heh." The balding man gave a worried smile. Bradly didn't smile, so he changed it to a worried frown as he dipped his pen into the inkwell. "How do you spell *Sauron?*"

"*Saur* as in *dinosaur*," said Mak-Thar. "*On* as in *on the job.*"

The worried man began scratching in the ledger. He was sort of making letters and sort of making crude sketches of letters.

"Would you like me to do that?" Mak-Thar offered.

"Oh no!" said the little man. "No, I'm in charge of personnel, and writing in the book is my job. We all have to do our assigned jobs, otherwise I'd be out of a job."

"It's nice to have a good job," said Fred.

"It's essential," said the balding head of personnel. In shaky, blocky handwriting, he wrote S A U R O N T H E J O B — T O R T U R E R. If calligraphy was an art, this guy was making stick figures.

Fred was a little worried about Mak-Thar being assigned to torture people. He hoped the dungeons were empty.

Mak-Thar continued to play the part of the confident, bossy cleric. "This is my acolyte, Belladonna. Two *L*s, two *N*s. She will be assisting me."

The head of personnel began laboring on Nightshade's fake name. "I'm afraid we cannot assign you an assistant at this time."

"I think you can," insisted Mak-Thar.

"Not at this time," insisted the head of personnel.

"I think you will find a way to help the head torturer," insisted Mak-Thar.

"Perhaps when more essential openings are filled," insisted the head of personnel.

Mak-Thar looked to Bradly.

Bradly shrugged. "We're shorthanded. Most of our people are out in the field right now."

"What do you grow?" asked Fred.

Mak-Thar scowled. "He means they are out pillaging the countryside."

"Oh," said Fred. So they were out in *other people's* fields.

"This one's dumb enough to be a guard," said Bradly. "Should we have him report to the sergeant-at-arms?"

"I'm not done with *her* yet." The head of personnel had written BELADONA TOOLS TOONS—, but he hadn't given her a job assignment.

Bradly looked her up and down. His eyes narrowed. "There's something familiar about you."

"I don't think we've met," said Nightshade. She pushed back her hair to show Bradly that her ears were round, like a human's. Fred thought that was pretty smart. The last time Bradly had seen them, Mak-Thar had been a mule and Nightshade had been an elf. So by showing off her ears, Nightshade was making herself harder to recognize.

Fred wished he looked different from last time, too, but Fred was always just Fred.

Bradly squinted at Nightshade's chest. This worried Fred. Was Bradly able to recognize women by their chests? Was that harder or easier than recognizing women by their ears?

"Who painted that?" asked Bradly, pointing at Nightshade's painting that really did look like a snake's head.

"I did," said Nightshade.

"You painted your own uniform?"

"Yes. Is that a problem?"

"I didn't have an official tabard for her," said Mak-Thar. "So I asked her to paint her own."

"That's very good work," said Bradly.

"Yes, it is," agreed the head of personnel.

"Thank you," said Nightshade.

The head of personnel came to a decision. "Report to Miss Purslane and tell her you are the new laundry and uniforms assistant."

"Actually, I was hoping for something a little more glamorous."

"Go!" said Mak-Thar. "Evil demands absolute obedience!"

Nightshade stuck her tongue out at him. Then she rolled her eyes and said, "Okay. Where's Miss Purslane?"

"Bradly can show you the way," said the head of personnel.

"'Bradly'!" exclaimed Nightshade. "That's it. It was on the tip of my tongue."

"What was on the tip of your tongue?" asked Bradly.

"Your name."

"So we *have* met? Were you one of those women who ran screaming when we burned down the village of Littlebrook last fall?"

"No, I'm from Watergate."

"Oh."

"Sorry I missed it," said Nightshade. "It sounds ... evil."

Bradly shrugged. "Yeah, it was pretty evil, I guess."

The bald man took out some blotting paper and tried to soak up the ink splotch that he'd made in the middle of Nightshade's job assignment.

"Are you sure you don't want someone else to write in the book?" asked Nightshade. "I could be your scribe or something."

"No, I already have your assignment written down," said the head of personnel—even though what he had written down was now an illegible blot. "Off you go."

"This way," said Bradly.

They left.

"And what's your name?" asked the head of personnel.

"Fred," said Fred. He did not say, *Fred, just Fred.* He did not say *Fred, F-R-E-D.* Fred had figured out how this guy's head worked, and he did not want some weird name appearing in the official register.

The man wrote $FRED-GUARD$ and said, "Report to the sergeant-at-arms."

"Will do," said Fred.

Apparently, their plan had worked. Cool!

Fred clasped Mak-Thar on the shoulder and said, "Good luck."

"*Evil* luck," said Mak-Thar. "This is a temple of *evil*."

"Right," said Fred.

"Wrong!" insisted Mak-Thar.

Fred exchanged a glance with the head of personnel and assured him, "He'll fit in just fine."

CHAPTER FOURTEEN: IN WHICH FRED MAKES FRIENDS AT THE EVIL TEMPLE.

FRED DIDN'T KNOW where to find the sergeant-at-arms, but he knew where to find some guards. He went back to the entrance.

"Hi. The bald guy said I can be a guard, so I guess we're on the same team now."

Dumpling woman and long-necked man eyed Fred suspiciously.

"You're awfully big for a guard," said long-necked man.

"Thank you!"

"I'm Evelyn," said dumpling woman.

"They call me Goose," said long-necked man.

"Oh!" said Fred. "Because of your neck?"

"It's short for Goosifer," said Goose. "What about my neck?"

"It's so graceful," said Fred.

"Oh," said Goose.

Fred asked, "Is there somebody off duty who can show me around?"

Confused, Evelyn looked out at the water and trees. "Why would you want to look around? It's a swamp."

"Around the temple," explained Fred. "I should probably find out what I'm supposed to be guarding."

"Oh," said Evelyn. "I guess that makes sense. Goose can show you around."

"What if we're attacked?" asked Goose.

"Then I'll run inside and scream for help," said Evelyn, "same as I'd do if you were here. Go on. Sam will understand."

"Well ... all right," said Goose. To Fred he added, "I have to do what she says. She has seniority."

Fred smiled.

"So ... um ... how long have you been guarding Curate Sauron?"

"Seven years," said Fred.

"Y-years?" asked Goose.

Fred nodded. Fred probably wasn't old enough to have been a professional bodyguard for seven years, but he was much bigger and stronger than Goose and Evelyn, so he knew they would not call him on it.

"Well, um, follow me, please." Goose hunched his shoulders and led Fred into the temple. There would be no question about which of them had seniority.

* * *

It turned out there were four jobs a guard could have. "Front door" was considered the worst because you had to stand outside in the weather and there was always a chance that something might decide to attack you.

"Dungeon duty" was useless. You just sat in a chair outside the prison cells waiting for someone to sneak into the temple, hit you over the head, steal your keys, and free the prisoners. Occasionally, you had to give the prisoners a bowl of gruel or carry an emptied bowl back to the kitchen. It was damp and dark in the dungeon, and Goose didn't even bother taking Fred down. He just waved at the stairs and said, "Roberto's down there now. He's the only one who can stand it."

"Patrol" was kind of what Fred and Goose were doing. The guard on patrol walked through the hallways, past all the closed doors.

"Never open a door," Goose advised. "There's always an evil cleric behind it, and evil clerics hate to be interrupted."

Goose walked more quietly when they passed closed doors, and he wouldn't resume his tour-guide talk until the door was safely behind them. Fred thought that working for evil clerics might have its downside.

Fred got lost pretty quick, but he realized he could orient

himself by looking up at the dome. On the outside edge of the temple, the red granite dome was only a few feet above the tops of the walls. As Goose's tour went on, the dome above climbed higher, so Fred knew they were getting closer to the middle of the temple.

Near the center, they walked along a hallway that curved, suggesting that they were outside the wall of a huge round room. The entrance to this room had a guard on either side.

Goose waved. "Hey, guys!"

The guards glanced sideways. One of them said, "Hey, Goose."

She put just enough politeness in the greeting to make it clear that she was only answering to be polite. She stood as tall as Fred, but she wasn't stocky enough to wear all that armor. She looked dangerous, though. With a little less iron on her body, she might be viper quick.

"This is Fred," said Goose. "He's the new guy."

"Hi." Fred waved.

"Hey, Fred." This time her voice was casual, with just a hint of *Don't mind Goose; the rest of us are cool.*

"Greetings, Fred," said the other guard. "My name is Quigly." He smiled with all his teeth, as though he were a knight posing for a portrait with his foot on the head of a vanquished dragon.

"Pleased to meet ya," said Fred.

"I'm Kayla," said the woman. "What brings you to our little swamp?"

"I walked," said Fred.

Kayla's attitude changed from casual friendliness to mild concern. "I mean," she said, speaking more slowly, "why do you want to be a guard?"

"He came with a curate." Goose wanted these two to know he had information. "And watch out for that guy! Evelyn just asked a few questions, and he threatened to cause her light wounds!"

"Sounds like a dastardly fellow!" said Quigly with a smile.

"Fred was his bodyguard," said Goose.

"Does that pay good?" asked Kayla.

Fred shrugged. "It buys food and ale. Once I'd bought my armor, I pretty much had everything I needed."

This was the truth. Fred hadn't bought anything important for years. Most of his gold pieces went into the Fighters' Guild pension fund.

"Well, you could use an upgrade," said Quigly.

"I could?" asked Fred.

"Or at least you could spend a little money on armor polish."

"Oh," said Fred. In his line of work, shiny armor was a disadvantage—unless you were fighting a medusa.

"Don't mind Quigly," said Kayla. "He wants to be a paladin."

"I do not!" Quigly's voice was intense and quiet. He glanced through the doorway he was guarding. Inside was an immense round room lit by braziers of flaming oil. A small group of clerics huddled around an altar. The room was huge, so the clerics were some distance away. None of them looked up from their work.

"I'm just as evil as the next man, make no mistake." Quigly's voice regained its haughty tone. "But if there were an evil counterpart to the paladin, then I would certainly qualify."

"There must be evil paladins," said Kayla. "Otherwise, who would the good ones fight?"

"Fred would know," said Goose. "He's been a guard for seven years."

"Ah!" said Quigly. "A man of the world?"

Fred shrugged. "You could say that."

Fred was a man, and he'd been born in the world. It didn't seem like a great accomplishment, but Quigly seemed impressed by his modesty.

"So tell me, dear fellow, *is* there such a thing as an evil paladin?"

"I don't know," admitted Fred. "Ma—" (Oops. Don't call him *Mak-Thar*.) "Master Sauron would know." (Good save.) "Anyway, I've never met one."

Quigly looked at Fred's muddy boots. "And you seem so well traveled."

"I get around." Again, this did not seem like a big accomplishment. Pretty much anyone in this swamp had traveled a long distance to get here, unless he was a lizard man.

Quigly observed, "It almost sounds like a step down, coming to work here."

"Well, apparently the temple needs a torturer," said Fred. "And Master Sauron is happy to help."

Quigly's nose wrinkled, but his face looked more sad than disgusted when he said, "Ah, yes. Those miserable wretches in the dungeon. I suppose someone had to deal with them sooner or later."

"I guess it's sooner," said Kayla. "Will you be sharing dungeon duty with Roberto?"

"I don't know," said Fred.

"Fred doesn't have an assignment yet," said Goose.

"Ask to be a ceremonial guard," said Kayla.

Quigly raised his eyebrows. "My dear colleague! Are you trying to rid yourself of me?"

Kayla cupped her hand beside her lips and whispered, "Quigly thinks everything is about Quigly."

Despite the whispering, Fred had the impression that she wanted to be overheard—especially because she was pointing the thumb of her other hand at Quigly.

Quigly pursed his lips and said, "Really!"

"I'm actually hoping to rid *you* of *me*," said Kayla. "If Fred takes this job, maybe I can go back on patrol."

"You don't like being a ceremonial guard?" asked Fred.

"It's extra prestige," admitted Kayla, "but not extra pay. The patroller at least gets to walk around."

"But the pomp, my dear! The circumstance!" Quigly shook his head. "You would miss it."

"No I wouldn't," said Kayla. "I'd be walking past it every ten minutes. I'd get regular doses of your melodious voice, while skipping the bits where we stand at attention and my butt falls asleep."

"Don't be crude," suggested Quigly.

"See?" said Kayla. "He's so sanctimonious. Definite paladin material."

"You jest," said Quigly, glancing over his shoulder again, "but it will be my head if someone overhears you."

"What are they doing in there?" Fred asked.

Quigly grinned. "'Tis a dark and sinister ritual!"

Goose's eyes went wide.

Kayla shook her head. "They're working on the accounting."

Quigly nodded. "As I said."

One of the clerics dipped a quill into a sticky substance on the altar and then made a mark in a ledger.

"They have to do the accounting in blood?" Goose asked.

"Yeah," said Kayla. She seemed unimpressed. "It makes them feel like they're doing something evil. Really, though, they're just trying to add up how much food the temple ate last week."

Quigly said, "Considering that all our food comes from pillaging the countryside, perhaps the accounting truly *is* evil."

"I suppose," said Kayla. She did not sound convinced.

Fred poked his head into the chamber. A giant snake stared down at him. Fred had faced a large number of scary things in his life, and there was now little that could startle him, but even Fred felt his heart race as he looked up at those shining green eyes and silver fangs.

The snake was not real. Fred was mostly sure of that. And after a few seconds, he had his heart back under control.

The snake was made of black granite, the same as the floor. Perhaps the two were one stone. If so, it was a monumental monolith. The head reached halfway toward the dome, and the lifeless eyes gazed down on the chamber with malice.

At the altar below the snake, the clerics were oblivious, arguing over what was to blame for the declining grain shipments. Their voices were softened by draperies of dark green cloth that covered the chamber's walls. Gold-inlaid designs carved into the granite floor defined concentric circles radiating from the chamber's center, and Fred now had a better idea of what *inner circle* was supposed to mean.

"They say if you meet Toxia's gaze, she will insinuate her venom into your soul," Goose warned him.

"They say a lot of things," Kayla observed.

"It's just a statue," said Fred.

"It is and it isn't," said Quigly. "I should think that a man who has been in Toxia's service for seven years would know more about the power of idolatry."

"I mostly do the sword stuff," said Fred. "Master Sauron is the one who knows things."

Quigly was not just trying to scare him. Quigly actually believed the statue had some sort of power. Fred didn't know about that, but he knew Goose was wrong. Fred had met the statue's gaze, and his soul was unharmed. Toxia's green eyes were as lifeless as stone. They *were* stone. Each eye was an emerald nearly as big as Fred's head.

Fred had the feeling that this was the sort of information that would interest Wren.

CHAPTER FIFTEEN: IN WHICH HELEN, WREN, AND TWILIGHT GET TO KNOW EACH OTHER WHILE SWEATING IN A SWAMP.

DRAGONFLIES DANCED IN THE SUNLIGHT. The air was thick with the scents of decaying trees and mule dung. Yellin' Helen wiped the back of her hand across her brow to keep the sweat out of her eyes.

Throughout the swamp, insects buzzed and frogs argued. In the distance could be heard the thrumming of a woodpecker banging his head into a tree. Occasionally something would plop into the water. Sometimes it was a frog, sometimes it was a turtle. Sometimes it was something larger, and Helen wondered if that could be a lizard man.

This was lizard man territory. The thing about adventuring was that you were *always* in the territory of something—usually several somethings. Right now, she was in lizard man territory, giant deadly snake territory, harmless frog territory, harmless-unless-you-lick-it frog territory, and evil cleric territory ... although she wasn't sure about that last one.

"What are you thinking?" asked Twilight. "If I may ask."

Helen hadn't been thinking. She'd been listening. But she told him what her next thought would have been if he hadn't interrupted: "I'm wondering what's in it for the lizard men."

Wren rolled over and sat up, blinking in the light. She looked cute. Helen always looked terrible after a nap until she had brushed her hair into submission, but Wren looked cute with a few locks out of place.

Twilight didn't seem to notice Wren. He was pondering Helen's question. "Perhaps the lizard men think cooperation is preferable to war."

"But why wear the uniform?" asked Helen. "Suppose a group of barbarians decided to live in an elven forest. Maybe you would let us move in, but I can't imagine you would all strip down to loin cloths."

"Apparently, the lizard men are subservient," said Twilight.

"Yeah. And I don't see why. They must outnumber the evil clerics."

"Good point." Twilight thought a moment. "I suppose I'll regret speculating—because the answer will turn out to be something stupid like, 'It says so on page 517 of *The Adventurer's Guide*,'—but perhaps the clerics are in a position of power."

"*The Adventurer's Guide* doesn't have 517 pages," said Wren.

"So which page explains why the evil clerics have power over the lizard men?" Twilight asked.

Wren shrugged. "There's not a lot of info specifically on evil clerics. We know clerics can have any alignment, and we know they can be NPMs. But there's nothing about evil clerics that makes them different from good ones."

"Except that they're evil," said Twilight.

"Except that," agreed Wren.

"Evil clerics have armies," said Helen. "And the lizard men don't."

"Ah," said Twilight. "So that puts the lizard men at a strategic disadvantage."

"The lizard men are fighting each other," said Wren.

"Are we sure?" asked Twilight.

Wren nodded. "Some eat the clerics. Others wear the uniform. They can't be on the same side."

"I'm not so sure," said Twilight. "They could be *pretending* to go along with the evil clerics, while harvesting them for food."

"So what's-in-it-for-the-lizard-men is lunch?" asked Helen.

Wren frowned and shook her head. "If they were all on the same side, they wouldn't have to boil clerics in a tunnel. I imagine you could eat a cleric just about anywhere in this swamp, and as long as you weren't in sight of the temple, no one would ever know."

"I'll keep that in mind," said Helen.

"Are you a cannibal?" asked Wren. "I apologize for not stating this earlier, but I won't adventure with someone who's a cannibal."

"Helen was jesting," said Twilight.

"So was I," said Wren. "I was doing the voice."

"What voice?" asked Helen.

"Mak-Thar's voice."

"Oh," said Helen. "I thought you were having trouble speaking because you had swallowed a gnat."

"That's not Mak-Thar's voice," said Twilight. "His voice sounds more like this: 'Although cannibalism may seem to be an efficient solution to the rations problem, the party as a whole is actually *losing* meat, once you take into account the expected value of the Hunting Table.'"

"That's brilliant!" said Helen.

Wren sighed. "It's easy to be entertaining when you have high charisma."

"I apologize," said Twilight. "I was not trying to show you up.

I just wanted to make fun of Mak-Thar behind his back."

Wren grinned. "That's mean. Are you evil? I apologize for not stating this earlier, but I won't adventure with someone who's evil."

Twilight looked confused.

"I think she's still trying to do the voice," Helen explained.

"Ah," said Twilight.

"Stupid low charisma," said Wren.

"*Mak-Thar* doesn't think you have low charisma," said Helen.

"That's the nice thing about people with limited social skills," said Wren. "They're somewhat forgiving of other people with limited social skills."

"I'm curious," said Twilight. "If you think Mak-Thar has limited social skills, why did you put him in charge of the people who are trying to talk their way into the temple?"

"Because Nightshade is a baby and Fred is stupid. Also, Mak-Thar is the only one of us fussy enough to pass as an evil cleric."

"That last I will grant you," said Twilight. "And the first. But Fred's not stupid."

"Wren thinks everyone is stupid," said Helen. "She's like Mak-Thar in that way."

"I don't think *you're* stupid," said Wren.

"You don't?"

"You're one of the smartest women I know. ... I mean, maybe you don't have the same sort of smarts we have in the Thieves' Guild, but honest doesn't mean stupid."

Helen said, "Fred's honest."

"But he's not bright," said Wren. "He wouldn't have known how to build this sleeping platform. He wouldn't have realized a fireball could create a dry hillock for the mule to stand on."

Helen shrugged. "Fred knows Fred stuff."

Wren was skeptical. "What kind of stuff is that?"

"Just don't underestimate him," said Helen.

"Are you two a couple?" asked Wren.

"What? No."

"Okay. I wasn't sure if maybe there was something going on that I wasn't picking up on."

"We're buddies," said Helen.

"Oh," said Twilight. He'd just realized something.

"What?" asked Helen.

"You didn't say, 'We're *just* buddies.' You said *buddies* like it was a very important relationship."

"It is." In the adventuring business, no one was more important than your buddies.

"That's how Fred introduces you," said Twilight. "He calls you 'my buddy from the Fighters' Guild.'"

"Yeah. And?"

"That's not how he introduces me."

"You're not in the Fighters' Guild," said Helen.

"I'm just his friend," said Twilight. "'Buddy' is something different, isn't it?"

"Um ..." Despite the log platform she was sitting on, Helen suddenly felt like she was on unsteady ground.

Wren grinned. "Twilight's jealous!"

Helen saw that as a good-natured ribbing, but Twilight didn't take it that way. He took her seriously.

"I think I *am* jealous."

"You're his buddy, too," said Helen. Fred and Twilight had been through a lot together. She knew Fred valued Twilight's friendship deeply.

"Gee," said Wren. "And here I was afraid that the boys would be fighting over *me*."

"No one's fighting," said Helen.

"True enough," said Wren.

"I'm sorry," said Twilight. "I shouldn't let it bother me."

"It's not a big deal," said Helen. "Fred and I have been on a lot of adventures together, that's all." And they had hung out in taverns and at the Fighters' Guild. Helen went on adventures with lots of different people, but Fred was the one she looked for when the adventure was done. He was just good to hang out with.

Wren smiled and touched Twilight's arm. "Tell us how you and Fred met."

"We met in a bar," said Twilight. "As I understand it, any other way of meeting is considered quite unusual."

"That's just the way people meet around *here*," said Helen. "Out on the steppe, we usually meet our buddies in mortal combat."

"So you met in a bar," said Wren, "went to a dungeon, and it was friends at first sight?"

"Well, there's a little more to it, of course."

"We have time," said Wren. "Tell us the story."

* * *

Twilight told the story of Fred's adventure to the Dungeon of Doom. Helen had heard the story already, but Twilight's perspective was—well, it wasn't the way Fred told it. In Fred's story, it started out as an easy dungeon crawl and an opportunity to show a new adventurer how to have a good time. In Twilight's story, it had been a fierce struggle for mortal souls.

On multiple occasions, Fred had been "grievously wounded" and only "the grace of the goddess Selene" had saved his life. Twilight, too, had been wounded, "attempting to fight alongside this fortress of a man." For Twilight, the adventure had been him and Fred against the world.

About halfway through the story, he seemed to remember that Mak-Thar had a crush on Wren, and he started adding details to make the mage look good. Wren stayed interested in the story, but Helen couldn't be certain Wren was interested in Mak-Thar. Other women seemed so good at picking up on that sort of thing, but Helen had to devote most of her senses to staying alert for lizard men.

Twilight did not quite tell the whole story. He got to the part where he and Mak-Thar worked together to take the Amulet of Spring, and then Wren interrupted with questions.

"Do you still have the amulet?"

"Yes," said Twilight. "As a matter of fact, I am wearing it now."

"Can I see it?" asked Wren.

Twilight looked embarrassed. "Not very easily. It's sewn into my shirt."

"Oh," said Wren. "Because you thought I would steal it from you?"

"Well ..." said Twilight.

"Hey!" said Helen. "We've been over this. There is no way I'd ask you to adventure with someone we can't trust."

"I was not worried so much about you, Wren, as about your colleagues in the Den of Thieves."

"That makes sense," said Wren. "No offense taken."

Helen grinned. "Does that mean you'll take off your shirt and show us the amulet?"

"No," said Twilight.

Wren said, "Some people are more modest than you, dear."

"She just wants to make personal comments about my chest," said Twilight. "I shan't give her the satisfaction."

"Let's send her out foraging," said Wren. "Then you and I can look at your amulet together."

Twilight asked, "How did this suddenly become a game of Make the Male Uncomfortable?"

"It has nothing to do with you being a male," said Helen. "You're just fun to tease because you're Twilight."

Twilight pursed his lips like he'd swallowed a sour pickle. After a moment, he said, "Thank you, Helen. You also have many unique qualities that I appreciate."

Wren laughed. "You're just encouraging her."

"I suppose you're right."

"So ignore her a moment, and tell me what the amulet does."

"I don't know," said Twilight.

"Really? You've never used it on anything?"

"How does one 'use' an amulet?"

"Okay. Fair point. If it's an Amulet of Protection, you just wear it and it protects you. But an Amulet of Spring ... maybe you could use it to make seeds sprout."

"Or turn the ground to mud," Helen suggested.

"Or summon daffodils," said Wren.

"Or call down a wet and bitter wind that chills your enemies to the bone."

"You and I have different ideas of spring," said Wren.

Helen said, "When it's springtime on the steppe, I wear twenty pounds of fur."

"Really?" asked Wren. "How come I've never seen that in a Nycadaemon Knickers ad?"

Twilight suggested, "'Thanks to Nycadaemon Knickers, this stinky yak pelt doesn't chafe my delicate skin.'"

"Cute," said Helen. Actually, her spring robe was a bear pelt, and the reason it didn't chafe was because she wore the fur on the inside and kept it clean and brushed. It *did* stink though—especially after she greased it to keep out the blowing rain.

Wren asked, "How about you, Helen? Why did *you* come to civilization and start adventuring?"

Helen shrugged. "Lots of barbarians come to Basetown."

"You don't seem like the type of woman who follows the crowd, dear."

Helen shrugged again.

Wren turned to Twilight. "I've never been able to get anything out of her. Has she told *you* her back story?"

"Occasionally she and Fred have shared stories from their past."

"Their *past* past? Or just 'in a previous adventure' type stuff?"

"Just adventures," said Twilight. "I don't think Fred has a *past* past. At least, his past doesn't include anything more interesting than raising chickens."

"Helen has some dark trauma," said Wren. "All women do."

"Really?" Twilight looked shocked.

"All the fighters do," Wren clarified. "A woman doesn't need dark trauma to become a *mage*. But to pick up a sword and start lopping off heads? Yeah. Has to be some dark trauma. That's why she's angry all the time."

"But she's *not* angry all the time," said Twilight. "She's not even angry *most* of the time. In fact, I doubt anyone has ever seen Helen angry and lived to tell about it."

Yes! Thank you, Twilight. Helen was trying to make the same point by sitting still and calm with one eyebrow raised, but sometimes it's nice to have a talkative elf friend make your points for you.

Wren was either oblivious, or she was trying to be annoying. She didn't let up. "Don't let her calm exterior fool you. Underneath that, she's a cauldron of boiling rage."

Twilight said, "I'll agree that Helen is fierce. But that's not the same as angry."

Wren shrugged. "Whatever you call it—fierce, angry—the point is that some man wronged her. She picked up his sword and took revenge. And ever since then, she's been Yellin' Helen."

"It's my own sword," said Helen. "My dad had it forged for my twelfth birthday."

Twilight eyed Helen's sword. "You must have been a very tall twelve-year-old."

"He said I would grow into it. I did."

She must have looked silly. Even at the time, she'd felt ridiculous trying to swing this heavy slab of metal over her head. But when it had slipped from her weak grip and nearly impaled her younger brother, her mom had just smiled and encouraged her to keep practicing.

And so Helen had practiced. Every day. Her wrists grew strong. Her arms grew big. Her back became muscular. The heavy slab of metal became her weapon—and then her body became her weapon, and the sword was just a part of her.

Her brother had watched her practice. Every day. And Helen had always made him watch from a stone's throw away, because she was pretty sure she couldn't throw her sword that far—at least, not accidentally.

Three years after Helen's twelfth birthday, her brother had received his own sword. Shyly, he had asked if Helen would like to spar, or if she preferred that he stay a stone's throw away. And Helen had sparred with her brother, because her sword had become her hand, and losing her grip had thus become impossible.

Wren interrupted Helen's thoughts. "That's your back story? You became a warrior just because your dad gave you a sword?"

"Yup," said Helen. "That's pretty much it."

Chapter Sixteen: In which Fred fits right in.

THE GUARDS HAD A TINY BARRACKS in a back corner of the temple. Bunks were stacked four to a wall. It was so cramped they could smell each other breathing. Fred was telling a story:

"… So I says to Helen, 'You know who we need on this job? We need Stinky La Foote.' And Helen says, 'Nuh uh,' because she's worked with Stinky before and she knows he's crazy.

"But that was the thing, right? If you want to steal a giant's nose ring, who can you get to reach inside there except the craziest half-pint you know?

"Helen had to give in. So it was her, me, and Stinky—and I have to tell you, those two got along so much better than you would think. Helen is always good company, of course, and Stinky is just a riot. Whenever we ran into trouble—like an orc patrol or a horde of zombie goblins—those two would charge right in, and it was so funny watching long-legged Helen try to outrun a three-foot-tall half-pint that sometimes I couldn't even get in on the fight because I was too busy laughing.

"Anyway, after a few of those fights, we get to the giant's cabin, and it was like this doll house, but in reverse, right? Like if it were a normal cabin, we would have to be the dolls.

"We'd planned to climb in through the open window, but no one had any rope. So Stinky says no problem, we'll just walk around the house and look for another way in. At the back of the house, he finds this path, and the path leads to a hole in the wall, and we squeeze through the hole and find ourselves inside the giant's cabin right next to this slab of wood with an enormous wedge of cheese.

"And I'm thinking, 'That's odd. Why did the giant put a wedge of cheese on the floor?' And Helen's thinking, 'Danger! Danger! Avoid the cheese!' because Helen is way smarter about these things than I am.

"But Stinky—he's not thinking at all. He charges up to the wedge of cheese and *snap!* he's caught. A giant metal bar has flipped out of nowhere and pinned him to the board. And Stinky ... well, it's like he doesn't even *notice*. He's still reaching for the cheese, like he'll somehow be able to shove it in his treasure sack.

"And the giant says, 'Aha! Got you, you little varmint!' Which was surprising, because I'd been expecting something more like, 'Fee, fie, foe, fum,' you know? But he doesn't say 'Fee fie.' He says 'Got you.' So then we're in for a fight.

"Helen draws her sword and keeps the giant dancing. She's swinging at his shins, trying to buy us time to get away. And I'm thinking it's up to me to get Stinky out of the mousetrap—or whatever it was—not even giant rats are that big.

"But Stinky doesn't wait for me to figure anything out. He just draws his sword and charges.

"Now keep in mind that a spring-loaded metal bar is pressing into Stinky's butt, pinning him to a slab of wood about the size of a coffee table. Stinky can't see the giant—his face is pressed to the wood. But even so, he somehow manages to draw his sword, stand up, and charge—yes, charge—in the general direction of the giant.

"Well, when the giant sees his own mousetrap charging at him, he squeals and kicks the thing away. The mousetrap, cheese, and Stinky all go flying through the air and out the open window.

"Helen grabs my hand, and while the giant is still watching to see where his mousetrap will land, Helen and I are sprinting back out through our mouse hole. We found Stinky outside, pried him out of the trap, and ran back to Basetown as fast as our legs could carry us. Stinky was limping a little, but he ran pretty fast, too. Never did get that nose ring."

Quigly shook his head. "That is the most preposterous tale I have ever heard."

Kayla elbowed him in the ribs—or rather, because they were both still armored, she cowtered him in the cuirass, which is basically the same thing.

"It was certainly amusing!" Quigly amended. "I merely said it was preposterous."

"Yeah," said Fred. "Stinky is a preposterous kind of half-pint."

"Tell us another one!" said Goose.

"It's time for bed," said Kayla.

"It can't be time for bed," said Goose. "Roberto's not here yet."

"Roberto has dungeon duty," said Kayla. "When we have prisoners, he works both shifts."

Quigly curled his upper lip. "Because those layabouts on the night shift are afraid to get their tabards dirty."

"So are you," said Kayla.

"So am I," admitted Quigly. "And now, I plan to lay about."

"It's 'lie'," said Evelyn.

"What's lie?" asked Quigly.

"Layabouts lie about."

"Hm," said Quigly. "So they do. Five points for Evelyn."

"Points?" asked Fred.

"He's just jesting her," said Kayla.

Quigly said, with great importance, "Evelyn, you now have five points. If you get to one thousand, I'll let you be a ceremonial guard."

Evelyn frowned.

"A thousand points sounds like a lot," said Goose. "Is he being mean?"

"*Mean* means *base and ignoble*," said Quigly. "I am haughty and condescending. That's the opposite of mean."

Fred was pretty sure he knew what *mean* meant, and he was pretty sure Quigly was being it.

"He's being a jerk," said Kayla. "Like always. Evelyn, if you want to be a ceremonial guard, just ask Sam. I'm sure he can find something else for Quigly to do."

"But a man of my qualities!" said Quigly. "I'm sure my talents would be wasted at any other post."

Kayla said, "You've just admitted that your talents would be wasted at any job that isn't ornamental."

"Some were born to labor," said Quigly. "Others were born to be admired. I know my place."

"Speaking of places," said Fred, "which bunk's mine?"

Kayla said, "You can sleep in Roberto's bunk, if you don't mind the smell of dungeon fungus."

"He should sleep below my bunk," said Goose. "He's the new guy."

"He can sleep in my bunk," said Evelyn.

They all looked at her, and her eyes went wide. "I mean—I'd move, if he wanted a bottom bunk. I didn't mean—"

Quigly grinned. "Evelyn! You cagey little vixen!"

"Just so everything is clear," said Kayla, "no one shares a bunk with anyone, ever. This is not the Temple of Chaos."

"Do guards share bunks in the Temple of Chaos?" asked Goose.

"Who *knows* what they do there?" said Quigly. "It's not even a real temple."

"I hear it pays pretty good," said Kayla.

"Chaos is not even a real religion," said Quigly. "It's just an excuse to justify doing whatever you want."

"Right," said Kayla. "Whereas we evil people get to do whatever we want without justification."

"Ah, fair point," said Quigly.

"So …" said Fred. This might get him into trouble and blow up the entire adventure, but he had to know. "What made you all decide to be evil?"

"I'm not evil," said Kayla. "I'm neutral."

Quigly said, "Kayla was fifth-in-command at the Cathedral of Neutrality in Watergate."

"Impressive," said Fred.

"Boring," said Kayla. "I was bored and poor. They couldn't afford to pay me. Do you know what a neutral fundraising drive sounds like? 'Brothers and sisters, please empty your loot sacks to aid our neutral cause! Right now, starving children are knitting stocking caps for blind widows who sold their hair to pay off the mortgage on the hospital at the Temple of Good. Ignore them! We owe our neutral guards three months of back pay.' When I heard this temple was hiring, I signed up right away."

"What about you, Evelyn?"

"Oh, I'm evil," said Evelyn. "It's in my blood."

"Evelyn's father was a temple guard," said Quigly.

"And *his* father," said Evelyn. "And *his* father. I'm fourth-generation evil."

She sounded more dedicated than evil, but Fred didn't want to judge.

"I'm evil because they were the only ones who would let me hold a sword," said Goose.

Fred looked expectantly at Quigly. Quigly didn't answer. The supercilious grin left his eyes, and for a moment, his face seemed hard as stone.

No one else seemed to notice—except possibly Kayla, who asked, "And what about you, Fred? No offense, but you seem a little too jolly to be hanging out with a guy like Sauron."

At the mention of Mak-Thar's fake name, Evelyn shivered.

"Aw," said Fred, "he's not such a bad guy once you get to know him."

"He's *much* worse than Quigly," said Evelyn.

"Oh sure!" said Fred. He had to agree, because Mak-Thar was supposed to be evil. That obviously made him more evil than Quigly. Fred hadn't been sure how to read Quigly's stone-hard face, but it hadn't said, *I am very evil.* It had said, *Never ask me that again,* which was a different thing.

Fred said, "Once you work with a guy for a little bit, you kind of figure out how to stay on his good side. Or … maybe his neutral side, I guess."

"So how did you meet him?" asked Goose.

"We met in a bar," said Fred. "He offered me a job. It sounded like fun, so I took him up on it."

"Wow," said Goose. "And he let you hold a sword?"

"I already had the sword," said Fred.

"Ah, the advantages of wealth!" Quigly slapped Fred on the back. "Eh, my boy?"

"Yeah," said Fred, because it *is* nice to own your own sword.

* * *

In the end, Fred decided to take a top bunk that belonged to someone on the night shift. Kayla told him it would probably be okay, but Fred wasn't sure if that meant it would *really* be okay or if she just wanted to see him get into a fight with someone from the night shift. Fred woke up early, before the night shift arrived at the barracks, and went to the cafeteria for breakfast.

Fred was polishing off his second bowl of gruel when Evelyn sat down across from him.

"Sleep well?" she asked.

"Yeah," said Fred. Near the top of the wall, he'd been sleeping in the open air underneath the temple dome, and he'd been a little worried about being landed on by bats. But as far as he knew, it had been a bat-free night.

"Why do we sleep in our armor?" he asked.

"We must be ever-vigilant," said Evelyn.

"Oh," said Fred. He was pretty sure he hadn't been ever-vigilant—not in his sleep—but maybe vigilant meant something else.

Fred noticed a haunted-looking man walking away from the kitchen window with three bowls of gruel.

"We can have thirds?"

"You want thirds of *gruel?*" Evelyn looked where Fred was looking. "Oh. That's just Roberto. He's getting gruel for himself and the two prisoners."

Ah. So Roberto didn't have thirds; he had three firsts.

But Fred was hungry, so it was worth a try. He picked up his bowl and left the table. As he approached the kitchen window, he caught a whiff of moldy leather—Roberto was gone, but his scent lingered.

Fred asked for thirds. The cook gave him a funny look, but she dished up thirds. Fred thanked her and returned to the table.

An armored man about Fred's size had joined Evelyn. His square jaw was covered in three days' worth of salt-and-pepper stubble. Fred nodded and sat down next to him.

The armored guy asked, "What's your name, recruit?"

"I'm Fred."

The guy didn't reach out to shake hands, so Fred didn't either.

"I'm the sergeant-at-arms, but you can call me Sam for short."

"Oh," said Fred. "I didn't know *Sam* was short for *sergeant-at-arms*."

"It is if I say it is."

So that was how things worked around here. "Nice to meet you, Sam."

"Nice? It's not supposed to be *nice* to meet me."

"Um ... *mean* to meet you?"

"Are you giving me lip? I don't take lip. Evelyn, tell Fred I don't take lip."

"Sam doesn't take lip."

Fred understood that Sam did not take lip. But he felt that he, too, should have the right to not take lip. This refusal of lip should go both ways.

Fred put a hand on Sam's armored shoulder and said, "You seem to be on edge, Sergeant. Were you out on a mission yesterday?"

"Didn't get back till three in the morning," said Sam. "And I'd like nothing better than to chew you up and spit you out, so don't cross me."

Well, Fred *was* going to cross him. That was just the nature of the adventure. But Fred didn't need to cross Sam *right now*. "Sounds rough," said Fred. "Did you lose many?"

"We didn't lose any," said Sam. "But we didn't *find* any, either."

"Six clerics are missing," Evelyn explained.

"Missing from where?" asked Fred.

"From the new construction site," said Evelyn. "We're supposed to have a barracks, a training ground, and everything."

"But the lizard men are behind schedule," said Sam. "The Council has been sending out clerics to manage the workers, but now six clerics are missing, including the assistant supervisor."

"That's rough," said Fred.

"They were last seen leaving the site and heading back towards the temple," said Sam. "At least, that's what the forelizard says, but I don't trust that guy."

Fred nodded to indicate that he, too, would not trust the forelizard.

"How long have they been gone?" asked Fred.

"Four days," said Sam.

"And how far away is the construction site?"

"Ten minutes."

"Ah."

"We *did* find tracks yesterday," said Sam. "But they disappeared into the water, and my scouts don't smell as good as you'd think."

Fred lowered his nose to his collar and sniffed his own tunic. Yeah. It could use a wash.

"They don't smell as *well* as you would think," Evelyn said. She wasn't correcting Sam; she was explaining to Fred. "Our scouts are lizard men, but they aren't much better than humans."

Sam looked Evelyn up and down. "You've been paying attention."

"Yes," said Evelyn. "A good guard is supposed to pay attention."

"How would you like to go out with the search party today?"

"I'd love to go out with you!" said Evelyn. Then her eyes grew wide and she looked embarrassed, but Sam was oblivious to any double meaning.

"Great," said Sam. "I'll put Fred on front door."

"Really?" asked Evelyn.

"Really," said Sam.

"I'll tell Goose!"

"Goose is *not* invited."

"I know, and I want to rub it in."

Sam watched her leave the cafeteria. "She's not a bad kid. But she sure *tries* to be, and I guess that's all you can hope for."

Fred lifted his spoon.

"Why are you pointing your spoon at me?"

"It's like raising my glass," explained Fred. "Except I don't have a glass. I have a spoon."

"Well, eat up. Your shift starts in twenty minutes." Sam got up, causing Fred's bench to bounce.

Fred wondered if he'd have to stand guard for twelve hours straight, or if he might be allowed to answer calls of nature. That was the neat thing about adventuring—you never knew exactly what would happen.

Fred had nearly finished his third bowl of gruel when he realized that a search party looking for missing clerics might make life difficult for his friends who were hiding in the swamp.

CHAPTER SEVENTEEN: IN WHICH HELEN, WREN, AND TWILIGHT GET SO BORED THAT THEY GO LOOKING FOR ADVENTURE.

AS SOON AS THE SUN got high enough to shine on the swamp, the log platform started heating up. Snakes can sense heat somehow, and one would occasionally slither out of the cool water and climb onto the platform to sun itself. Helen would whack it in the head with a cudgel she had carved from a tree branch, and then she would have something to do for a while. She tanned the skins—maybe she could sell them in Basetown?—and laid the meat out in the sun to dry. Dried snake meat tastes real good when the alternative is dried frog.

Helen was filleting her eighth snake when Twilight asked a question she had been expecting for quite some time:

"How long should we wait?"

Wren shrugged. "It takes time to case the joint."

"But how can we be certain they are still 'casing the joint'? What makes us think they have not 'blown their cover'?"

Wren asked, "If they'd been caught, wouldn't we have heard Mak-Thar's fireball?"

"Not from here," said Twilight. "Perhaps they are just being thorough, but I was expecting them to be back by now."

Wren said, "They have to stay in place until we do the job. That's what the inside man does, see? He stays inside."

"Then how do we get their information?" asked Twilight.

"Mak-Thar will figure something out," said Wren. "He's very smart."

Twilight gave Helen a look. Helen shrugged and gave it back to him.

"What was that about?" asked Wren. "Mak-Thar's smart, isn't he?"

"Yeeesss?" Twilight sounded torn between vouching for his friend and telling the truth.

Wren said, "That was the least-confident yes I have ever heard."

"Mak-Thar is mage-smart," said Helen.

Wren raised an eyebrow. "And that means … ?"

Twilight said, "It means that if the solution involves setting an elaborate trap, casting a spell, or starting a fire, Mak-Thar is your man."

"Sounds good," said Wren.

"If the solution involves simply walking away from the temple for an hour, it might not occur to him."

"Oh," said Wren.

"But he has Fred with him," said Helen.

"That's not reassuring," said Wren.

"Well," said Twilight, "their skills *are* complementary. I suppose Fred might realize he needs to come visit us."

"Sure he will," said Helen. "You can count on Fred. You just need something to distract you until he comes."

"Like skinning snakes?" asked Twilight.

"Works for me," said Helen. "But if you're bored, we could look for an adventure."

"An adventure while we're already on an adventure?"

"Sure," said Helen. "I do it all the time."

"We could look for the lizard man lair and steal their treasure," said Wren.

"That sounds good," said Helen.

"That sounds terrible," said Twilight. "In the first place, we could all be killed. In the second place, a successful theft would alert our enemies to our presence."

"What's the third place?" asked Helen.

"Isn't that enough?" asked Twilight.

"I suppose," said Helen. The excuse sounded kind of weak with only two places.

"We could scout to see where the walkway leads," said Wren.

"It leads to the temple," said Helen.

"Yes, dear. But when you walk the other direction, it must lead somewhere else."

"Probably the hills," said Twilight. "When we were last exploring this corner of the world, the evil clerics had wagons rolling through the hills carrying grain to the temple. The walkway explains how they got the grain here without losing their wagons in the bog."

"So it's a wagonway?" asked Helen.

"I think so."

"All right," said Helen. It was probably wide enough to be a wagonway.

"That makes sense," said Wren.

"Yes, it does," said Twilight. "And I find that suspicious. So much of this setup—an evil temple miles away from civilization—just looks like an excuse to give the crazies in Basetown a place to adventure. But when you look at it the right way, sometimes some of it makes sense."

"It *all* has to make sense." Helen was annoyed by Twilight's insistence that the world merely followed stupid rules in The

Adventurer's Guide. "I mean, sure, the temple is just here to give us something to attack. But the people in the temple still have to worry about where their food comes from, how they're going to recruit people, and how to get along with the locals."

Twilight cocked his head like a bewildered robin. "Did you just say it was both things?"

"What things?" asked Helen.

"Are you saying that the world is designed for adventures, *and* that it makes sense? Are you saying the world was built for us, and everyone else is expected to deal with it as best they can?"

"Something like that," said Helen.

We are people of the sword, her uncle had said, *and this world was created to be our domain. Why would there be a world of battles if we were not meant to fight them? Why would the gods create us in this place if we were not meant to conquer it?*

That had been his call-to-arms speech, just before they had set out to plunder the southern villages. A woman in body, a girl in mind, Helen had been thrilled by the chance to test herself against warriors who were really trying to kill her.

Her brother had tagged along, wearing a sword he didn't know how to use and a pair of boots that Helen had outgrown. He wanted to follow in her footsteps, but the best he could do was wear her boots.

Helen soon discovered that her uncle was right about the people in the villages: They were weak. None of them could stand up to Helen. Sometimes they ran, sometimes they fought, but they were never a match for her skill and ferocity.

The pillaging went on for months. Helen thought it was glorious, but her parents and her siblings grew tired of killing. Eventually, even Helen began to realize that she was fighting people who had never done anything to *her*, except defend themselves against her extended family.

Looking back on it now, Helen had to admit that rampaging across the countryside—fun as it was—might have been somewhat evil.

She'd been indifferent to good and evil in those days. The strong won. The weak perished. That was the barbarian code. Barbarians weren't supposed to worry about good and evil. And as long as Helen had her sword in hand, she felt she was being the woman she had been created to be.

There was no defining moment of conscience. There was no moment when she had looked into her opponent's eyes and asked herself the difference between a warrior and a murderer. There was simply five months of battle, each day a little less satisfying than the one before, until the day they tangled with a tribe of devil worshippers who took her brother's leg.

"I'm liking this idea," said Wren. "We might be able to turn it into a backup plan."

Twilight shrugged. "At the very least, it could give us some context for what is going on around here."

"What do you think?" Wren was talking to Helen. Helen hadn't been listening.

Helen said, "If it will get us up and moving around, I'm all for it."

* * *

Sneaking through the swamp was better than skinning snakes. And Helen had to admit that Wren had picked the right team. Even moving through water, Wren stepped gracefully and quietly. Twilight made little mincing elf-steps from tussock to tussock—as though he thought that would save his new green elf pants from getting wet—but they were *quiet* mincing elf-steps. Twilight was one with nature, like a fastidious deer.

Helen picked up the trail not far from the door to the dwarf tunnel. The surviving lizard men had run straight for the swamp, and their footprints were quite clear in the mud at the edge.

"Can you track them through water?" asked Twilight.

"Of course," said Helen. "And so can you."

"I would expect their tracks to blend in with their natural habitat."

"But you've tracked deer in the forest," said Helen. "Everything leaves signs of its passage."

"I suppose that's true. I confess I don't have much experience tracking sentient beings."

Helen asked, "Does *sentient* mean *lives in swamp?*"

Twilight said, "I don't have experience tracking in swamps, either. Will you show me what to look for?"

She did.

Twilight was a good tracker. And tracking in the swamp could be quite easy. The water was still, so a track in the water did not get washed away. The trick was to scan the clear places ahead of you before your own tracks made the water murky. Twilight's reluctance to get his ankles muddy really helped him there.

The lizard men had the opposite philosophy. Whenever they saw deep water, they went straight for the middle of it. Twilight and Helen walked around the deep water, but they could always find the tracks again on the opposite side.

The trail led them to the decapitated remnants of a huge hollow tree. Densely packed mud suggested that the lizard men had spent quite a bit of time inside before they had decided what to do next.

The trail leaving the hollow tree was fresh. The lizard men had left this hideout within the last few hours, marching somewhere with a purpose.

Helen, Twilight, and Wren followed.

"Are we heading toward the temple or away from it?" Wren asked.

"The temple is over there." Helen pointed.

"How do you do that?" Twilight asked. "My sense of direction comes from my awareness of all living creatures. But you just point and go."

"There's a ball of yellow fire in the sky," said Helen. "Once you realize that, it's kind of hard to get lost."

"The sun moves," said Wren.

"Yeah, but I know how to dance with the sun."

"Cheek to cheek?" asked Wren. "Or is the sun more of a line dancer?"

"It's a path," said Twilight, pointing ahead. The tracks they were following headed straight for it.

"Let me go ahead," suggested Helen. Lizard man paths were full of tracks, and she did not need extra feet confusing the trail. Helen left the others and watched her quarry's tracks closely, looking for a hint about which direction they had chosen.

The rearmost lizard man had cut the corner, leaving a tail mark curving onto the path. "They went that way."

"Should we follow the path?" asked Twilight. "Or should we take a parallel course?"

"Let's stay in the trees," said Wren. "If no one sees us, we can choose to avoid a fight."

"I hope we can avoid a fight regardless," said Twilight. The elf hoped the lizard men might become allies against the temple. Helen thought that was unlikely, but she was willing to watch Twilight try to convince them. When his plan failed, she would be ready to kill them.

The nice thing about monsters was that you could count on them to attack you. That was what made them monsters. Sometimes they attacked and then died; sometimes they attacked and then ran away. Either way, it was a clean victory.

Fighting people wasn't like that. People might fight or they might beg for mercy. Taking stuff from people who were too afraid to defend themselves just seemed mean. Helen was glad she didn't do that anymore. She fought because the gods had put her in the world to fight, not because she needed to rob farmers of their turnips.

* * *

They caught up to their quarry sooner than they had expected. A group of naked lizard men stood in the middle of the trail talking to a group of lizard men wearing the temple uniform. Helen wasn't sure what this meant for Twilight's plan. Were the two groups in cahoots? Were the naked lizard men trying to persuade the others to leave the temple? Or were the naked lizard men the last of the resisters, now begging to rejoin their tribe because Helen had killed too many of them?

Well, it wasn't like she'd had a choice. The lizard men had not said, *Oh, hi. We're eating evil clerics right now, but if you'll wait until after lunch, we'll join you and help you overthrow the temple.* No. They had drawn weapons and attacked.

And Helen had been fine with that. When you tried to figure out *why* monsters did what they did, things got too complicated. Fighting was better because it was simpler.

She wondered if she would feel differently if lizard women bought Nycadaemon Knickers.

"It just sounds like a bunch of hisses," said Wren. "Do either of you speak lizard man?"

Twilight shook his head.

"Figures." Wren frowned at the hissing monsters. "Hey! I'm pretty good at *written* languages. If you write down what they're saying, there's an eighty percent chance I can read it."

Twilight made his skeptical face. "I don't see how I can write it down if I don't know what they're saying."

"Can't you cast some elf spell to learn what they're talking about?"

"If you really want to know," said Helen, "you could just ask them."

Wren said, "I think they might resent the interruption."

"Oh!" said Twilight. "I think I have a plan!"

"Cool," said Wren. "What's the plan?"

"I can talk to the tree."

Helen was confused. "How can a tree help us against the evil temple?"

"The tree can tell us what the lizard men said." Twilight pointed to a scraggly black thing with peeling bark and stunted gray leaves. "Once they are gone, I shall commune with that tree and ask what it overheard."

"What if the tree doesn't speak lizard man?" asked Wren.

"Nature speaks all languages and none," said Twilight.

"And that means ... ?"

"I don't care what it means," said Helen. "Even if that tree *did* have information, how could we trust it to tell us the truth?"

"It's a tree," said Twilight.

"That tree looks like a liar," said Helen.

"But—"

"We're doing this my way." She raised her voice. "Hey! Do you mind speaking the common tongue? We're trying to overhear your conversation."

Wren shook her head. "Don't improvise, dear. You don't have the talent for it."

The lizard men immediately drew their weapons—mostly clubs, knives, and spears. They peered into the trees, but they hadn't seen Helen yet.

"Over here." Helen waved. "See? We're too far away to hurt you. We just want to talk."

Actually, they were easily within range for Twilight's and Wren's bows, but why split hairs?

The naked lizard men recognized her and started hissing again.

"Speak common!" Helen shouted. "We can't understand you."

One of the tabard-wearing lizard men said, "Give me one reassson we ssshould not kill you where you ssstand."

Helen had a good answer for that: "Because we stand far away, and it would be a lot of work to walk over here."

"Not for usss."

Oh, right. Lizard men were *really* fast in the swamp. She remembered that from last time.

"Okay," said Helen. "How about this, then? If you attack us, I'll cut you all down."

"And you sssay you come in peasss."

"Doesn't mean I have to leave in peace," said Helen.

"Excuse me," said Twilight. "I'd just like to say that I appreciate the restraint you have shown so far, and if we continue listening to each other, we may be able to find some common ground."

"Thisss isss *our* ssswamp. We will not ssshare with you!"

Twilight looked worried. "When I said 'common ground' I was speaking metaphorically."

The lizard men looked confused.

"They can only understand half of what you say," Helen told him.

Wren asked, "If you don't share with humans, why are you sharing with the temple?"

"Mind your own busssinessssss!"

"Stupid low charisma," Wren muttered.

"No, that was a good question," said Twilight. "You've hit a nerve. They all want to know what you said, and now he has to explain it to them."

Indeed, the leader did seem to be doing some explaining, and by the time he was done, some of the naked lizard men were looking at them with curiosity.

Helen called, "What if we told you we're here to overthrow the temple?"

"If you help us, you won't be slaves anymore," called Wren.

"We are not ssslavesss! We are free lizard men. And loyal. Very, very loyal to the temple." He gestured to the naked lizard men. "They are loyal, alssso. They sssimply ... lossst their clothesss ... to ... mothsss?"

"Moths ate their clothes?" asked Helen.

"Yesss. Mothsss."

Did this guy really think the naked lizard men were loyal? No. He was covering for them. Did he know they had eaten clerics?

"Maybe we should have asked the tree," Helen admitted.

"No," said Twilight. "This is more informative. I think the tree would have been a better liar."

"Anyone would be a better liar than this guy," said Wren.

"Okay," Helen called. "We get it. You guys are totally loyal. But if you happen to find any *disloyal* lizard men, be sure to mention that we hate the temple, too. It's time for that pile of rocks to fall."

"Is that it?" asked Wren.

"I think that's it," said Twilight. "They are not in a mood to negotiate right now, but if they want to move against the temple, they know they have allies."

"We're going now," called Helen. "See? We leave in peace."

"We ssshall track you down, kill you in your sssleep, and boil your bonesss!"

"Hey, I can do that, too!" said Helen. "Are you guys good to eat?"

There were a lot of angry hisses, but none of the lizard men left the trail. Helen had given them a lot to talk about.

CHAPTER EIGHTEEN: IN WHICH OUR INSIDE PEOPLE COMPARE INFORMATION.

FRED STOOD GUARD for about an hour. Once he realized that no one was coming to attack the temple, he forgot about the "guard" part and just stood. "Standing guard" for an evil temple was a lot like "taking a watch" for an adventuring party, except that he could do it in the daytime.

Every so often, Bradly came by to check on them. Apparently, that was Bradly's job. There wasn't much to check on, though. Fred and Goose were supposed to be standing around, and they did so.

Fred wouldn't like a job where he had to watch people stand. It seemed like the sort of thing that might get tedious after a few weeks. Fred thought maybe he should hide around the corner so that Bradly would have something to do on his checkup, but he had sense enough to realize that keeping Bradly on his toes would not be helpful to Wren's heist plan.

Goose would get very tense when Bradly came by. His armor would clink as he tried to stand up straighter, and his long neck would grow even longer.

Fred wanted to relieve the tension with a little small talk. He wanted to ask if Bradly missed traveling with his wandering party of evil clerics. But he didn't ask, because he thought that might remind Bradly that Fred had killed him.

Fred had been on guard duty for about four hours when a lizard man crawled out of the swamp and onto the walkway. The monster stopped in full view of the temple, staring at them.

Goose watched Fred to see how he would react, but Fred stayed calm. He did not put a hand on his sword. The lizard man was wearing a green-blob tabard, and Fred knew that meant he was supposed to be an ally. Also, there was no reason to draw when the lizard man was still so far away.

Seeing that Fred would not put on a show, Goose went into the temple and came back with a tall, thin woman. Fred thought he recognized her from the accounting ritual the day before.

The woman swept past Fred without even seeing him. With purposeful strides, she approached the lizard man, who waited nervously.

The cleric stopped, and the end of her snake staff hit the walkway with an imperious thud. She hissed. The lizard man hissed back, but politely.

The two held some sort of conversation about something. Then the lizard man bowed, and the woman returned to the temple.

"What was that all about?" Fred asked, when both the cleric and the lizard man had gone.

"I don't know," Goose admitted. "Sometimes it seems like the lizard men just like to talk. But they don't talk to us guards. Anyway, if Bradly catches us talking about the lizard men, we'll be in trouble."

Fred kept quiet when Bradly was around. He didn't want Goose in trouble. And really, it was probably best if Fred didn't get into trouble, either.

By midafternoon, Bradly was scowling at him anyway. Bradly was now certain that he knew Fred from somewhere, but he still didn't know where.

Every so often, Fred would remember that he was supposed

to come up with a plan for warning his friends that Sam and Evelyn were searching the swamp. But then he would forget again—because, really, Fred was not a tactical mastermind.

So he still did not have a plan when the night shift showed up. Fred didn't see the night shift coming. One moment, he was watching dragonflies. The next moment, a voice behind him said, "You can stand down now, boys. It's time for the *men* to take over."

The speaker was a lean and wolfish fellow who was old enough to grow a beard, but young enough that his beard was his biggest accomplishment in life so far. It was one of those patchy beards, thin in odd places—as though the beard had grown itself, and the guy's face just happened to be underneath it at the time.

"Yeah," said the shorter, scrawnier one. "Hurry to your beds before it gets dark."

This guy had a raspy voice, like he was trying to get over puberty but his throat wouldn't let him. He had to be exactly Goose's age, but obviously he thought that being on the night shift made him tougher. Judging by size, Fred figured Goose could dump this guy on his butt before he could even draw his sword, but Goose didn't look ready to fight.

Fred wasn't going to fight, either. He was a fighter, but he was a fighter who spent a lot of time in taverns. And guys who take offense at every little thing don't get to finish their mug of ale.

He held out his hand and said, "Hi. I'm Fred."

"I'm Ike," said the guy with the patchy beard. He seized Fred's hand.

Ike's grip was tight, and a hundred contingencies flashed through Fred's mind. If Ike tried to pull him off balance, Fred could twist his hand free. If Ike tried to push him, Fred could sidestep and use Ike's leverage to throw him onto the steps. If Ike went for an armlock, Fred could draw that knife in Ike's belt and stab him in the arm. In that one instant of handshake, Fred knew that there were a hundred ways he could take this guy down and humiliate him in front of the two younger men.

Fred grinned and said, "Pleased to meet you, Ike."

Ike let go.

"Fred slept in your bed last night," said Goose.

Ike's eyes flicked between Fred and Goose. Goose was definitely trying to start a fight. But Fred wasn't. And he had convinced Ike not to start a fight, either.

Ike said, "Mind your own business, Goose, or you'll see what happens to *your* bed when *you're* not there." He briefly met Fred's gaze and added, "Kids."

"Kids," Fred agreed cheerfully. "Come on, Goose. Let's get supper."

"It'll just be gruel again," said Goose.

"A man with his own sword has to eat," said Fred. "Eating keeps you strong."

Fred led the way into the temple and nearly ran over Bradly. The low-ranking cleric jumped out of the way and shouted, "Watch where you're going!"

"Sorry," said Fred. "I didn't see you there."

Bradly looked him in the eyes, and Fred thought that maybe this time Bradly would remember. But he didn't. He just said, "I've got my eye on you, Fred. You can't hide behind Curate Sauron forever."

Fred couldn't hide behind Mak-Thar at all—the mage was too skinny. But Fred just smiled and gave Bradly a little salute. Then he headed for the cafeteria.

* * *

The cafeteria was much more crowded at suppertime, but—as Goose had said—the meal was the same. Fred took his bowl of gruel and found a seat next to Nightshade.

Mak-Thar was already seated opposite, watching the pale paste drip from his spoon.

"I hope you had a better day than we did," said Nightshade.

"I got to guard the temple," said Fred. "But nobody attacked us."

"Well at least you didn't have to paint uniforms all day," said Nightshade. "I swear, if you give me a paintbrush tonight, I'll be painting snake heads in my sleep."

"Kind of a rough day?"

"Yeah. I mean, I like roleplaying as much as the next chick, but to roleplay all day? Miss Purslane isn't even fun to talk to. She's gotta be, like, ninety-seven. She can barely hear."

Fred had to admit that he, too, would have liked to see a little more action.

Fred asked, "How was your day, Mak— Sauron?"

Nightshade giggled and said, "Ah'm Conner Mac Sauron of the Clan Mac Sauron!"

"You're Belladonna," said Fred. "*He's* Sauron."

"I was doing the— you know, the thing."

"Don't do the thing," said Mak-Thar. "Especially not if it makes you giggle."

"Oh, right!" said Nightshade. "No giggling. Don't want to blow our cover. Hee hee! Don't you think it's cool that I get to say, 'Blow our cover'?"

"Very cool," said Fred. He actually didn't care about thieves' cant, but if it made Nightshade happy, he wasn't about to discourage her.

"They're already suspicious of us," said Mak-Thar. "Probably because I asked about their vacation plan."

"Why would that make them suspicious?" asked Nightshade.

"I don't know. They told me I needed to work here at least six months before I ask about things like that."

"So how was work?" asked Fred.

"Awful," said Mak-Thar.

"Mak-Thar had to torture people," said Nightshade.

"Oh," said Fred. Yeah, that *would* be pretty awful. "Shouldn't we leave, then? No one should be tortured just so we don't blow our cover."

"Well, to tell the truth," said Mak-Thar, "I *didn't* torture anyone. I just pretended."

"How do you *pretend* to torture people?" asked Nightshade. "Do they pretend to scream?"

"As a matter of fact, yes." Mak-Thar dropped his spoon and pushed his bowl away. "Look, it was horrible, okay? I walked down to the dungeon thinking, 'I can do this. I'm neutral, and they're only NPMs.' Then the guard opened the door to the first cell and showed me a little boy."

"A little boy?" asked Fred. "Why did they throw him in prison? What did he do?"

"He didn't do anything," said Mak-Thar. "They just threw him in prison because they are evil."

"That's mean!" said Fred.

"Duh," said Nightshade.

"And his puppy looked up at me with the saddest eyes—"

"Wait," said Nightshade. "The little boy had a puppy?"

"Yes. And I've never been much of an animal person, but now that I've actually *been* an animal, apparently I've gained the Kind to Animals disadvantage. I couldn't hurt them."

"So what did you do?" asked Fred.

"I told the guard that the boy was obviously young and impressionable, and that my torture would be far more terrifying if he first heard the screams from the adjacent cell."

"Oh," said Fred. That sounded harsh.

"Then when the guard turned his back, I gave the dog an iron ration and told the boy not to worry. I have *no* idea why I said that."

Nightshade grinned. "Because you're a good guy like us!"

"Not so loud! I'm Sauron the Evil. Anyway, the guard took me into the next cell, and when I saw who was in there, I told the guard to leave and shut the door."

"Who was in there?" asked Nightshade.

"A little girl," said Mak-Thar.

Nightshade's eyes widened. "No way!"

"With a kitten."

"No way!"

"And the kitten had a ribbon around its neck. And hanging from the ribbon was a little wooden heart-shaped pendant. And written on the heart were the words *From Grandma*."

"No way!"

"I didn't torture them, either," said Mak-Thar.

"Well, of course not," said Fred.

"Instead, I taught them how to scream like they were being tortured."

"Really?" asked Nightshade.

"Yes. We put on quite the act. Then I went next door and taught the little boy and the puppy the same trick."

"Cool!" said Nightshade.

"So that's my new job," said Mak-Thar. "Instead of studying Lightning Bolt, I have to spend the day listening to children and pets scream on cue. I need ear plugs."

"I can get you some beeswax from the supply cabinet," said Nightshade.

"I would be most grateful."

"It's not locked, so I don't think I can get XP for opening it. But maybe if I try to steal it while Miss Purslane is in the room it will count as a Pick Pockets attempt."

"It's probably best to wait until you are unobserved," said Mak-Thar. "It will count as earned treasure either way, and your Pick Pockets skill has only a twenty percent chance of success."

Nightshade's face drooped. "I know. And the really sad thing is that it's my best skill. Except for Climb Walls."

"Speaking of climbing walls," said Mak-Thar, "have you noticed that there is no ceiling? Some clerics lock their doors, but you could easily get into any room just by climbing in from any place adjacent."

"Yeah, that's cool!" said Nightshade. "I'm gonna loot the whole place tonight!"

"There's a night patrol," said Fred. "I think the night shift might have more guards than the day shift."

"Oh, right," said Nightshade. "They work at night, because everything here is so evil and dark! Except our tabards, which are dishwater gray. I hope I never see another tabard again."

"What's your job tomorrow?" asked Fred.

"Probably painting more tabards," Nightshade admitted. "I wish I could get out of it."

"How much paint do you have left?" asked Mak-Thar.

"I don't know. Some. Less than I had when I started. Why?"

"Perhaps you could run out."

"Run out of paint?" asked Nightshade. "Or run outside?"

"Both," said Mak-Thar. "Say you have run out of paint, and you need to make some more. This requires natural pigments, which you can find only in the swamp."

"Oo! I get it! A lie!"

"Yes, Nightshade, a lie. And it will be especially convincing if you *actually do* run out of pigment."

"A true lie! I read that those are the best kind."

"Yes," agreed Mak-Thar. "Once you are outside, I need you to deliver this to Wren."

He passed her a piece of paper. Nightshade looked around to see if anyone was watching. Then she tucked the paper inside her sleeve. She grinned. "This is so romantic."

Mak-Thar looked confused. "Romantic like *The Three Musketeers* or romantic like *When Harry Met Sally*?"

"I was thinking girl-boy romance. Not boy-boy."

Fred asked, "If there's three of them, wouldn't that be boy-boy-boy?"

"There are four of them," said Mak-Thar, "and no it would not. Nightshade— Um, Belladonna, I hope you meant *romantic* in the sense of *adventurous* and not in the sense of … um …"

"Kissy-kissy?" suggested Fred.

Bradly happened to walk past right then. He scowled. But he'd been scowling all day, so Fred couldn't be certain Bradly had overheard.

Mak-Thar ate a spoonful of his gruel. Once Bradly had left, he put his spoon back in the bowl.

"I just handed you a map," said Mak-Thar.

"Oh," said Nightshade. "You're sure it's not a love letter?"

"It's on graph paper," said Mak-Thar.

"You know," said Fred, "it's just as easy to imagine you writing a love letter on graph paper as it is to imagine you writing a love letter at all. Maybe easier."

"That is called the conjunction fallacy," said Mak-Thar.

"What is?" asked Fred.

Mak-Thar ignored him. "I have mapped seventy percent of the upper level. I also mapped all of the dungeon level, but it's not very big and there's nothing worth stealing. The real goods are in the central ceremony room. The statue of Toxia has giant emerald eyes."

"Wow!" said Nightshade. "How cool is that!"

"I hope it's cool enough to satisfy Wren and Helen," said Mak-Thar. "I do not relish the thought of spending more time in the dungeon. The sooner we get done with this adventure, the better."

"Right," said Nightshade. "So that's our plan. I'll run out of pigment, pretend to get some more, and take your map to Wren."

"Yes," said Mak-Thar. "And it would help if you actually came back with more pigment. That would make the ruse more credible."

"Right. Got it."

"Good."

"And um ..." Nightshade hesitated.

"Yes?" asked Mak-Thar.

"Well," said Nightshade, "if you have trouble sleeping and decide to write a love letter, I can take that to Wren, too."

"Eat your gruel."

CHAPTER NINETEEN: IN WHICH TWILIGHT IS DISMAYED.

HELEN HAD A SENSE of this place now. She could hear the wingbeats of the raven flying overhead to survey her drying snake meat. She could spot the sparkling dragonflies dancing in the distance. She could smell the coolness of the water as the morning sun warmed the log platform. She could feel the eyes of the snakes gazing longingly at the platform onto which none of them now dared climb.

Helen was also aware of her companions—and not just because they hadn't changed their underwear. Everyone had to stay quiet and respectful so they could continue to peacefully share their tiny living space. In their stillness, they had become part of the swamp. Helen could see them with her eyes closed.

Twilight was no longer trying to make conversation. He was meditating—communing with his goddess—and Helen could feel his energy reaching out to all living beings.

Perhaps Helen, too, was meditating. Though she was a vigorous woman, she knew how to accept stillness. Though she loved making noise, she knew how to listen.

A sparrow gave the first warning—a shrill little *pip* that was passed along by another sparrow and echoed by a thrush in a nearby nest. The next warning was the sudden silence of the frogs. In that silence, Helen heard a gentle sloshing sound, and she knew that was no lizard man.

"With panther-like grace, Nightshade sneaks through the swamp, catching her comrades completely by surprise."

Twilight opened his eyes. "Nightshade's coming."

"I know," said Wren. "I have a four-in-six chance of being able to hear her."

"No way," said Nightshade, who was still fifty yards distant and hidden by the trees. "I'm totally moving silently here. You won't know a thing until I'm right behind you."

Wren shook her head. "Footpads."

"Don't worry," Nightshade assured them. "I'm not gonna backstab you or anything. I'm just sneaking up for practice."

Wren and Twilight grinned at each other, and Helen felt herself grinning, too. Helen was glad to hear Nightshade's voice. That probably meant she was really desperate for the waiting to end, but maybe it also meant she actually *liked* Nightshade, at least a little bit.

A short while later, Nightshade came into view, and Twilight called, "Nightshade! We're completely surprised to see you."

"As my thief walks into camp, you notice she has paint on her fingers." Nightshade held up her fingers.

"Green nail polish?" Twilight asked.

"It's paint," said Nightshade. "I've been painting snake heads on serapes—except they're not called serapes; they're called tabards. Miss Purslane has a word for everything."

"And who is Miss Purslane?" asked Twilight.

"Head laundress at the temple," said Nightshade. "I'm her assistant, in charge of uniforms. Oh, by the way, if you use Miss Purslane's special soap, the paint stays in the uniform for at least seven washings."

"You have used your time well," said Twilight. He was still grinning.

Wren asked, "Whatcha got for us, Nightshade?"

"Besides laundry tips," said Helen. "Although, those are good, too."

"I," said Nightshade, "have a map." She produced a piece of paper with a flourish.

Wren took it and unfolded it. It was covered in little squares.

"It's Mak-Thar's map," Nightshade admitted. "But *I* brought it. We asked ourselves, who's the one person who could possibly sneak this valuable information out of the temple, and of course, we decided on me."

"Won't you be missed?" asked Wren.

"What if Miss Purslane needs to starch a collar?" asked Twilight.

"She thinks I'm going out to look for paint," said Nightshade. "By the way, do we still have some?"

Wren said, "I think the party paint is in Mak-Thar's backpack."

"We have party paint?" asked Helen.

"We have party everything," said Twilight. "Don't you remember Mak-Thar's shopping expedition?"

"Oh yeah."

Nightshade said, "I told Miss Purslane that making paint was part of my Painting proficiency. But now I'm worried that maybe it isn't."

"I know how to make a green paint from natural pigments," said Twilight. "I should be able to show you how."

"Will that use up a proficiency slot?" asked Nightshade. "I need to keep one slot open for Beast Riding in case I capture a pegasus."

"I'll talk with the Guild," said Wren. "Pretty sure they'll let you fold it into your Painting proficiency."

"Cool!"

Wren examined Mak-Thar's map. "Oh, this looks good. Is there any way to come in through the top?"

"It's pitifully easy," said Nightshade. "The walls don't touch the dome. So you can climb into the temple from pretty much anywhere on the outside. Also, there's no ceiling."

Wren looked thoughtful. "So we can also climb out if we need to get away in a hurry."

"Yeah!" said Nightshade. "And you should be able to run around on the tops of the walls, if you have Acrobatics."

"That's like having fleas," said Helen.

"Except they can jump higher," said Twilight.

"What?" asked Nightshade.

"I think they're making a joke," said Wren. "But with low charisma, I can't always tell."

Twilight said, "We are making a joke and we're hilarious. But tell us, dear Nightshade, what of our friends? How do Fred and Mak-Thar fare?"

"Fred's okay, of course. He's not doing a very good job of roleplaying, but no one seems to care. Mak-Thar though …"

"Yes?" asked Twilight.

"He has to hang out with the prisoners, and I think that's got him a little down."

"What?" asked Wren. "Why does Mak-Thar have to hang out with prisoners?"

"He was acting all tough when we got to the temple," said Nightshade. "And I think he overdid it. They're making him be the head torturer." She put a hand on Wren's shoulder and looked Wren in the eyes. "But he's not actually torturing anyone. Mak-Thar is very sweet."

"Um … thank you for the information?"

"Who are the prisoners?" asked Twilight.

"Oh, it's so over-the-top evil you wouldn't believe it," said Nightshade. "The first prisoner is a boy with a little puppy, and the other prisoner is a girl with a kitten."

Twilight got a look of horror on his face. "Did you say there's a puppy?"

"Yeah."

"Does it have big, mournful eyes?"

Nightshade shrugged. "Probably. Mak-Thar said it had 'the saddest eyes,' but he didn't say if they were big."

"We have to get in there," said Twilight urgently. "We have to stop them right now!"

"Stop them from doing what?" asked Helen.

"It's not obvious?" asked Twilight. "They're going to kill the puppy!"

"Right now, they just want the kids tortured a little bit," said Nightshade. "Mak-Thar's been teaching them to scream on cue."

But Twilight was unwilling to let his idea go. "No, they're going to kill the puppy! There's no reason for a puppy to even be in this story unless the bad guys demonstrate how evil they are by killing it."

"Whoa!" said Nightshade. "That's harsh!"

"Evil is ugly," said Twilight. "This must be stopped."

"Wouldn't they kill the kitten, though?" asked Wren. "Wouldn't that be even more evil?"

"The kitten is wearing a ribbon," said Nightshade.

"No, they kill the puppy," insisted Twilight. "Reason being, everyone knows that boys are little scamps. The puppy is there to show that despite his mischief, he actually has a heart of gold. So first they get our sympathy that way, then they kill the puppy, and we're committed to the kid for the rest of the story."

"But this isn't a story," said Wren. "This is an adventure."

"An adventure that so far has been motivated only weakly," said Twilight.

Helen didn't know what he was talking about. Overthrowing a temple was its own reward.

"Once we've learned that they've killed the puppy," Twilight continued, "we'll be morally justified in doing whatever it takes to rescue the boy and the girl."

"Whatever it takes?" asked Helen. That sounded interesting.

"Oh," said Nightshade. "You're very genre-savvy."

"What does that mean?" asked Helen.

"It means we know they're going to kill the puppy," said Twilight. "And because we know, we can't in good conscience stand by and wait for it to happen. We have to pre-emptively rescue the puppy."

"Before it's killed, right?" asked Nightshade.

"Right."

"Good. Just wanted to be sure I was following."

Well, Helen wasn't interested in rescuing a puppy *after* it had been killed. So going in early sounded like the right thing to do.

"So this is a rescue now?" asked Wren.

"It can still be a heist," said Helen. She was fine with either or both, as long as it ended with going inside the temple and doing *whatever it takes*.

Nightshade said, "If you need something to steal, there's this snake statue with giant emeralds for eyes."

"That sounds good," said Wren.

"And the prisoners will probably give us XP," said Nightshade. "Maybe a reputation bonus if they turn out to be royalty, but I wouldn't count on that. Gotta be worth XP, though, right?"

"Let me think," said Wren, studying the map.

"Right!" said Nightshade. "Master plan! Should we act it out while you tell us what to do?"

"That won't be necessary," said Wren.

"Oh wait," said Nightshade. "There was one more thing, but I can't remember … Oh yeah! Fred says they're looking for us."

"What?" asked Wren. "Who's looking for us?"

"The temple guards," said Nightshade. "Well, maybe they aren't looking for *us*, but they're wandering around the swamp looking for those clerics that were eaten, and Fred thinks they might find our tracks."

Wren looked to Helen. "Will they find our tracks?"

"I don't know," said Helen. Their tracks were obvious, but most people were very bad at seeing the obvious. "I suppose it depends on whether any of the guards are trackers."

Wren considered this. "Maybe it won't matter," she decided. "We know the layout. We know their weaknesses. We have people on the inside. We're ready to move. By the time they realize we've been here, we'll be gone."

"Yeah!" said Nightshade. "We'll disappear like cats in the night!"

"Except it's daytime," said Helen.

"Do cats disappear at night?" asked Twilight.

"Who cares?" Wren looked at Helen and smiled. "Let's go overthrow that evil temple."

CHAPTER TWENTY: IN WHICH FRED GOES ON HIGH ALERT.

GUARD DUTY WAS BORING. It was Fred's second day on the job, and he was really glad he was actually a fighter on an adventure and not a guard like Goosifer, who had to stand here and stare at the swamp every day.

Goosifer was here because the temple let him have a sword. He never got to draw it, but maybe that didn't matter. Maybe he was the sort of fellow who just wanted to *pretend* to be a fighter. That wouldn't be good enough for Fred. He had to be a *real* fighter. Guards had boring stories.

So there I was, standing in front of the Evil Temple of Evil, when suddenly, three lizard men crawled out of the swamp. Instantly, I did not draw my sword. Then I did not charge. Instead, I just kept standing there.

After a while, some clerics came to talk to the lizard men. Then the clerics went back inside, and the lizard men left. I kept standing there, because that was my job.

No, that wouldn't do at all. Complaining about work is not

the same as telling a story, and no one would want to hang out with someone who couldn't tell the difference.

Guard duty made Fred's neck itch. It wasn't a real itch. It was just the idea, in the back of his mind, that a good guard could never be a comfortable guard. A good guard should be, well, on guard, and Fred had discovered that being on guard did not suit him.

He had a lot of time to think about it, and eventually he realized that he hated being on the defensive. On an adventure—even on the most boring dungeon crawl, where the mage was forcing him to walk only sixty feet per turn—Fred was the one taking action. Even when he walked into an ambush, it was the other guys who had done the waiting. Fred could *react*. Reacting was okay. But *waiting* to react was ... well, it just wasn't Fred's style.

You'd think that after watching the swamp for four hours, Fred would have started feeling sorry for himself, but he didn't. He felt sorry for Goosifer. Fred was actually quite lucky, because he knew Nightshade was out in the swamp giving the others the inside info. Fred wasn't sure what would happen next, but he knew it would be interesting.

* * *

The first interesting thing that happened was that Nightshade came back and winked at him. That was probably a secret sign. Fred thought it was pretty cool to have a secret sign.

After Nightshade went inside, Goosifer asked, "Why did the cleric wink at you?"

"I don't know," said Fred. "Maybe she had something in her eye."

"You two aren't a couple, are you?" Goosifer seemed worried. "I'm pretty sure that's not allowed."

Fred and Nightshade would be doing lots of things in this temple that weren't allowed—things much more exciting than a wink.

"Don't worry about it," suggested Fred.

Goosifer did worry about it, but he didn't say anything more.

The next interesting thing that happened was that Sam and Evelyn showed up with four lizard men. The group had been searching for missing clerics, but of course they didn't come back with any, because the missing clerics had been made into cleric noodle soup. Sam hadn't figured that out yet, but he wasn't looking slump-shouldered and dejected. He was looking agitated—he walked like he had a newt in his pants.

Sam hissed something at his lizard men, and they spread out along the walkway, facing back toward the swamp.

"I'm putting the guard on high alert," said Sam. Then he spat on the walkway. Fred wasn't sure why he did this, but it probably had something to do with being a tough guy. Fred flexed his biceps to show it was possible to be a tough guy without being unsanitary.

Sam called, "Evelyn, you're in charge of this squad. Don't let anyone past you."

"Right, Sergeant."

Sam scowled at Fred, then went inside.

As soon as Sam's footsteps had faded into inaudibility, Goosifer asked, "Why are we on high alert?"

"We found tracks," said Evelyn, very pleased to have been part of a discovery so important.

"The missing clerics?" Goosifer asked.

Evelyn shook her head. "Adventurers."

"Adventurers?" Goosifer asked. "Here? What would adventurers be doing in a swamp?"

"Well, there's nothing here but us," said Evelyn. "So obviously we've been quested."

Goosifer swallowed a long swallow that took a long time to descend through his long neck. Fred had the impression that Goosifer did not want to be quested.

"Maybe we'll be okay," Fred suggested. "Maybe they'll avoid us and try to sneak in through the back door."

"There is no back door," said Evelyn.

"I was speaking metamorphically," said Fred.

Evelyn looked confused. "You were speaking like a rock that has been transformed by intense heat and pressure?"

Now Fred was confused.

One of the lizard men looked over his shoulder, and he, too, appeared confused.

"I don't think they'll come this way," said Fred. "I think they're trying to be subtle."

Evelyn shook her head. "Adventurers are never subtle."

"Have you fought them before?" Goosifer asked.

"My grandpa told me stories," said Evelyn. "His temple was attacked three times, and he was killed every time."

"Ev-every time?" Goosifer asked.

Evelyn nodded. "After they raised him the third time, he put in for early retirement."

Fred asked, "Did adventurers kill your father, too?"

Evelyn rolled her eyes. "No. He came to work drunk one night, and the clerics sacrificed him. They said it was to teach him a lesson, but there's not much you can learn after a wolf has eaten your liver."

"A wolf ate his liver?!" Goosifer asked.

"Yeah. Dad worked for the wolf-cult that was behind that lycanthropy outbreak in Basetown." Evelyn shook her head. "Those guys were crazy."

"So nothing at all like the Cult of Toxia," Fred suggested. He was hoping Evelyn would say something reassuring. He didn't like to see Goosifer so worked up.

Evelyn looked from Fred to Goosifer. "Look, I'm not trying to scare you guys, but you should have known that temple guards don't have it easy. My dad always said you should never work for an evil temple unless you're in it for the death benefits."

The wild look in Goosifer's eyes suggested that he was not, in fact, in it for the death benefits. Fred really hoped his friends were planning to be subtle.

Chapter Twenty-One: In which Yellin' Helen is Subtle.

STEALTHY AS A SMILODON, Yellin' Helen glided toward the evil temple. Her bare legs slipped through the water leaving scarcely a ripple. A rope trailed behind her, slithering like a water snake.

Sneaking up on the temple in the noontime brightness, Helen felt exposed. But she was a professional underwear model. She was always exposed.

Helen reminded herself that she was sneaking up to the rear wall of a windowless building. No one could see her except the dragonflies.

The lake surrounding the temple was shallow enough for wading, but just barely. Only Helen's long legs kept her from dunking her brand-name knickers. Finally, she reached the granite foundation and pulled herself out of the lake.

Helen sat down gently, so as not to clank her metal butt against the stone. Dangling her legs off the edge of the granite slab, she inspected the damage.

Not bad. Only four leeches.

After scraping away the leeches, Helen got to her feet and examined the plaster wall looming above her. It hadn't loomed when she'd been standing on the lakeshore with Wren and Twilight. Now, however, it loomed. Helen thought this might be an optical illusion, but Fred always called them *tickle illusions*, so she wasn't sure.

Helen scanned the wall for handholds. There were none. That was okay—Wren had sent her with a grappling hook—but handholds would have been quieter. Helen tossed the grappling hook, and it caught on the top of the wall with a noise that sounded like *Chthink!*

Anyone who heard that noise would say, "What was that?" Then they would listen a little while, in case they heard the noise again. All Helen had to do was outwait them.

Helen waited. A snake slithered toward her, attracted by the rope she had dragged across the lake. The snake's eyes met hers, and Helen grinned. The snake slithered over its own tail and swam away.

The trick for outwaiting someone is to wait as long as you think the other person has waited and then count to ten. Helen kept losing count somewhere around five, so by the time she got to eight, she knew she had waited long enough. Helen jerked on the rope and anchored the grappling hook.

She nodded to Wren across the lake.

Wren and Twilight applied steady tension to the rope, gently lifting it out of the water. The resulting ripples were soon swallowed by the duckweed. Wren and Twilight secured their end of the rope around a branch at just the right height for short people.

Twilight went first. He seized the rope, hooked his ankles around it, and sloth-crawled toward the top of the temple wall. He wasn't a very experienced adventurer, but he had a natural grace that made it seem as though he did this sort of thing every day. Only an elf could move that well in pants that tight.

As soon as Twilight reached the top of the wall, he disappeared by dropping into the room on the other side.

"Eek!" said a voice in the room. It was Mak-Thar.

Twilight said something Helen couldn't hear.

Mak-Thar said something about taking 1d6 damage for every ten feet fallen. Twilight said something dismissive. No one raised an alarm, so Helen nodded to Wren.

Wren crossed the lake as easily as Twilight. She was a pro with years of training.

She was also a pro with special climbing claws, which she strapped on as soon as she reached the top of the wall. Her descent on the opposite side sounded like an infestation of Rats comma Giant, but it was swift, and no one raised an alarm.

After seeing Wren and Twilight work the rope, Helen was glad no one was watching to compare her technique. Helen jumped, grabbed the rope, dangled there for a second, hooked her legs over it, and wiggled her fat butt up to the top of the wall.

No, that wasn't fair. She should be more positive about a butt that had sold so much underwear. "Whatever your size," she murmured to herself, "you're the right size for Nycadaemon Knickers."

Helen slipped over the wall, dangled at full length, let go, and hit the floor with bending knees.

"And now you!" said Mak-Thar. "It's 1d6 damage for every ten feet fallen, you know."

"I'm a barbarian," said Helen. "Those numbers mean nothing to me."

"Now that you mention it," said Twilight, "I've been meaning to ask you …"

"Yes?" asked Helen.

"If numbers mean nothing to barbarians, how could you be given a sword when you turned twelve?"

Helen scowled at him. What made him think he should question her back story?

"We have shamans who count for us."

"Ah," said Twilight. "Thank you. All is now clear."

Helen nodded to indicate that the matter was now settled. But she had not given Twilight a straight answer. The truth was that Helen's family had not needed to consult the shaman. Her little brother knew how to count.

He could go all the way to twelve without using his fingers. It was freakish. No one liked to talk about it much. But maybe they should have encouraged him to study with a shaman instead of letting him tag along while they plundered villages. Maybe things would have gone differently.

Wren said, "We should get going before someone finds us in their linen closet."

"Nightshade is watching outside," said Mak-Thar. "She will warn us if anyone comes. However, I am worried about Fred. He has been unable to leave the front door, so Nightshade was not able to tell him his part of the plan."

"He'll be fine," said Helen.

Fred's job was to make trouble if all hell broke loose—the sort of job that any member of the Fighters' Guild could handle without being told. Helen was more worried about her own job.

"Nightshade found you this," said Mak-Thar, handing Helen a bundle of cloth. "She says it's a dress, but I think it's actually a large robe."

Helen slipped it on. "How's it look?"

"I can barely see you," said Mak-Thar. "Should I light a torch?"

"You look like you're wearing a sack," said Twilight. "I'm sure Nightshade could have found something that fit better than that."

Nightshade's voice came from the other side of the door. "There's not much on the 'Big and Tall' rack, okay?"

"Wait a minute," said Helen. She drew her knife and sliced off the bottom of the robe to give it a knee-length skirt. Then she picked up the scrap piece and sliced off its hem, which she tied around her waist. "Now what do you think?"

"Wow!" said Wren. "That's amazing!"

Twilight nodded. "But the effect is kind of spoiled by the way your broadsword sticks out of the collar."

"It's not a broadsword. It's a humongous sword."

"Oh."

"But since I'm a humongous broad, it's easy to get confused."

Wren giggled.

Twilight said, "Um, that's not what I meant."

"You're right, though," said Wren. "Helen will have to lose the sword, or it will give the game away."

"What?" asked Helen.

"You're supposed to be a doting aunt," said Wren. "Doting aunts don't carry swords."

"Mine does," said Helen.

Wren shook her head. "This isn't the steppe, dear. If you want this to work, you need to play your part."

Helen did want it to work. At least, she agreed that they needed to rescue the kids from the evil temple. But Wren's plan was all subtlety and secrecy, and Helen had the feeling that she wouldn't get to tear this place apart unless something went horribly wrong. So even though she was going along with the plan, she was also hoping something would go horribly wrong.

"Give the sword to Mak-Thar," said Wren. "He's already carrying so much stuff that no one will notice." Mak-Thar still had his overstuffed backpack, his belt with many pouches, and his ridiculous amount of rope coiled over his shoulder.

Twilight asked, "And no one has commented on the fact that a humble brother of the temple walks down the hallway outfitted for a major expedition?"

Mak-Thar shrugged. "Perhaps they think it's strange, but they don't dare say anything. I'm the head torturer."

Helen took off the dress so she could unbuckle her sword. She sighed. Sometimes she really hated being a team player.

"Mak-Thar, hold out your arms."

The mage did so.

Helen wrapped the straps around Mak-Thar's chest and arranged the scabbard so that it nestled in between his backpack and his left shoulder. She buckled it on him.

"How's that?" she asked. "Too loose? Too tight?"

"It is somewhat heavy," said Mak-Thar. "But it does not weigh enough to move me up into the next encumbrance category."

"That means it's just right," said Twilight.

It wasn't right, though. No one who fought like Mak-Thar should be carrying a blade that nice. Helen ignored the pang of separation anxiety and put her dress back on.

"Much better," said Twilight.

Wren shook her head. "Even an old sack looks good on you. How do you do it?"

"Truly," said Twilight, "were I not an elf, I would be most enraptured by your appearance right now."

"What does being an elf have to do with it?" Wren asked.

"We cannot allow ourselves to be attracted to humans," Twilight explained. "That would essentially be a death sentence. When an elf's spouse dies, the elf dies of grief."

"Wait, what?" said Nightshade, still on the other side of the door. "No one ever told me about that."

Twilight rolled his eyes. "I'm sure 'Arctic elves' are different."

"Oh, yeah. That's probably it."

Helen looked at Mak-Thar. "So we're ready?"

"Yes," said Mak-Thar. "We should go now, before the end of the turn. I don't know the encounter probability in this linen closet, but in the rest of the temple, it seems to be quite high."

* * *

Wren and Twilight went off to do their heist thing. Nightshade left to go tell Fred the plan. This left Helen and Mak-Thar in charge of the rescue mission.

Mak-Thar led Helen through halls that smelled of torch-smoke and boiled flour. Dirty plaster walls boxed them in. The dome high overhead made her feel like a lump of meat in a covered stew pot. How much pressure would it take to blow that lid off? Could Mak-Thar do it with a fireball?

Three clerics stepped into the corridor. Helen reached for her sword and grasped empty air. Her sword was no longer on her back.

Mak-Thar, in the lead, did not hesitate. He continued toward the clerics as though he did not even see them. Two of the clerics stepped aside, but the third held her ground with her snake staff squarely in Mak-Thar's path.

"Brother Sauron," she said, "who is this person you have brought into the temple?"

Mak-Thar stopped and drew himself up haughtily. Helen stopped with her hands at her sides so she wouldn't reach for the humongous sword strapped to Mak-Thar's back.

"Sister Malicious," said Mak-Thar, "are you questioning my authority to torture the prisoners as I see fit?"

The cleric's eyes narrowed. "What does *she* have to do with *your* job?"

"Simple," said Mak-Thar. "This is the children's aunt. She asked to visit them, and I agreed on the condition that she be forced to watch the torture. I'm sure a woman of your fine sensibilities can see how the presence of a loving relative will make the torture much more evil."

"But how did any relatives escape the massacre?"

"I cannot say," said Mak-Thar. He turned to Helen and raised an eyebrow.

Helen gritted her teeth. What she really wanted to do was draw her sword and hack these people up, but she wasn't supposed to do that unless her "cover" was "blown". Until then, she had to be subtle.

"I escaped by running," said Helen. "Your troops were so busy massacring that they didn't have time to chase everyone down."

Sister Malicious grinned. "But you seem to be in our power now."

"I'm just here for a visit," said Helen.

"Lock her up," said Sister Malicious. "She can't be their aunt. The children are not related."

Mak-Thar looked shocked. "Of all the audacious lies!" He reached for Helen's arm, but then thought better of it. Instead, he just pointed. "Walk in front of me, you— you false aunt! I'll soon discover who you *really* are."

Helen shrugged and pushed past Mak-Thar and the clerics. Mak-Thar followed along behind.

"Search her clothing before you lock her up," called Sister Malicious as Helen and Mak-Thar continued along the hallway. "She's probably hiding a file or some lockpicks."

"Sister Malicious thinks she runs the place," Mak-Thar grumbled, once they had left the clerics safely behind.

"Does she?" Helen asked.

"Not by herself," said Mak-Thar. "In theory, the temple is governed by a council.

"Well, I hope I didn't cost you a promotion," said Helen.

"You jest," said Mak-Thar. "In truth, I can hardly wait to get out of here. I never imagined that being evil would be so ... so ... suboptimal!"

Helen didn't know what that word meant—not exactly. But she knew Mak-Thar considered it an insult.

"This is a perfect example," said Mak-Thar. "They have you at their mercy, and now they could try to convert you, or they could kill you and animate your corpse in an interesting way. Instead, they just want you locked up in the dungeon, where you'll contribute nothing to the temple while eating their food! I should be out in the swamp, using my cleric spells to intimidate the lizard men, but instead they keep me in the dungeon, where I have to torture children just so a guard can hear them scream." Mak-Thar shook his head. "It's a waste of resources."

"Nightshade said that you aren't actually torturing anyone."

"I don't actually know any cleric spells, either. I'm talking about the principle. Ah. Here we are! Let me go ahead again, and this time, do try to look more like a doting aunt."

Mak-Thar led her down a set of stairs carved into the damp stone. Despite flaming torches, the temple was darker down here, and it smelled of moldy despair.

The plan was simple. Wren said it was so simple, even a barbarian could handle it. Mak-Thar would introduce Helen as the children's aunt. Helen would act harmless until the jailor let his guard down. Then Helen would sucker-punch him, and they would take his keys.

Helen had offered to decapitate the guard, but according to Wren, decapitation wasn't subtle.

The problem with Wren's plan was that it required Helen to act harmless. Helen was a model, not an actor.

Of course, it was dark down here, which might hide the bloodlust in her eyes. Her skirt might conceal the fact that her legs were always in a combat stance. But fighters can spot fighters. If they exchanged one glance, her "cover" would be "blown". And then ... well, then she'd get to tear this place apart, which was what she had wanted to do ever since she saw it. Helen grinned. Things were about to get interesting.

They stepped into a small antechamber and found the guard standing at attention in front of the keys to the jail cells.

Mak-Thar was confused. "Roberto? Why aren't you sitting in your chair?"

A fungus-scarred chair held together with rusty wire sat in a lonely corner. Its empty seat was well-polished.

"The guards are on high alert," Roberto said. "A patrol found tracks left by adventurers."

So Roberto was ready for her. Helen didn't mind. In fact, she was glad. That made this a fair fight.

But Roberto wasn't fighting. He hadn't recognized that Helen and Mak-Thar were adventurers. Helen met his eyes, and she realized that Roberto was not really a fighter. He was just a miserable man who spent all day sitting in a moldy dungeon. This place smelled of mold and despair because *Roberto* smelled of mold and despair. This was his smell, and this was his place.

Helen had been all ready to hurt this guy, but now, looking into those miserable eyes, she wasn't so sure.

CHAPTER TWENTY-TWO: IN WHICH MANY THINGS HAPPEN AT ONCE.

FRED HAD DISCOVERED that being on high alert was a lot like standing guard, except that Goosifer was standing up straighter. Evelyn seemed tense, too, her eyes scanning the swamp for any sign of attack.

Fred was a little uneasy about standing guard with four lizard men. It was weird to be on the team with the monsters. But then, Fred wasn't actually on this team, was he? He was just *pretending* to be on this team until someone told him to stop.

Nightshade had winked, but that wasn't the same as telling Fred to stop pretending. In fact, near as Fred could tell, it was the opposite. It was sort of like saying, *Hey, we're doing a great job of pretending to be on the same team as these evil guys!*

If Nightshade had said that out loud, it might have made Goosifer suspicious. So the wink was much better. Fred decided that Nightshade was pretty smart. At least about some things.

They had been on high alert for only ten minutes when Bradly came to check on them.

"Hi, Bradly," said Fred. "You're early."

"Don't talk to me!" said Bradly. "You're supposed to be on high alert!"

"Oh, right," said Fred. "Sorry." He pretended to watch the swamp like Evelyn was doing.

Bradly stood very close and squinted at Fred's face. "There's something wrong about you, Fred."

Fred remembered that this was an evil temple, where wrong was right, so he said, "Thank you."

One of the lizard men looked over his shoulder, as though wondering if he had heard correctly. It was the same lizard man as last time. Apparently, he understood something of the common tongue.

"Are you disrespecting me?" asked Bradly.

The lizard man went back to looking down the walkway. Evelyn was *very* focused on the swamp. Poor Goosifer just stood there and gaped.

"I thought I was being friendly and polite," said Fred.

"I told you not to talk to me!"

"Okay," said Fred. "But when you're talking to me, it seems rude not to answer."

"You think you can get away with that just because you have a sword. Well, I'm not afraid of your sword! I—"

Bradly stopped and looked closely at Fred's sword.

"There's something familiar about that sword. Let me see the blade."

Bradly didn't look like the sort of man who could recognize swords by their blades. On the other hand, that blade had been the last thing he had seen before he died.

Fred's thoughts were interrupted by Nightshade, who appeared in the entryway and said, "Excuse me. I need to talk to Diabolicus Maximus."

"What?" Bradly turned.

"It will only take a second." Nightshade pointed at Fred and wiggled her finger.

Fred took a step toward Nightshade, and Bradly put a hand on Fred's chest. Fred allowed himself to be stopped by Bradly's puny hand.

Bradly said, "She doesn't give you orders. I do."

Fred wasn't sure anyone could give him orders. Fred often did what people asked, but that was because Fred was a nice guy.

Nightshade rolled her eyes. "Gee, Bradly, it will only take a second."

"If you need to talk, you can talk right here."

Nightshade shook her head. "It's private. I have a private message from Curate Sauron."

Bradly studied Nightshade's face. "There's something familiar about *you*, too."

"Duh. We met, like, day before yesterday." Nightshade pushed back her hair to remind Bradly that she had human ears.

Bradly shook his head. "No, there's something about your voice. I've heard it before. ... And that sword ... The two of you together ..."

Poor Bradly. It must be frustrating to *almost* remember the circumstances of one's own death. Fred watched as Bradly's mind struggled. He couldn't see Bradly's mind, of course, but he could see Bradly's forehead, which bore a confused frown.

Suddenly, the frown deepened, as though Bradly's memory had given him an answer that he could not believe. Then the eyes widened, and Bradly looked from Fred to Nightshade and back.

"You're—"

Bradly was struck by two arrows, a crossbow bolt, and a magic missile.

"What?" said Bradly. "Not again!" Then his eyes went dead and he slumped to the ground.

Fred had been expecting a fight as soon as Bradly announced that Fred and Nightshade were imposters. Since Bradly hadn't announced that yet, this attack seemed early. Nightshade looked totally surprised, so Fred knew that *she* hadn't shot Bradly—and she certainly had not shot him four times. The lizard men and the temple guards had no bows. That meant—

"Ha! We have surprise *and* initiative. I cast Sleep before they can raise the alarm."

Six people Fred had not seen coming were now standing on the walkway. The speaker was a woman in a violet and crimson robe.

("Ew!" said Nightshade. "Those colors do *not* go together.")

Fred thought the mage's name was Antarea. Helen had been on an adventure with her once or twice.

"Wait," said a man in a simple brown frock over a suit of spiked armor. "Let me cast Hold Person at the same time, in case your spell doesn't get them all."

Antarea frowned. "I think I have to act first."

"*I'm* going first," said a scruffy-looking half-pint. He charged.

Fred wasn't thinking as quickly as things were happening. Fortunately, he was *acting* quickly. He already had his sword drawn, and he had stepped in front of the lizard men to defend them and everyone else from the attacking adventuring party ...

... For that's what it was. Six people had shown up in the middle of the walkway and shot Bradly four times. The magic missile had come from Antarea. The arrows were from an elf in the back and the thief whose friends called him "Louse". Fred was surprised to see that the crossbow was held by Ludo, their erstwhile mountain guide. There was a brown-frocked cleric whom Fred did not know. And leading the charge was Fred's old friend, Stinky La Foote.

"Stinky!" said Fred. "Are you on an adventure, too?"

The half-pint stopped his charge and skidded to a halt just out of reach of Fred's sword.

"Hey, Fred. Whatcha doing?"

Fred shrugged and gestured with his sword. "Just guarding this evil temple."

"Yeah," said Stinky. "That's what it looks like you're doing, all right. ... But *why?* Aren't you supposed to be looting it?"

"Hey," said Louse. "Nobody told me we were going to fight Fighter Fred."

"We must uproot evil in all its forms!" said the brown-frocked guy.

"I don't have to," said Louse. "I'm neutral."

"I'm neutral, too," said Antarea. "Is this guy somebody special?"

"He's a pretty good singer," said Ludo. "And I don't think he's supposed to be working for an evil temple. Maybe he's possessed by demons."

Stinky cocked his head to one side and looked up at Fred. "Are you possessed by demons, Fred?"

"Don't think so."

Louse turned to Antarea. "I don't think we want to fight Fighter Fred. We should convince him to join us."

Behind Fred, one of the lizard men hissed. Then all four jumped into the water and started swimming away.

"Damn!" said the cleric. "Now we've wasted our surprise attack!"

"That's okay," said Antarea. "We get plus two to hit fleeing opponents."

"I don't think we should shoot them in the back," said the cleric, with some regret. "I might lose favor with my god."

"They said, 'It's time,'" said the elf. "I wonder what *that* means."

"That means it's time to fight," said Stinky, waving his sword. "What do you say, Fred? Want to help us kill these guys?"

Fred looked over his shoulder. Evelyn and Goosifer were staring wide-eyed. Neither had drawn a sword. Fred really didn't want to help the adventurers chop them up.

Nightshade was watching him, ready to follow his lead.

"Run away!" Fred shouted, and he charged into the temple.

* * *

"Roberto," said Mak-Thar, "this is Harmless Helen. She's here to visit the children."

Roberto looked confused. "The dungeon doesn't get visitors."

Helen shrugged. "Well, there's a first time for everything."

"Why is someone showing up to visit the children as soon as the temple goes on high alert?" Roberto asked. "Don't you think that's suspicious?"

"Yes, I see your point," said Mak-Thar. "I didn't know the temple was on high alert until you mentioned it. You're expecting adventurers?"

Roberto nodded.

"How many?" Mak-Thar asked.

Roberto frowned. "I don't know."

"But you're sure it was more than one?"

"I suppose so."

"Well, Helen is alone. So that means she's not a party of adventurers. Besides, whoever heard of an adventurer called 'Harmless Helen'?"

"I've never heard of *anyone* called 'Harmless Helen'."

"Yes," Mak-Thar agreed. "That settles it."

Roberto looked from Mak-Thar to Helen, trying to read their faces in the feeble torchlight. Helen folded her hands and looked down at her skirt, trying to look harmless. Roberto came to a decision.

The guard removed his chair from its dingy corner and set it beside Helen. "It will take me a moment to unlock the door. Please sit down."

Helen thought that request was a little odd, but she was supposed to be harmless, not suspicious. She sat down.

Helen's armored butt clanked against the wood.

Roberto's eyes met hers. He had heard the sound, and he was not surprised. He had been expecting it. Roberto knew she was an adventurer.

Roberto stepped between Helen and Mak-Thar and drew his sword. Helen swivel-stepped off the chair and raised it as a weapon. Roberto rammed his sword through Mak-Thar's chest.

Mak-Thar's eyes opened wide with surprise.

Leaving his sword in the body of the mage, Roberto grabbed the keys and tossed them to Helen. "Let's get these kids out of here!"

* * *

Fred ran through the hallways of the evil temple. Nightshade, Goosifer, and Evelyn kept pace.

"Who were those guys?" Goosifer asked.

"Stinky, Louse, Antarea, Ludo, and two people I don't know."

"What are they doing *here*?" asked Nightshade. "This is *our* adventure."

"I guess they must have heard rumors about the evil temple," said Fred.

"Well, sure," said Nightshade. "But those rumors weren't for NPMs."

They ran past the stairs to the dungeon.

"Oo," said Nightshade. "Helen and Mak-Thar are down there. I'd better tell them what's up." She headed down the stairs.

"We'll keep running," Fred said to Evelyn and Goosifer.

The two guards nodded.

Fred followed the route Goosifer had shown him on his first day. He wanted to warn Kayla—and even Quigly—before the adventurers showed up.

"How do you know those people?" Goosifer asked.

"Why did Belladonna say, 'This is our adventure'?" Evelyn asked. "And whom was she warning?"

Fred thought those were pretty good questions. "I'll tell you if we get out of here alive."

"If we want to go out, why are we going farther in?" Evelyn asked.

They came to the wall around the temple's inner chamber. Fred followed its curve and finally stopped running when he saw Kayla and Quigly standing in the middle of the corridor, swords drawn.

Fred sheathed his sword. Quigly relaxed and sheathed his own sword.

Kayla did not relax and did not sheathe her sword. Instead, she asked, "How many?"

"Six," said Fred. "And trust me, you don't want to fight those guys."

"Maybe not," said Kayla, "but it's our job. Has someone woken the night shift?"

"I think Sam was going to do that," said Evelyn.

"Fred knows the adventurers!" said Goosifer.

"Are they powerful enough to take us down?" asked Kayla.

Fred wasn't sure. He'd never seen Kayla in a fight.

"If they get this deep," said Evelyn, "it means they've gone through the night shift and all the clerics."

"That's a dilemma," said Quigly. Although he still had that jovial note in his voice, Fred could tell he was sincere when he said, "As a ceremonial guard, I am sworn not to leave this post. But I can't very well stand here while intruders are slaying our leaders and our comrades in arms."

"Right," said Kayla. "Okay, as ranking member of the day shift, I'm taking command. Fred and Quigly, you're with me. Goose and Evelyn, guard this doorway with your lives. Let no one in or out."

Quigly raised an eyebrow. "I say, that's a bit drastic, don't you think? If the adventurers make it this far, Goose and Evelyn should run away."

Kayla was surprised. "You think they should desert their post?"

"They have already done so once," said Quigly. "So they are well practiced. Furthermore, the curse on the idol should make it able to defend itself."

Kayla glanced into the inner chamber. Fred followed her gaze. Wren was climbing up the side of the giant snake statue.

She pulled a rag out of her sleeve and polished a scale. Kayla seemed not to see her.

"Okay," said Kayla. "I suppose it should be okay for you to run from danger."

"Right," said Quigly. "So guard this doorway, but not with your lives. And don't let anyone in or out unless it looks like they mean to kill you."

"What about the cleaning lady?" asked Goosifer. "Can we let her out?"

"Of course you can let the cleaning lady out," said Quigly. "She's not anyone."

"That's our plan, then," said Kayla. She looked at Fred. "You ready to do this?"

Fred had been hoping that he could convince Kayla and Quigly to run away with him. But maybe they would be convinced once they saw what Stinky and Antarea were doing to the temple.

* * *

Helen caught Roberto's keys. "So that's it? You were on our side all along?"

Mak-Thar drew his dagger and stabbed Roberto twenty-two times in the chest. "Die! Die! Die! Die!"

Helen dropped Roberto's chair, stepped into the melee, and seized Mak-Thar's wrist.

"Die! Die! Die!" Mak-Thar screamed, arm pumping so hard that he was lifting himself off the floor. Helen held fast as Mak-Thar's scrawny wrist jerked in her grip.

Wide-eyed, Roberto stepped out of Mak-Thar's reach. The guard's breastplate bore twenty-two gouge marks, but apparently the dagger had not pierced the half-inch of hardened leather.

Mak-Thar, on the other hand, was definitely pierced. Helen could see the point of Roberto's sword poking out through the back of Mak-Thar's robe, pushing his pack a handsbreadth away from his back.

"Why isn't he dead?" Roberto asked.

"Die! Die! Die!"

"Mak-Thar?" Helen's hand was actually getting tired! "Mak-Thar, it's okay. He's on our side."

"He stabbed me!"

"Yes," said Helen. "Because he thought you were an evil cleric."

"Why isn't he dead?" Roberto asked again. He reached for his scabbard, but the gesture was futile—his sword was still in Mak-Thar.

Helen kept her voice calm. "Mak-Thar, I think you might need a healing potion."

Mak-Thar stopped shouting, but his eyes were still wide. "It— hurts— to— breathe!"

"Yes, um ..." Helen really wished Twilight were here. There was probably a right way to do this, but Helen didn't know it. "Where's your healing potion? I know you're carrying one."

Mak-Thar was carrying everything else. He had to have a healing potion.

With his free hand, Mak-Thar patted one of his pouches.

"Right," said Helen. "I'm going to get your potion for you, but first, I want you to drop the dagger."

"What dagger?"

"The one in this hand. The hand I'm holding. Drop the dagger."

Mak-Thar dropped the dagger.

Helen let go of his wrist. Mak-Thar's arm remained raised, muscles tensed, as though it had been petrified.

Helen slipped the potion out of the pouch and popped off the stopper. She pressed it into Mak-Thar's less-tense hand, waiting patiently until his fumbling fingers wrapped around it.

"I want you to drink that," she said. "On three, ready? One. Two."

Helen yanked Roberto's sword out of Mak-Thar's chest. The backpack thumped into place against the mage's back.

Helen turned to Roberto. "Three comes next, right?"

Roberto nodded.

"Three," said Helen. "Drink, Mak-Thar." She helped him raise the potion to his lips.

Mak-Thar drank. His knees buckled.

Helen swept out a foot, grabbed Roberto's chair with the toe of her boot, and kicked it under Mak-Thar's collapsing body. The mage sat down.

Helen found a rag hanging on a nearby hook and wiped Mak-Thar's blood off Roberto's sword. It was a small weapon, easy to wield one-handed in close quarters. Such a sword would not be Helen's first choice, but it was sturdy and well cared for.

Helen still had the ring of keys around the crook of her elbow. Roberto seemed to realize that Helen had the things he was supposed to be guarding and the thing he was supposed to guard them with. Helen and Mak-Thar were between him and the stairs.

"Who are you people?"

"I'm Helen," said Helen. "But I'm not really harmless. This is Mak-Thar. He's ... a mage." Mages were either harmless or mutual assured destruction. Helen felt no need to explain that at this time.

"He stabbed me!" said Mak-Thar.

"Yep," said Helen. "And you stabbed him. So we're even, right?"

Roberto looked worried.

"He's a traitor!" said Mak-Thar.

"He's *our* traitor," said Helen. "He didn't mean to stab *you*. He thought he was stabbing an evil cleric."

"So he's not an evil cleric?" Roberto asked.

"Nope. Just an overwrought mage."

"Hey, guys! Guess what's happening?" Nightshade came down the stairs. "Oh, you still haven't knocked out the guard."

"He stabbed me!" said Mak-Thar.

"Ouch," said Nightshade. "So why hasn't Helen killed him yet?"

Helen hadn't killed him because he was just a confused and moldy man who really didn't want to be imprisoning children.

As a barbarian, she had killed a lot of people who really didn't want to be where they were. In fact, everyone who saw Helen charging at them did not want to be where they were. But this time ...

"I hope I'm not getting civilized."

"You're wearing a dress and everything," said Nightshade.

"Who are *you*?" asked Roberto.

"I'm Belladonna, Miss Purslane's new uniform assistant."

Helen said, "She's Nightshade. She's another adventurer."

"Wow! Way to blow my cover! I've been roleplaying for *three days*, and you just ruined everything!"

"Relax," said Helen. "Roberto's on our side."

"Oh, okay. Cool. I came down to warn you that there's an adventuring party in the temple. I mean, someone else besides us."

"Who?" asked Helen.

"Some chick with bad color sense, our dwarven guide, an elf, a cleric, that half-pint Fred is always going on about, and my friend Louse."

"Louse is *your* friend, too?"

Nightshade shrugged. "We're not like besties or anything, but we're in the same guild."

Another adventuring party in the temple? That was bad timing. Or maybe it was good timing.

"Did you say Stinky La Foote was with them?"

"Yeah, that's the guy."

"We'd better get these kids out of here," said Helen. "Things are about to get really messy."

Chapter Twenty-Three: In which more things happen at once.

Fred ran through the temple with Quigly and Kayla. Kayla knew some shortcuts, and unlike Goosifer, she wasn't afraid to open closed doors.

They ran through a darkened bedroom where someone was snoring.

"Adventurers!" Kayla shouted. "All clerics evacuate!"

They ran into a conference room where four clerics were studying a map of the temple. Buttons were scattered across the map, and a thimble marked a place near the entrance. One of the clerics looked up, saw the three of them, and moved a button from one place to another.

"All clerics get out!" said Kayla. "Leave the tactics to the guards!"

They ran into a room where four clerics were playing pinochle. Kayla snatched their score sheet off the table and said, "Get out of here! Adventurers are ransacking the temple!"

As they sprinted down a corridor, Fred checked over his shoulder to see if any clerics were following them. He saw none. Maybe they were bad at reacting to the unexpected. Maybe that was why they had guards.

Fred admired Kayla's attention to duty. She'd joined the evil temple for the money, but she wasn't going to hide when things got tough. Kayla was going to fight—even though she was terrified.

Fred had never cared about being brave. He had run away in fear many times. But Kayla was running *toward* her fear, just because someone had paid her to do so. And Quigly—well, he looked like he was going to be sick, but he was right on Kayla's heels.

This wasn't about doing evil deeds or acting in the service of Toxia. They were running to defend the temple because they were guards, and defending temples is what guards do. Fred was a fighter, and his job was to fight temple guards.

Fred had always liked the idea of everyone doing their job. He had gone far in his career simply by adhering to that basic principle. But now that he was on the other side of the adventure—on both sides, really—he suddenly wondered if there wasn't a flaw somewhere. He had a feeling that if Kayla did her job and Stinky La Foote did his job, then someone he liked would be killed.

They ran past the entrance. Bradly's body lay on the walkway outside.

Fred stopped and called, "Kayla, come back here! You guys should run away."

Kayla and Quigly stopped and turned to look back at him.

"We can't desert," said Quigly. "Not when the temple needs us most."

Fred said, "After Stinky La Foote gets done with this place, there won't be a temple. This is the best time to desert."

"What about your curate?" asked Kayla. "You're supposed to be his personal bodyguard. Are you just going to leave *him* to die?"

Fred was pretty sure Mak-Thar could take care of himself. But he was also pretty sure that Mak-Thar could take *better* care of himself when Fred was there.

"Okay," said Fred. "That's a good point. Let's go save Sauron."

* * *

Once again, Helen had her humongous scabbard on her back. Her humongous sword was in her hand.

Normally, she liked to hold her humongous sword in two hands, but her other hand was holding a puppy. That hand was wet, and not because the puppy was sweating.

Mak-Thar was almost back to normal. He was explaining to Roberto how hit points worked.

"So you see, even though you impaled me, your shortsword can never do more than six points of damage. Perhaps eight or nine with strength bonuses, but that's still not enough to kill a fifth-level mage."

Helen led the way up out of the dungeon. Three steps from the top, she stopped. Torchlight was flickering in the corridor ahead, and she could hear a different conversation:

"Is that a side passage, or is it stairs going down?"

There was a rustle of paper. "It must be stairs going down. My map doesn't have room for a side passage."

Helen recognized that voice. That was Antarea, a mage who had taken charge of the party on several of Helen's adventures.

Antarea was the sort of woman who always carried a pouch of change to ensure that the treasure could be divided evenly. Her maps were always accurate, her back was always straight, and her fingernails were always lacquered immaculately. Because Helen was a professional model, Antarea had often pestered her for makeup tips. Helen had felt obliged to give her some, even though she didn't know that much. On their last adventure, someone had pointed out that Helen did not actually wear any makeup. Helen had been so embarrassed that she hadn't spoken to Antarea since.

Yellin' Helen's boldness and courage were legendary among the members of the Basetown Fighters' Guild, and Helen was glad that none of her colleagues were on the stairs with her at that moment, because the sound of Antarea's voice made her shrink back in fear.

Some chick with bad color sense. Yeah, okay, in retrospect, Helen could see why basic-black Nightshade might describe Antarea that way. But Helen would have described her as *The woman it would be most awkward to meet at the top of the stairs of a dungeon.*

Helen turned and whispered to Roberto, "Does the dungeon have a secret exit?"

Roberto shook his head.

Nightshade's forehead wrinkled, and she was about to ask a very inconvenient question when a booming voice broke into the conversation in the corridor above.

"You dare to defile our temple? Now you shall feel Toxia's venomous wrath!"

A few smaller voices chimed in with "Yeah!" and "Get lost, losers!" And one said, "Aw, I wanted to give the speech."

The man who had been asking Antarea for directions answered the challenge in a sanctimonious tone of equal volume: "Lay down your arms, foul denizens of this place most vile! For if you oppose us—"

But he was interrupted by Stinky La Foote, whom Helen knew as a half-pint of action. With a ferocious battle cry, Stinky charged past the top of the stairs, heading toward the booming evil-cleric voice.

"Fear me!" shouted the evil cleric, and underneath the echoes of his voice, Helen heard Stinky's boots skidding on the granite floor.

With a terrified wail, Stinky charged past the top of the stairs in the opposite direction.

So Stinky was not, in fact, immune to fear. Someone at the Fighters' Guild was going to lose a bet.

"Damn. They've got spells," said Antarea's sanctimonious cleric. "Remove Fear!"

Once more, Stinky's boots skidded on the granite.

"Hey!" said Stinky. "What's the big idea?"

The half-pint ran past, charging at the evil clerics again.

"It's my turn!" said the one who had wanted to give the intimidating speech. "Fear me!" he squeaked.

Stinky's boots skidded, and he ran back toward the adventuring party.

"Remove Fear!" shouted Antarea's cleric, and Stinky charged the other way again.

"As amusing as it is to watch half-pint ping pong," said a voice with a dry elven accent, "maybe we should *all* attack."

Two arrows and a crossbow bolt whizzed down the corridor after Stinky. Helen turned and backed everyone four steps down. Clerics shouted curses of the non-magical kind. Adventurers' boots pounded past the stairs.

Once Helen was certain that Antarea's shapely red leather boots had passed down the corridor, she gave the word: "Go!"

Helen bounded up the steps two at a time. She took up a position between the battle and the stairway as Nightshade cajoled the children to make a run for it. Roberto came next, gave a guilty glance at the embattled clerics, then followed along behind the children. Mak-Thar came last, carrying the kitten.

One of the clerics saw him and shouted, "Sauron! Save us!"

Mak-Thar raised his free hand to cover his face and hurried after Roberto.

Fortunately, no one from Antarea's party looked back. They were too busy fighting the clerics. The wooden snake staffs had come to life—of course—and were writhing about the adventurers' ankles. Waist-high and full of rage, Stinky La Foote was hacking at the serpents slithering along the floor. Ludo's arms were pinned to his sides by the coils of some sort of python. Antarea's cleric was pummeling an evil cleric into submission. That elf who liked to hang out with Antarea was shooing snakes away from the mage's feet while she readied a spell. Louse was standing thirty feet behind the battle, nervously shooting arrows into it.

Helen kind of wanted to help, but joining the fight now would be really awkward. Adventuring parties were supposed to stay out of each other's way. And, while she probably needed to stop avoiding Antarea, this did not feel like the best time to renew their acquaintance. Also, she'd have to explain why she was wearing a dress. And holding a puppy.

Yellin' Helen ran away from the fight.

* * *

Fred followed Kayla and Quigly through the halls of the temple. The nice thing about Kayla and Quigly was that their armor was as heavy as Fred's. He didn't often get to run with people who were as slow as he was.

A door opened and Sam stepped into the hallway. Kayla barreled into him and they both went sprawling.

Quigly and Fred stopped.

Those two guys from the night shift followed Sam into the corridor. The patchy-bearded one—Ike—said, "Ha! Told you the day shift would be running away."

Quigly pointed in the direction they had been running. "That's not away." He pointed back toward the entrance. "That's away."

"Well, you were still running."

Fred said, "Hello, Ike."

Ike looked away and mumbled, "Hello, Fred."

Kayla helped Sam to his feet. "Sorry, Sergeant. I wasn't expecting you to pop out like that."

"Why aren't you at your post?"

Kayla looked at Quigly, then met the sergeant's eyes. "We left Goose and Evelyn to guard the chamber. We figured you'd rather have us up front. The kids would just get themselves killed."

"They're *supposed* to get themselves killed," said Ike. "That's the way this works."

The look on Kayla's face said that she knew guards were supposed to get themselves killed, and unlike Ike, she knew that did not only apply to guards like Goosifer and Evelyn.

Sam said, "I suppose we can wait to discuss the punishment for deserting your post until we know if any of us survive. Right now, I'm glad you're here. I assume you know we've been quested?"

Kayla nodded. "Fred told us."

Sam met Fred's eyes and did not look glad to see him. "How many are there?"

"Six," said Fred. "And they are high level. Trust me, Sam, the only way to keep your people alive is to get them out of here."

"Well, I'm glad that the man who's been here three days already knows exactly what to do," said Sam. "You know, if you'd fought them off at the entrance, we wouldn't be in this mess. But we're in it. And now, you're going to help clean it up." Sam drew his sword and gestured down the corridor. "You can go in front."

So Fred went in front. Normally, he was happy to be in front, but he didn't like having Sam and Ike behind him.

They weren't running now. They were advancing cautiously. But because they were temple guards and not adventurers, they didn't have to advance at the ridiculously slow pace of sixty feet every ten minutes. Fred just tried to walk quietly, and that was good enough.

There was some sort of battle in the distance—voices shouting, the clang of metal on metal. Fred also heard the clang of metal on stone, as someone repeatedly struck the floor with a shortsword. He guessed that was Stinky.

Before they could get close to the battle, they heard a voice that sounded like it was about sixty feet away, coming around the corner just ahead. Sam put a hand on Fred's shoulder, and they all stopped.

"Then Nightshade, with the aid of Mak-Thar's carefully drawn map, will lead everyone to the exit point."

Quigly murmured, "That definitely sounds like an adventurer."

Ike said, "Shut up, Quigly. We know what an adventurer sounds like."

Ike was scared.

"Do you really?" asked Kayla. "How often have you been quested, Ike?"

Sam said, "You will all now quit bickering and behave as a single, well-trained combat unit. That's an order."

Nightshade came around the corner.

"It's one of ours," said Ike's raspy-voiced buddy.

"I don't recognize her," said Ike.

"She came with Fred," said Kayla.

Nightshade was followed by a boy, a girl, and Roberto.

Fred could feel all the guards relax.

"Where are you taking the prisoners?" asked Sam.

Nightshade stopped narrating her action. Roberto gave a guilty start.

"We're taking them ..." said Nightshade, "... for a walk. Because the ... air in the dungeon ... is too ... evil? ... And ... that's bad because ... we like evil and we're afraid they might be enjoying it too much."

Mak-Thar came around the corner. Fred could feel all the guards tense up.

"Who are you?" Mak-Thar demanded.

"I'm the temple's sergeant-at-arms! Who the heaven are you?"

"I am the temple's torturer," said Mak-Thar. "Thanks to your security breach, Sergeant, I am forced to relocate my prisoners to the swamp. When will you have this situation under control?"

"That's the curate that came with Fred," said Kayla.

"But the cute cleric was talking like an adventurer," murmured Ike.

"Yes, something's fishy," Quigly agreed.

Then there was an awkward pause, as the night shift and the day shift realized they were agreeing with each other.

Sam called, "I can't help but notice that you are carrying enough equipment for a major mountain-climbing expedition."

"Well," said Mak-Thar, "I do like to be prepared."

Yellin' Helen came around the corner, wearing a dress and carrying a puppy. She stepped past Mak-Thar and held the puppy out to the little boy. "Hold this. I think there's gonna be a fight."

"Who is that?" asked Quigly.

"Why does she have a humongous sword?" asked Ike.

Kayla asked, "Fred, is there something you want to tell us?"

Was there something Fred wanted to tell these people? He had pretended to be one of them, but did he really feel bad about it? Fred realized he didn't.

He hadn't really lied to them. He had mostly been himself. He was a guy with a sword hanging out in an evil temple. They were guys with swords hanging out in an evil temple. So, sure, he had pretended to be one of them, but he kind of was. Everyone here would have fit in perfectly fine at the Fighters' Guild—even Ike and his raspy-voiced buddy.

Fred didn't think he had really betrayed these people. At least, he hadn't yet.

"All I wanted to say," said Fred, "was that you guys should get out of here. I'm sorry you wouldn't listen."

"Egad!" said Quigly. "It was a ruse!"

Quigly looked down the corridor at the little girl holding Nightshade's hand and the little boy holding the puppy. Then he smiled, and in that smile, Fred saw admiration. "You risked your lives putting on this elaborate ruse just to free two helpless, impoverished children!"

Actually, no. Fred was here simply because Helen wanted to

be here. And Helen was here to tear the place apart. Her humongous sword was in her hands. On her face was a heavy-lidded smile, like the smile of a hungry smilodon ready to wake up from its nap and start killing things.

Fred was standing between Helen and the temple guards, and Helen's face said all hell was about to break loose.

And in that moment, while the temple guards were still realizing that Fred was not really a guard and Helen was sinking gently onto her back leg in preparation for a crazed barbarian rush, something scratched against the wall.

And then there were more scratchings. And suddenly dozens of clawed feet were climbing up the outside wall, and monsters started dropping into the corridor.

Fred and the guards found themselves surrounded by lizard men.

Chapter Twenty-Four: In which quite a bit of hell does, in fact, break loose.

THIS ADVENTURE was becoming complicated. Yellin' Helen, barbarian warrior of the plains, was accustomed to battles that had only two sides, whereas this adventure had enough sides to be a square or a heptapebbelgon or something.

On any other adventure, when you met guards in the hall, you attacked. But on this adventure, Fred was with the guards.

On any other adventure, when lizard men started raining down, you attacked. But on this adventure, maybe the lizard men were her allies. At least some of them.

This adventure was so complicated that even the lizard men had two sides.

"They shouldn't be able to drop like that," said Mak-Thar. "Not without taking damage."

One of the lizard men dropped directly in front of Nightshade. He wore a temple uniform, which meant he was an enemy. But Nightshade was also wearing that uniform, which meant she could pretend to be the lizard man's friend.

The lizard man bared his teeth and waved his club. That meant he was hostile. But if he was reacting to Nightshade's *uniform*, then he was hostile to the *temple*, in which case he was an ally. This was a mess.

"Stand back!" said Mak-Thar. "I'm going to cast Edwin's Weird Dweomer!"

Nightshade said, "But *Fred's* in there!"

Fred was in there, somewhere—somewhere beyond the dropping lizard men. Helen hoped he could make more sense of this than she could, but she knew he couldn't. He was just Fred. She hoped he didn't get killed before he figured out which side he was on.

The lizard man threatening Nightshade said, "We will be your ssservantsss no more!"

He ripped off his uniform and urinated on it.

"Ew!" said Nightshade.

Helen was not an expert on lizard man customs, but she was getting the impression that the lizard man had decided to turn against the temple. She stepped forward and said, "We're not actually with the temple. We're the ones who spoke with you in the swamp."

Mak-Thar gave a little bow and said, "I am Mak-Thar the Magnificent. Although I wear the garb of the temple, I am actually rescuing these two children."

He gestured at the children, and the kitten in his sleeve said, "Mew!"

Nightshade took off her temple robe, revealing her smart little black outfit with the flouncy leather skirt. "I'm Nightshaaade! My cleric tabard was only a disguise. I'm actually a thief!"

The lizard man squinted. "I don't know any of you. Where'sss the female with two armorsss?"

Helen sheathed her sword and ripped off her dress—literally. She just tore it open with both hands and let the tatters fall to the floor.

The lizard man's eyes widened. *Now* he recognized her.

"You! You killed my brother!"

"Probably," Helen admitted.

"I will boil your bonesss and roassst your younglingsss!"

"Oh," said Nightshade. "For a second, I thought we were going to talk our way out of this one."

The lizard man hissed something, and those who had been waiting for his signal attacked.

Helen drew her sword and stepped between the lizard men and her friends.

"Protect the mage!" shouted Mak-Thar, half a beat late.

"I wish I'd brought my bow," said Nightshade. "Do you have a dagger I can borrow?"

But Helen didn't need Nightshade's help. These lizard men were full of fury but short on skill. With a swipe, Helen disemboweled two who had underestimated her reach. She fell back a step to dodge a club, drove her swordpoint into a scaly thigh, kneed one in the stomach, spun to elbow one in the face, reversed her pivot to pierce a throat, and suddenly she was through her line of lizard men and behind the ones who were attacking Fighter Fred.

They did not see her coming, and they did not last long.

* * *

Fred had not realized that so many lizard men could live in one swamp. And he'd never seen lizard men drop from the ceiling before. Of course, the temple didn't really have a ceiling, so he wasn't seeing it this time, either. But the temple did have corridors, and the lizard men definitely had them trapped in one.

Kayla was fighting by Fred's side, and she was doing a pretty good job.

"Where'd you learn to fight like that?" he asked. "Did the Cathedral of Neutrality get attacked a lot?"

She gave him a wide-eyed panicked look and nearly got skewered by a lizard man's spear.

Fred chopped the spear in half, feinted at the lizard man

threatening him, and punched Kayla's lizard man in the head. Kayla's lizard man went down, and she stabbed him in the chest.

"Sorry," said Fred. "Didn't mean to distract you."

Apparently, this was her first battle. She'd just been really well trained.

Fred and Kayla dared not let any lizard men past them. They were protecting the backs of the guards who were fighting the lizard men on the other side. And with any luck, the guards were still alive and protecting Fred and Kayla's backs. Fred could see why mages always liked to have an empty dungeon behind them. Fighting with nowhere to run was inconvenient.

Then, quite unexpectedly, a lot of lizard men started falling down dead. Within fifteen seconds, Yellin' Helen killed everyone that Fred and Kayla had been trying to fight.

Helen and Kayla locked gazes for a moment—it reminded Fred of the time Ike had tried to crush his hand—then Kayla turned and called, "Quigly! You've got space to retreat!"

"A paladin never retreats!"

"You're not a paladin!"

"Excellent point!"

The raspy-voiced kid who hung out with Ike got clubbed in the knee and fell down. Ike bent to help him and got clubbed in the head. Fred thought he saw Sam's body, already down, somewhere among the legs of the lizard men who were pressing in on Quigly.

Fred stepped in to help.

He lopped off a scaly arm and stabbed another lizard man in the face. The wounded monsters retreated, and Fred lunged at the next rank. Quigly kept pace, and together they drove the lizard men back just enough that Kayla could grab the raspy-voiced kid and pull him out of their way.

Fred glanced down at Ike and saw that Ike was not getting up—at least not until some evil cleric came by and Raised him.

Quigly was holding his ground, but there was strain on his face. He had not been in as many battles as Fred.

"You should swap out with Helen," Fred suggested. "She and I can hold this corridor while you guys get away."

Fred blocked a club, stabbed the one threatening Quigly, and sliced open a lizard man's leg.

"I shan't abandon this temple!" said Quigly. "I swore an oath!"

The dome above was suddenly lit by the orange glow of a nearby fireball.

"Maybe this is your chance to reconsider," suggested Fred.

Mak-Thar said, "According to my map, there's no easy path to the exit from here. And I fear that Antarea's fireball may have complicated things further."

"Good thing we have a backup plan," said Twilight. The elf's voice came from the top of the wall the lizard men had so recently climbed over.

"Twilight!" said Mak-Thar. "I can't remember when I've been so glad to see you!"

Fred would also have been glad to see Twilight, but he was busy trying to keep a lizard man from bashing Quigly's head, so he had to settle for being glad to *hear* Twilight.

"Hey, Twilight!" Helen called. "I was afraid you were going to be left out of this one."

Mak-Thar said, "Fred, Twilight has lowered two climbing ropes. If the other NPM fighter is also sworn to defend the temple, ask her to take your place so you can escape with us."

"We're all going," said Fred. "Send the wounded guy up first."

"That will take two extra rounds," said Mak-Thar.

"We'll hold them," said Fred. "Right, Quigly?"

Quigly grunted as a club glanced off his shoulder. Fred stabbed that lizard man in the armpit, and his own lizard man tried to sneak by. Fred tripped him, stabbed him in the back of the neck, and fell back one step.

Quigly fell back with him.

"How are they going to withdraw from the fight?" Kayla asked. Her voice was now coming from the top of the wall.

"Trust Fred," said Helen. "He's gotten out of worse scrapes than this."

That was probably true, but Fred was having difficulty coming up with an example. He risked a glance over his shoulder. Mak-Thar and Nightshade were climbing up the ropes. Everyone else had already escaped.

"You're next, Quigly," Fred said. "Run for the nearest rope."

Quigly seemed reluctant.

From the top of the wall, Kayla called, "The fire's starting to spread."

"You go," said Quigly. "Perhaps 'tis best I die here."

Fred punched a lizard man in the nose. Do lizard men have noses? He punched a lizard man in the nostrils.

"But what if 'tis not best?" asked Fred.

"My life is not worth yours," said Quigly.

Fred jumped to avoid a lizard man's attempted leg sweep.

"I'm not planning to die here," said Fred. "Please go. It will be a lot easier to save myself if you're not in the way."

Kayla called, "And I need someone to be my character reference when I apply for my next job!"

"Well," said Quigly, "I suppose this isn't the first time I've done something I'll never live down." Quigly left.

And now it was just Fighter Fred, all alone against a horde of lizard men. The blows came faster than he could think, so he just relaxed and let his blade flow where it needed to be. Clubs splintered against his sword. His feet glided swiftly as a spider's. His shoulders turned to let a blow slide off his armor.

Then he was running away, and only then did he realize that he had a brilliant plan. Two ropes hung down into the hallway. Quigly and Twilight watched from above with anxious faces. Fred ran past the nearer rope, leapt, and seized the next rope, swinging away from the lizard men ...

Huh.

He'd expected to swing higher than that.

As Fred hung there, not even halfway up the wall, he realized he did not have a brilliant plan.

Fred swung backwards into the lizard men. A club bounced off his spine. Then his butt hit the lizard men like a battering ram.

Not checking to see how many he had stunned, Fred climbed desperately, hand over hand, until he was at the top of the wall.

Gasping, Fred looked down on two dozen disappointed scaly faces. Then one of them shrugged, and they walked off to find someone else to eat.

"That was well done!" said Quigly. "Please forgive me for doubting you. This is the first time I've met a professional hero."

Fred was a professional fighter. He wasn't sure he was a hero.

Smoke was billowing above a fire in a corridor beyond the one he could see down into. Screams echoed from the direction the lizard men were heading. Sam's dead body lay on the floor below, staring up at him angrily. Ike lay still and face down.

Fred sighed and climbed down a rope to the foundation outside the temple walls. Everyone seemed glad to see him, even the moldy guy.

Fred met Helen's eyes and asked, "Has the temple been overthrown enough?"

Helen shrugged. "I suppose."

"So this was a vengeance quest?" Kayla asked.

Helen opened her mouth to reply. But then she had second thoughts. Instead of answering, she said, "Let's go find Wren."

"I'm still trying to splint this knee," said Twilight, who was working on Ike's raspy-voiced buddy. "I'm finding it difficult to make a splint without any pieces of wood."

"Doesn't Mak-Thar have any?" Helen asked.

"I don't believe so," said Mak-Thar. "Let me check my equipment list." The mage pulled his notebook out of its pouch.

"You have a list of everything you're carrying?" Kayla asked.

"Of course," said Mak-Thar.

Quigly eyed Mak-Thar's enormous backpack. "How else could he keep track of it all?"

"Oh!" said Mak-Thar. "I may have just the thing!" He removed his pack and started rummaging through it.

"Why are we binding wounds on NPMs?" Nightshade asked.

"Because it's the decent thing to do," said Twilight.

In an undertone that he hoped no one else heard, Fred

asked Kayla, "What's that kid's name, anyway?"

"I don't know," she murmured. "He's just that raspy-voiced kid who hangs out with Ike."

"We'll have to stop calling him that," said Fred.

Kayla looked grim. "I know. Poor Ike. I never thought I'd feel sorry for someone on the night shift."

"Aha!" Mak-Thar emerged from his backpack. "The telescoping ten-foot pole! I knew it would come in handy."

So they busted up the telescoping ten-foot pole and used the pieces to splint the raspy kid's knee. The children watched with interest, while Twilight carefully explained each step of the procedure. Even so, Twilight worked swiftly, and he finished the splint just as Wren came walking around the corner.

She was empty handed.

"Aw," said Nightshade. "She didn't get the gems."

"What gems?" asked Quigly in a tense voice. "Why would the cleaning lady get gems?"

"She's not really a cleaning lady," said Nightshade. "She's actually the master thief of Basetown, cleverly disguised."

Wren wasn't really disguised. Nor was she the only master thief in Basetown. But Nightshade's version sounded cool, so Fred figured she was justified in letting her facts get a little fuzzy.

"I'm confused," Kayla admitted. "Is this a rescue mission, a vendetta, or a burglary?"

Fred shrugged. "It's just an adventure."

"It was a little bit of everything," said Wren. "My original objective was profit, but when our inside man discovered rug rats in the slammer, we found a way to take them along for the ride."

Nightshade quivered with delight. "Thieves' cant is so cool!"

"So who are our new friends?" Wren asked.

"This is Kayla," said Fred. "She's a guard. This is Roberto. He was guarding the dungeons, but it looks like maybe he wants to quit."

Roberto nodded.

"This is ... the Raspberry Kid. He's considering new career options."

"Hi," said the raspy-voiced kid.

"And this is Quigly. He wants to be a paladin, but he's afraid he's too evil."

Quigly looked at his vambrace. "Is my heart on my sleeve?"

"And these are the imprisoned children," Fred finished. "But I don't know their names yet."

"I'm Tabitha," said the little girl. "My mommy called me Tabby, but now I'm an orphan."

"That's great," said Wren.

Everyone looked at her.

"What?" asked Wren. "Most everyone in the Thieves' Guild is an orphan. *I'm* an orphan. It's a great career move."

Twilight said, "I do hope you aren't implying you orphaned yourself as a career move."

"No, I just grew up on the streets. Parents unknown. That sort of thing."

"So maybe you're secretly a princess!" said Nightshade.

Wren nodded. "See? Nightshade gets it."

"I'm Rutherford," said the boy. "I'm an orphan, too."

"And do you have a nickname?" Wren asked.

"No," said Rutherford.

"Would you like one?" asked Wren.

"No," said Rutherford.

"You'll get one anyway," said Wren. "Think about what you want to be called."

"I want to be called Rutherford."

"Well, good luck with that," said Wren. "Um … Mak-Thar?"

"Yes?"

"Can you, um, tell me our current financial situation?"

"That depends," said Mak-Thar. "Did you get the gems?"

"If she had them, wouldn't we see them?" asked Nightshade. She held up her hands as though encompassing an object about the size of Rutherford's head. "Aren't they about this big?"

Mak-Thar looked embarrassed. "It's just that high-level thieves have ways of hiding things on their person."

"Mak-Thar thinks maybe Wren has the gems in her bra," Helen said.

Nightshade and Kayla giggled.

"That's not true. I deliberately did not specify—"

Quigly said, "Please tell me you haven't stolen the Eyes of Toxia."

"I haven't," said Wren.

"Good."

"Does that mean you don't want a cut?" asked Wren.

"Ah!" said Mak-Thar. "'Our financial situation.' Yes, now I understand. The NPMs are just strays we picked up. As far as I know, none of them are expecting a share in the treasure."

"Treasure?" asked Rutherford.

"You don't get any treasure," said Wren. "You're a quest object."

"Wren!" said Nightshade.

"Well, it's true." Wren shrugged. "If you want a cut of the adventure, you gotta learn to do cool stuff. Like this:"

Wren reached for a rope that was dangling down from the outside edge of the dome.

Then she hesitated and checked with Twilight. "You set it up the way I asked?"

"I did," said Twilight. "How did you know the top of the dome would have vents?"

"There's always vents," said Wren. "Or tunnels. But I was betting on vents."

"I bet the vents are there to let the bats out," said Fred. "That's why none of them landed on my face."

Twilight looked puzzled. "I'm sure bats have lots of reasons not to land on your face, Fred. Vents are not required."

"Stupid low charisma," said Wren. "Now I've ruined the moment. Anyway, I don't have the Eyes of Toxia 'on my person', but I'm going to steal them right now."

Wren yanked on the rope dangling over the edge of the dome. For a moment, nothing else happened. Then the rope started falling, piling up in loops in the water below the granite foundation.

Wren held out her hand. "Mak-Thar, please hand me the butterfly net."

Mak-Thar reached into his pack, pulled out a butterfly net, and handed it to Wren.

Wren held out her hand again. "Mak-Thar, please hand me the telescoping ten-foot pole."

"Um ..." Mak-Thar stared wide-eyed at the remaining pieces of the pole, which lay scattered about their feet. "The thing is, you never told us what you needed it for, and ..."

Above them could be heard the sound of two very large rocks sliding rapidly along the outer surface of the marble dome.

"Oh," said Wren. She looked at the rapidly descending rope. She looked down into the water. She looked up at the dome ...

Two multifaceted emeralds, each the size of Rutherford's head, appeared below the edge of the dome and fell through a strip of blue sky.

Wren jumped, arm extended, butterfly net reaching, reaching, reaching ...

With a drastic splash, Wren belly-flopped into the lake and disappeared from view.

"Helen," asked Mak-Thar, "would you say Wren is the sort of person who will look back on this and laugh?"

"None of us will look back on this and laugh," said Quigly. He was horrified. "None of us will get out of this alive."

Fred remembered that Quigly had said the curse on the idol would make it able to defend itself. But he hadn't really known what Quigly meant.

As Wren's head emerged from the lake, spitting water and gasping for air, Fred's relief was overshadowed by the dread that rumbled in his bones.

No, wait. That wasn't dread. It was just a vibration. The pillars were rumbling against the stone foundation. Something was shaking the temple. And Fred realized that anything big enough to shake the temple was something very, very big.

"It's Toxia!" said the Raspberry Kid. "The statue has come to life!"

Chapter Twenty-Five: In which Fred has to do one more thing before he can run away.

"You've doomed us all!" Quigly shouted down at the wet and bedraggled thief. "Why did you have to take the Eyes of Toxia?"

"I'm a thief!" said Wren. "Taking stuff is what I do."

"Wow, this is so cool!" said Nightshade.

The temple reverberated with the sound of crunching plaster.

"Why is this cool?" asked Kayla, who clearly thought this was not cool.

Nightshade shrugged. "Just, you know, a cool plot twist. Aren't heist movies supposed to end with a cool plot twist?"

Except for the fact that this adventure was not, in fact, a movie, Fred thought Nightshade had a pretty good point. You could get lots of free drinks for a story about a giant snake statue coming to life.

"We're all going to die!" said the Raspberry Kid.

"Nonsense," said Mak-Thar. He reached into his pack and pulled out a funny iron triangle. He handed it to Rutherford. "Here. Climb up on my shoulders and hook that on the line overhead." He pointed at a rope that ran from the top of the wall to a tree branch on the edge of the lake. The rope was vibrating like a lute string thanks to all the rumbling coming from the temple.

Rutherford, who had spent quite a bit of time with Mak-Thar when the mage was pretending to torture him, did exactly as Mak-Thar asked. As a black granite tail punctured the wall and knocked out a nearby pillar, Mak-Thar calmly uncoiled the rope from his body and asked Rutherford to attach one end to the triangle.

"Why are you all watching the crazy man?" asked the Raspberry Kid. "I'm running for the walkway!" He stood up, fell over, and sat down.

"You have to be careful on that splint," said Twilight. "You don't want to reinjure yourself."

From inside the temple, voices shouted curses at the giant granite snake.

"This is a zipline," said Mak-Thar. "Observe."

Mak-Thar grabbed the triangle and glided gracefully off the edge of the foundation. He glided gracefully over Wren's head. He glided gracefully across the lake. As the rope went lower, he lifted his legs so he wouldn't get his boots wet. Then he dangled awkwardly, trying not to get his butt wet. Then his backpack overbalanced him, the line sagged, and his bare legs kicked uselessly in the air until he fell, only ten feet from shore, with a loud, muddy splat.

The kitten climbed out of his sleeve, sat on his head, and said, "Mew."

From the water below the temple's shivering foundation, Wren said, "Okay. I guess Mak-Thar and I are even. Helen, would you help me out?"

Helen lowered an arm, and Wren climbed out of the water.

Wren gave Helen a funny look and said, "So when you told me I should ask about Mak-Thar's knickers ..."

Helen raised an eyebrow.

"... how did you know he doesn't wear any?"

"Oh dear," said Twilight.

Helen snickered.

Wren shrugged uncomfortably and started wringing out her dress. "Well, he went right over my head. I suppose I should have averted my eyes, but—"

"Can I go next?" asked Rutherford.

"Great idea," said Wren.

Rutherford handed his puppy off to Twilight.

Fred had to admit this was a pretty cool way to make a getaway. Thanks to Mak-Thar's rope, they were able to pull the triangle back to their side. Then Rutherford went across kicking and screaming, but with a landing that was much better than Mak-Thar's had been.

"So that's it?" Kayla asked, as smoke started to billow out of the hole the granite snake's tail had made. "You just awaken an eldritch curse and leave?"

"Well," said Fred, "don't you think this is a good time to leave?"

"Some of your friends are still in there!"

"That's a different adventuring party," said Nightshade. "We have everyone we came with."

"Don't worry," said Helen. "They can take care of themselves."

Kayla gave Fred a hard stare. "Goose and Evelyn can't take care of themselves."

"Oh," said Fred, as another plaster wall collapsed with a crunch. "I suppose you're right."

Quigly asked, "Wouldn't they have died the instant the statue came to life? They say if you meet Toxia's gaze, she will insinuate her venom into your soul."

"Yeah, but how's she going to gaze without eyeballs?" asked Fred. "I guess Kayla's right. We have to go back for them."

"You want to rescue more NPMs?" asked Nightshade.

Not really. Fred wanted to escape on the zipline. It looked like fun.

"You know," said Helen, as Twilight started pulling the triangle back to their side, "this isn't exactly the fastest escape thingy ever. I bet we've got time to go look for your goose and still get back before it's our turn."

"He's not a goose," said Kayla. "His *name* is Goose."

"You have a friend named *Goose*?"

"It's short for Goosifer," said Fred.

"Really?" asked Quigly.

"You didn't know?" asked Fred.

Quigly shook his head.

Helen strode off toward the hole the giant statue had

knocked in the wall. Fred hurried after her. Behind him, Quigly said, "I can't believe I'm going into a burning building to save a man named Goosifer."

"And Evelyn," said Kayla. "You have to save them so you'll still have someone to look down on."

"Nonsense," said Quigly. "I look down on everyone."

Helen looked down at Quigly and frowned. "Is he going to complain the whole time?"

"Probably," said Kayla.

"At least we'll be able to keep track of him in the smoke," said Fred.

Helen drew her humongous sword and led them inside.

The first thing Fred noticed was that the temple was so smoky he couldn't see. The next thing Fred noticed was that the temple was so smoky he couldn't breathe. He reached out and grabbed Helen's elbow, letting her lead him until they were out of the smoke.

"Where'd your guard-friends go?" Helen asked.

"Quigly!" Fred called. "Kayla! Come this way."

A moment later, the pair emerged from the smoke. Quigly was coughing so hard he had to bend double to catch his breath.

In the distance, they heard a thunderous snapping sound. Kayla said, "Sounds like it just broke another pillar."

Quigly looked up at the huge stone dome overhead. It wasn't falling yet.

"The smoke is only going to get worse," said Helen. "Where do you think your friends might be?"

"We left them in the center of the temple," said Quigly.

"Kayla knows a shortcut," said Fred.

"So do I," said Helen, pointing to a huge gap in the plaster wall.

"Oh," said Fred. "Good point."

They climbed through the rubble and stepped over the dead bodies on the other side. Apparently, the four clerics had finally abandoned their pinochle game, but they hadn't gotten far.

"Don't linger over the dead," said Helen. "We need to hurry before the statue comes back this way."

In the distance, someone screamed.

Helen took off at a trot. Fred, Kayla, and Quigly had trouble keeping up.

Helen's sense of direction was good. She led them through broken walls and even a few actual doors. They swiftly found themselves in the center of the temple. It was difficult to recognize, because half the wall had been knocked down and the snake statue had slithered away. But at least the altar was still there, knocked askew. Its legs had scuffed the golden concentric circles in the black granite floor.

Helen fingered one of the dark green curtains hanging on the remnants of the wall. "Well, at least we know Antarea didn't get this far."

"Antarea was the mage who cast the fireball," Fred explained.

Kayla asked, "And we know she didn't get this far because ... ?"

"She would have taken these curtains," said Helen.

Quigly said, "If the adventurers did not come here, that suggests Goose and Evelyn would have still been at their posts when the curse took effect."

"Where are their posts?" asked Helen.

Quigly pointed to the pile of wood and plaster that had framed the doorway. Kayla was already moving chunks of wall, looking for any bodies that might be underneath.

Fred went to help. He grabbed the smaller chunks and passed them to Quigly, who stacked them out of the way.

Fred was helping Kayla with a particularly heavy slab when the sound of scrabbling claws reached his ears and a dozen lizard men emerged from a ruptured wall.

The lizard men hissed.

Quigly groaned. "Not another lizard man fight!"

More lizard men came through the wall.

"Let's run," suggested Fred.

"Good idea," said Helen. She started running.

"We can do that?" Quigly asked.

Fred met Kayla's eyes, and they both started after Helen, with Quigly close behind.

"I thought heroes never ran from danger!" Quigly said.

"We aren't heroes," said Fred. "We're adventurers!"

"Ah," said Quigly. "I confess this fine distinction has eluded me until now."

They rounded a corner and Helen slammed into a thief who had been running the other way.

"Hey! Watch where you're going!" said Louse. He picked himself up off the floor.

"Where's your party?" Helen asked.

Louse waved a hand vaguely.

"And you decided to go that way?" she asked.

Lizard men came around the corner, hissing and waving clubs. Louse took off in another direction.

"Follow that coward!" said Quigly, chasing after Louse.

They ran after Quigly, the lizard men close behind.

"This isn't the way out!" said Kayla.

"It's the path of heedless panic!" said Quigly. "Maybe it will lead us to Goose and Evelyn!"

Actually, it led to the barracks.

"In there!" said Kayla, and they all went in, except for Louse, who ran down the hall pursued by half a dozen lizard men.

Lizard men tried to get inside the barracks, too, but the wall was still intact, so the monsters had to come through the door. Every lizard man that tried to come in got his head whacked off by Helen's humongous sword. After two or three head-whackings, the remaining lizard men decided they'd rather chase after Louse.

Helen said, "Gee, I guess your good-for-nothing friend is actually good for something."

"Louse is good for lots of things," said Fred. "But this is the first time I've seen him be helpful in a fight."

"You have a friend named *Louse?*" asked Kayla.

"That's even worse than Goosifer," said Quigly.

"Hey!" said an indignant voice under Evelyn's bunk.

"Goose!" exclaimed Kayla. "I *thought* you might be hiding here." She knelt down. "But I didn't expect to find you under Evelyn's bunk. With Evelyn!"

"We weren't sharing the bunk!" Evelyn explained. "Because we were *under* it, not in it."

"Evelyn!" Quigly exclaimed. "You cagey little vixen!"

Evelyn and Goosifer crawled out from under the bunk. Kayla brushed a dust bunny from Evelyn's hair.

"Oh, more guards," said Helen. "For some reason, I thought 'Evelyn' was the name of the goose girl."

"Who are *you*?" Evelyn asked suspiciously.

Helen opened her mouth to reply, but Kayla interrupted: "We'll explain if we get out of here alive."

"That's what Fred said. Something odd is going on here."

With a booming snap, the giant snake statue took out another pillar.

"Are you referring to the adventuring party attack, the lizard man rebellion, or the spontaneous animation of the statue of Toxia?" Quigly asked.

"The adventuring party," said Evelyn. "I think Fred's in league with them. And bikini-chick is *definitely* in league with them."

"Helen's in a league of her own," said Fred. "And Kayla's right: This is not the best time for true confessions."

"No matter who Fred is working for," said Kayla, "he did come in to save your life."

"I think we should trust him," said Goosifer.

"Whom," said Evelyn.

"Trust Fred," said Goosifer.

"No. It's 'No matter *whom* Fred is working for,'" said Evelyn.

Fred was pretty sure he was working for himself, and it was time to get back to work. He climbed up to his bunk.

"Where are you going?" asked Goosifer.

"He's scouting," said Kayla.

"Oh."

Once on top, Fred stood on his bunk—a thing he had

never done before because his mother had told him not to stand on his bed. Being this high was kind of creepy. He looked out over the maze of walls and rubble and saw something even creepier.

Rising above the temple's walls was the face of a black granite viper. Though rough and hard as stone, the face was clearly alive. A shiny obsidian tongue flicked out between its lips. The face turned toward Fred and gazed on him with empty eye sockets.

The viper's mouth opened with a hiss, revealing gleaming silver fangs as long as swords. And Fred realized that deep in his heart he was a true adventurer, because he caught himself wondering how much they would pay for those teeth in Basetown.

But mostly he was wondering how they were going to get away.

"So what's the quickest path out of here?" he asked.

"You tell us," said Helen. "You've got the best view."

They couldn't see the snake, Fred realized. They couldn't see its scaly body undulating over the walls, smashing the timbers and crushing the plaster. They didn't know the snake was heading straight toward them, like a vengeful avalanche. But couldn't they hear its belly grinding against the granite? Couldn't they hear it smash through wall after wall, coming closer and closer?

"Is the snake coming closer?" Helen asked.

"Get out!" said Fred. "Get out, get out, get out!"

Standing on the top bunk, Fred knew he would be the last person out the door. So Fred didn't run for the door. As the snake smashed through the last wall that stood between Fred and oblivion, Fred stepped onto the wall of the barracks and ran sideways.

He did not go far.

Maybe he wasn't very graceful, or maybe it's just hard to balance on a wall when fifty tons of granite slams into it, but for whatever reason, Fred fell off, tumbling into the corridor below.

He landed on his shoulder, smacked his elbow, and rolled

until he thumped against the opposite wall. A massive body of stone was slithering past, inches from his head.

Fred got to his knees.

"Hey, Fred. Hop on!"

A small hand with a stout hairy forearm reached toward him. Fred jumped, grabbed the forearm, and pulled himself onto the back of the rampaging statue, right behind his buddy from the Fighters' Guild, Stinky La Foote.

"Cool ride, huh?" asked Stinky, his voice pitched high enough to be heard within the bass rumble of slithering destruction.

Fred crouched low and tried to maintain his balance as the snake negotiated a turn.

"What happened to Antarea and Ludo and the others?" asked Fred.

Stinky waved a hand vaguely. He didn't seem too concerned.

Daylight flashed ahead. The statue had broken through another exterior wall. Avoiding the lake, it made a sharp turn and headed back toward Fred and Stinky.

"Yee haw!" shouted Stinky. He drew his shortbow and shot an arrow that bounced harmlessly off the snake's forehead.

The head reared up, but the rest of the body continued to move toward the edge of the temple, and Fred and Stinky were pulled on by.

"Sharp turn!" yelled Stinky. "Get ready for some fun!"

"This is where I get off," said Fred. And truthfully, he would have gotten off there even if he hadn't wanted to, because the change of direction was forceful enough to throw him to the floor. Fred skidded across the granite so fast that his armor sprayed sparks. He came to a stop with his head and one arm dangling off the edge of the foundation.

Fred clambered to his feet, hoping to get some distance between himself and the part of the snake that was still going through the turn. But, you know, Fred couldn't move real quick—certainly not as quick as the tail end of the turning snake. The tip of the tail caught Fred right in the belt and sent him flying over the lake. His butt skipped off the water, and he flew some more. Fred counted three more skips before he finally slowed down enough to plow through the water and skid to a halt on the slimy lake bottom. When he stood up, the water was only knee deep, and the shore was only ten yards away.

Helen, Kayla, Quigly, Goosifer, and Evelyn emerged from the gap in the wall where Fred had just been standing. Helen pointed and, in a voice made faint by distance, said, "See? I told you he'd be okay."

Chapter Twenty-Six: In Which We Learn the Real Reason Yellin' Helen Hates Temples.

They did not linger. Although the curse of Toxia appeared to be confined to the site of the temple, no one—not even Helen—wanted to stick around long enough to find out what would happen once everything had been thoroughly destroyed.

They had just picked up Evenstar from the swamp camp when the ground shook from a terrific crash—the sound made by the temple's massive dome smashing into the granite foundation, splintering pillars and dooming anyone who might have been left inside. Someone suggested they continue on toward the mountains and drier ground, and even those who had not been dunked in the lake agreed with this plan most heartily.

At the edge of the swamp, they were still within the territory of the lizard men, so they decided the best thing to do would be to go through the tunnel and camp in the wilderness on the other side. And that's what they did, even though they had to put the Raspberry Kid on a litter and take turns carrying him.

Along the way, of course, Fred did finally tell Evelyn and Goosifer everything he had promised he would tell them. He even explained a few more things, like how he had gotten out of the temple ahead of them and how he knew Stinky. It was a long tunnel, and they had time for as many stories as people wanted to hear.

When they finally emerged from the darkness of the tunnel, it was dark outside, too. They camped in the forest. Helen made a campfire and handed out dried snake meat, which Twilight said was thematically appropriate. Fred didn't know what Twilight meant by that, but he did know it had been a long time since his morning gruel, and the snake meat tasted pretty good.

The children and the puppy fell asleep right away. Shortly after that, Antarea's party emerged from the tunnel. There were still six of them, so that was good. They all exchanged a few awkward greetings, and then Antarea's bunch continued on through the forest to camp some ways off.

"Better sleep on top of the emeralds," said Fred. "Louse likes to wander around at night."

Wren gave Fred a blank look. "The emeralds are lost in the lake, remember? Besides, Louse is too smart to move against me."

There were a lot of words people could use to describe Louse before they ever needed to use the word "smart", but Fred could see her point. Although Wren was not dangerous the way Helen was dangerous, she was high enough in the Thieves' Guild to be dangerous to Louse.

"I don't believe the emeralds are lost in the lake," said Twilight.

Wren shrugged.

"You pulled them out of the temple, so they must have been attached to the rope somehow. Which means you did not need to dredge the lake for them; you just needed to retrieve the rope. I assume you did so when the rest of us were distracted by the zipline—or by the giant serpent statue smashing through the wall."

Fred knew Twilight was right. There was no question in Fred's mind that Wren had come back with the emeralds. If her heist plan had failed, she would have been glum all afternoon. But Fred could tell she was satisfied.

"Perhaps Wren wishes to avoid discussing the emeralds at this time," suggested Mak-Thar. "Perhaps she is waiting for a moment that is more private."

"It's okay," said Kayla. "We aren't expecting a share. We're just grateful you got us out alive."

Goosifer asked, "Do you think it'll be okay if I keep the sword?"

"You can keep it," said Helen. "But you'd be stupid to wear it in Basetown until you learn to use it."

Evelyn frowned and didn't say anything. Fred could tell she wasn't sure whether she should be happy to be rescued or not.

"I'm still curious about this adventuring business," said Kayla. "I'm guessing it pays well?"

"Eh," said Helen.

"It pays great!" said Fred.

"It depends," said Wren.

"I am completely supported and outfitted via my adventuring income," said Mak-Thar. "It even covers guild dues, which in the Mages' Guild can be quite expensive."

"But you won't get paid for rescuing two orphans," said Kayla. "So why did you go after them? Is it because you're aligned with good?"

"I'm neutral," said Mak-Thar.

"Neutral people don't risk their lives just to be nice," said Kayla.

"They're heroes," said Quigly.

Fred wasn't sure about that. Sure, he'd sort of risked his life, but Fred never went on an adventure with mortality on his mind. He was usually pretty sure he would get out alive, and that wasn't in the same category as making a heroic last stand to save your friends, which was what Quigly had offered to do.

"But when you started this adventure," said Kayla, "you didn't know about the kids, and you didn't know about the emeralds. So why did you decide to quest us?"

"They explained that," said Quigly. "They ran across the temple last month, realized it was evil, and vowed to destroy it to protect the swamp."

"That's *his* reason," said Kayla, pointing at Twilight. "I want to know Helen's."

Helen worked her jaw like she was still chewing on snake meat. Finally she said, "I don't have to tell you anything." She thought a bit more and added, "I don't have to tell *any* of you anything."

Her attitude was hostile. And defensive. Fred didn't know what to make of that. When Helen was hostile, she was usually *offensive*. In fact, when Helen got *this* hostile, she was usually killing something.

But this was a different kind of hostility. She wasn't physically threatening. And that was even weirder, because Helen could be physically threatening just by being in the same forest with you.

"Helen," Twilight asked in a gentle voice, "is there something you *want* to tell us?"

Helen didn't answer.

Twilight asked, "Is there something you'd like to talk about with Fred? I'm sure we'd all understand if you need a moment of privacy."

"I'm not drunk enough to pour my heart out." She looked at Fred. "Not to any of you."

"What's going on?" asked Nightshade. "Everyone knows Helen wanted to do this because she hates evil temples. Why is this suddenly some big, serious thing?"

"Because Helen has a *reason* for hating evil temples," said Twilight. "A personal reason. And she can't tell us because she's afraid it will make her seem smaller in our eyes."

"It's a dark trauma," said Wren. "She was a victim of some horrible abuse. She never wants to feel that helpless again, so now she wields a bloody blade to wreak vengeance on the world."

"Oo!" said Nightshade. "That's a cool back story!"

Wren looked at Helen's eyes flickering with reflected firelight. "I'm right, aren't I?"

"No," said Helen. She sighed.

And Fred knew what this sigh meant. "She's half right?"

Helen shrugged. "Yeah. She's half right."

"Which half?" asked Nightshade. "The dark trauma, or the horrible abuse?"

"The helpless part," Helen admitted. "That's why I hate temples." She looked at Kayla. "Not just the evil temples—all of them. When I needed their help, they didn't help me."

* * *

I had a little brother. Sometimes I think of Fred as my little brother, but I had one on the steppe, too.

You can't understand. You didn't grow up there, so you can't understand. You'd see it as harsh. But if our way of life is harsh, it's only because the whole world is harsh. Snake eats mouse. Hawk eats snake. Death is what life *is*. And words like "good" and "evil" seem meaningless.

But barbarians are still *people*. We still love each other and mourn our dead. I loved my brother. And my brother looked up to me, even before I really knew how to wield my sword.

When he got a sword of his own, I would spar with him. I don't know, maybe I went too easy on him. Maybe he would have learned better if I— Well, I just don't know. By the time we were old enough to go on raids, I knew how to kill people, but he was still practicing technique.

Barbarians don't have technique. The things we do with our blades aren't tricks we learned and practiced. Our moves are pure expressions of our will. The snake doesn't practice striking. The hawk doesn't practice diving.

Well, actually, the hawk *does* practice, when it's young and stupid, before it really knows how to fly. But it doesn't truly become a hawk until it can seize its prey. It's not technique anymore. It's will.

So that's where we were when our warband took us on our first raid. I was a hawk. My brother was a fledgling. I loved slaughtering villagers. He hated it.

Yeah, that's right. We plundered villages, just like the soldiers from the evil temple do. We were hawks; they were mice. It all seemed so clean and natural.

The pillaging went on for five months, and I confess, even after five months of carnage, I was still enjoying it. I suppose the villagers would say I was a monster. And maybe I was. I didn't care.

And then we met the cultists.

They worshipped one of the bigger devils—I don't know which one. The name they called him sounded like a lot of bees buzzing against their tongues. They were nasty, and that fight was really fun, because I had become quite nasty, too. I liked proving I was nastier.

We fought so fiercely they ran away. Can you imagine that? We were so horrible that even devil worshippers ran away from us! And I felt like we'd really accomplished something, until I saw my brother lying there on the ground, bleeding from the stump where a cultist had hacked off his leg.

* * *

Helen stopped there. But Fred knew about stories, and he knew this story wasn't done.

"Did it get infected?" Twilight asked.

"No," said Helen. "We cauterized it."

Nightshade winced.

"My dad made him a peg leg, so he could hop along and watch us plunder more villages. But seeing him crippled ... well, my heart wasn't in it anymore. When we got near the town of Picklingford, my parents let me take him to the temple."

"What sort of temple do they have in Picklingford?" asked Kayla.

"A temple of good," said Helen. "I took my brother and all the treasure I had pillaged. We went into the temple and I begged them to grow my brother's leg back."

"But they couldn't take your money," said Twilight. "Because you had earned it by spilling innocent blood."

Helen shook her head. "No, it's dumber than that. They took

the money, no questions asked. They put him on the altar and did a bunch of holy things, but the ritual didn't work. He still had no leg. So they called in the high priestess. She tried to regrow his leg herself. Same result."

Helen wiped her hand across her eyes. "So then she asks me how he lost it. And I told her about the evil devil cultists. And she told me that evil people have temples, too. And they have altars. And they can't regrow legs, because they're evil. But what they can do is make dead bodies move around. The cultists had run away with my brother's leg. They'd taken it to their temple and sewn it onto a zombie or something. She couldn't regrow it because it wasn't gone yet. It was still running around somewhere. Undead."

"What a bizarre metaphysical conundrum," said Mak-Thar.

"So, wait," said Nightshade. "If your brother was still hopping around and watching battles after losing his leg, how did he die?"

Helen winced and tried to shake the pain out of her head. "He didn't really die. He became an accountant. He's working at that bank you wanted to rob."

Wren asked, "Your brother is an accountant at the Basetown Bank?"

Helen nodded.

"Do you think he can—?"

"No."

"Right," said Wren. "Sorry. Only a person with low charisma would try to take advantage of your tragedy."

"But ... it's not really a tragedy," said Twilight. "Is it? He's still alive, and he has a respectable occupation."

Quigly said, "Helen and I have just met, so I could be wrong about this, but perhaps in her worldview, a respectable occupation *is* a tragedy."

"I haven't talked to him since he moved to Basetown," Helen admitted. "To see him hopping around on a wooden peg—it reminds me of how I failed him."

"So instead of talking to your brother, you attack evil temples," said Twilight.

"Any kind of temple," said Helen. "I hate the evil temple for taking my brother's leg, and I hate the good temple for not fixing him. ... And I suppose I hate myself for not watching over my brother. I was so caught up in my bloodlust, I just forgot about him. When he needed me the most, I wasn't there."

Helen looked at Wren. "So you were right. I do have a lot of anger at the temples. They left me helpless. I do have a dark back story that made me become an adventurer. But that's not why I kill. I joined the Fighters' Guild to become *less* of a killer. You see, barbarians fight because they like fighting. Fighters, the good ones, fight to keep their buddies alive. I failed to protect my brother, so I found a career that would let me try again, protecting people like Fred."

CHAPTER TWENTY-SEVEN: IN WHICH OUR HEROES RETURN TO BASETOWN AND FRED'S NEW FRIENDS SEEK GAINFUL EMPLOYMENT.

FRED HAD ALWAYS KNOWN that Yellin' Helen thought of him as a little brother. Now that he knew why, some things made a lot more sense.

Leave it to Twilight to get that story out of Helen. There was something about that elf that made people willing to talk about their deepest, innermost feelings. Twilight could even get feelings out of *Mak-Thar*.

Fred had to admit that this adventure had given him some feelings of his own. Fighting temple guards was less fun once you'd *been* a temple guard. It gave a fellow a different perspective. Fred had always known that guards were just ordinary people doing a job, but being one of them had really driven that point home.

Of course, being an ordinary guy just doing your job was not a good reason to lock up little kids in a dungeon. That wasn't the sort of thing you should do even if some evil clerics asked you to. In fact, if an evil cleric asks you to do something, that's actually a clue that maybe you shouldn't be doing it.

Roberto had been a woodcutter in one of the first villages that got plundered. He went out to chop wood one day and came back to find everything burning. With no one to chop wood for, he was out of a job, so he decided to join the temple. They were hiring, and he figured that, as a jailor, he could make things a little better for any innocent people they imprisoned.

That had not worked out well. Fred and Helen had hoped that Roberto's part in the rescue would help him assuage his guilt, but apparently he still had bags and bags of guilt left to assuage.

Fred wasn't sure how to help him, but he did know a couple guys who had quit the Fighters' Guild to work on Basetown's many construction projects. The projects needed wood, and to get wood, you need to cut trees. So Fred was, at least, able to connect Roberto with a woodcutting job that would get him out in the sunshine.

Goosifer, Evelyn, and the Raspberry Kid were easier to help. They were perfect for the city guard. Fred put in a word with Cuthbert, mentioning that all three guards had survived an attack by lizard men *and* by an adventuring party. They were hired on the spot.

Quigly and Kayla were obvious fits for the Fighters' Guild. Fred gave them an official recommendation, but he wasn't certain they would join. Kayla was researching the pay at the temples in Basetown, and she had discovered that the Casino of Chaos paid its bouncers really well. Quigly was hanging around the Temple of Good and the Temple of Law, hoping someone would tell him he could still be a paladin.

Helen told them they could get day jobs *and* join the Fighters' Guild to do adventures on the side. After all, she was a fighter and an underwear model. When Kayla heard that, she wanted to know how much modeling paid.

Quigly assured Helen that he would take her advice under consideration. Quigly had listened *very intently* to Helen's story in the forest, and Fred could tell that Quigly, too, had some problems that he might be able to get over if he took up adventuring.

Wren and Nightshade took Tabitha and Rutherford into the Thieves' Guild. Twilight wasn't sure that was the *best* way to raise orphaned children, but Wren was so insistent about the career opportunities that they all acquiesced to her plans. Nightshade promised that if the kids didn't enjoy a life of crime she would find something else for them to do.

Twilight wasn't sure Nightshade was the *best* guardian for orphaned children, seeing as she was likely to be assassinated if she stayed in Basetown. But Nightshade insisted that she was disguised. Twilight said that painting one's hair green and walking with a limp was not a particularly good disguise, but Nightshade said it was, so they had to agree to disagree. Or they could argue. Twilight liked having someone to argue with.

Two days after their return to Basetown, a note came to the Fighters' Guild saying that Wren had sold the emeralds and she wanted everyone to meet and divvy. Helen had to do some shopping first. Fred went with her. After the shopping, they somehow found themselves walking through the Temple Square.

As they walked past the future site of the Temple of Law, Helen gazed up at the pillars and said, "We did it. We brought down an entire temple."

"Yep," said Fred, "we did."

They'd had help, of course. And it had mostly been the temple itself that had brought the temple down. But that was why adventuring was fun—you never knew quite how it was going to go.

They walked past the Temple of Good and Helen didn't even twitch.

"Does that mean you're done overthrowing temples for a while?" Fred asked.

Helen shrugged. "I don't know. I just know I don't have any urges to ransack anything right now."

"That's nice," said Fred.

"I think it's because of Roberto," said Helen. "He was a jailor in an evil temple, but when I looked into his eyes, I realized I shouldn't kill him. Once a person has realized something like that—well, it's a whole new world."

Fighter Fred and Yellin' Helen walked through the Temple Square without ransacking anything. Fred carried his treasure sack, because they were on their way to divvy treasure. Helen carried a present. Mak-Thar had said it could only be found in a rules supplement, but Helen had found it in a cobbler's shop.

Their meetup was not at the Den of Thieves—nobody was dumb enough to divvy treasure at the Den of Thieves. Wren had called for the six adventurers to meet at the Basetown Bank.

Helen was bringing her brother a boot.

The End

Acknowledgments

MUCH OF THIS STORY was inspired by the illustration D. A. Trampier did for the first edition *Advanced Dungeons & Dragons Players Handbook*. Some of the influence was conscious—like the idea of stealing a giant idol's jeweled eyes—and some was unconscious—like the lizard men.

If the architecture of the Evil Temple of Evil seems somewhat bizarre, that is because it is based on the Temple of Nyllyn, which was a dungeon I made when I was about fourteen. On the other hand, if the architecture seems practical and sensible, then I will claim that I carefully researched it, and you should totally go build a temple in a swamp according to the instructions given here. Let me know when you get the stone quarried, and I'll come help you raise the pillars.

Although these stories will always be inspired by Gary Gygax's Dungeons & Dragons, I have now spent so much time with these characters that they are beginning to inspire their stories themselves. Perhaps you have noticed that we are spending less time commenting on archaic rules and more time examining the characters' motivations. This was inevitable. I once told my wife that *Fighter Fred and the Dungeon of Doom* could never have a sequel, but the truth was simply that the sequels would have to be about more than the absurdity of living in a world based on a rulebook. Sometimes the stories are also about brothers, or camaraderie, or friendship.

Actually, all my stories are about friendship.

Speaking of Sierra, she was once again a great help to me in getting this book out, especially with her heroic efforts to read the entire thing to Linden and Zora during a long car trip. If you have enjoyed reading this series as much as I have enjoyed writing it, it is due to my family's constant encouragement and support.

About the Author

JASON A. HOLT writes from the viewpoint of Fighter Fred, but in real life, he likes rulebooks as much as Mak-Thar does. Jason has worked on over forty-two board games. In particular, he designed the English-language word list for Codenames and translated the rulebook for Galaxy Trucker.

His first game-based novel was *Galaxy Trucker: Rocky Road*, and he also writes the Edgewhen® fantasy adventure series.

You can find out more about Jason at JasonAHolt.com. He even has a mailing list that will tell you when you can expect his next book.

Made in the USA
Middletown, DE
01 September 2020